The Moscow Eccentric

Andrei Bely, 1913

THE MOSCOW ECCENTRIC

ANDREI BELY

TRANSLATED BY

BRENDAN KIERNAN

ILLUSTRATIONS BY KATYA KOROBKINA

Russian Life
BOOKS

Translation © 2016, Brendan Kiernan
Cover illustration by Katya Korobkina

ISBN 978-1-880100-47-9

Library of Congress Control Number: 2016952861

Russian Information Services, Inc.
PO Box 567
Montpelier, VT 05601-0567
www.russianlife.com
orders@russianlife.com
phone 802-223-4955

TRANSLATOR'S NOTE

I am pleased to present the first English translation of Andrei Bely's, *The Moscow Eccentric*. The novel's characters, plot, and imagery, call to mind, however improbably, a comic book: an absent-minded professor and a glamorous yet bumbling spy struggle over a powerful secret formula. Eccentric personalities, wild dialogue, improbable sounds, bristling images, and vivid colors fill each scene to bursting. Bely, however, does not sacrifice thematic complexity to cartoonish entertainment. He confronts some of the thorniest issues of his day, including the nature of individual consciousness and the essence of family, social, economic, and sexual relationships in Russian society on the cusp of WWI.

Bely challenges readers not only with ideas, but by presenting them in a unique and demanding format, a novel that he calls an "epic poem in prose format." *The Moscow Eccentric* is built on a rhythmic backbone of metered prose that supports a wondrous array of literary devices, both poetic and prosaic. Bely's language play is breathtaking. He is just as brilliant on a huge canvas depicting spectacular swaths of city life as he is in detailing the patterns of snow on a small stretch of sidewalk. He surprises and thrills readers with constant tonal and stylistic variation, moving effortlessly, for example, from lyrical descriptions of Russian nature to slapstick physical and verbal parody of its social milieu.

The Moscow Eccentric will appeal to a broad audience. If you are a fan of the Russian novel in particular or great literature from anywhere, you should read this book: it is an underappreciated gem. If you are a fan of Bely's poetry, Russian poetry, or poetry in general, you should read this book: Bely uses poetic tools, and in places pure poetry (some of it deliberately second-rate), to push the boundaries of prose. If you are a writer of any stripe, you will be amazed at what you find here and, just possibly, walk away thinking differently about the patchwork of sound and images in your own prose, be it fiction or not.

Readers will be happy to learn that *The Moscow Eccentric* (June 1926) does the job of any good introduction: it leaves them satisfied yet somehow eager for more. *Moscow Under Threat* (October 1926) and *Masks* (1928) are the second and third parts of the series. Bely never wrote an announced fourth installment.

BELY'S STYLE

Bely's style delights and confounds first-time readers. *The Moscow Eccentric* should be approached throughout with five key stylistic elements in mind. At one time or another, each of these elements may seem intrusive or overbearing, but taken as a whole, their interplay summons an imagined universe so vivid, so unique that readers quickly learn to balance the load.

RHYTHM

Bely called *The Moscow Eccentric* an epic poem in prose format. Its primary poetic rhythm, maintained throughout, is a repeating group of three syllables consisting of two unstressed syllables followed by one stressed syllable. This three-beat pattern is known as an anapest, or anapestic meter.

Throughout the translation, with limited exceptions, I treat this rhythmic backbone as the fundamental constraint in a multi-variable challenge. I subordinate grammar, syntax, word choice and all other elements of prose style to this most basic element. While remaining true to the logic and meaning of Bely's prose and trying to reproduce the sonic elements of the original, I strove to maintain, first and foremost, the underlying metrical beat. This decision means that word order has been altered more than it would have been otherwise; in places, clauses have been swapped within sentences; in some places clauses were conjoined and in others they were sundered to retain both the meter and clarity of expression. All of this "reconstruction" was done in an attempt to remain faithful to the guiding spirit of the original text.

SOUND

Bely carefully added rich layers of sound over the novel's rhythmic backbone. These sounds are both verbal and non-verbal. The non-verbal sounds include the noise of everyday life such as trains and automobiles, church bells, and nature's booms, groans, and pops such as the clank of sleet on a metal roof, the grinding of carriage wheels on cobbles, or the whistling of a storm in the trees.

The most common verbal elements of Bely's sonic smograsboard are alliteration and assonance. Sometimes he links together or emphasizes actions; at others, he seems more intent on setting the mood. Often, it seems like he is, simply, playing.

While Russian's vowels and consonants are, obviously, different from those found in English, the pronunciations of many are close enough that they can be matched for poetic purposes. Alliteration provides an illustration. Take, for example, the letter P, which has *broadly* similar pronunciations in both languages (though the oral mechanics can differ). Where possible, if Bely played with P's in a paragraph or on a page, I played with P's. Sometime, however, when Bely played with P's, I was forced due to the lexical constraints, to the next best choice, another labial consonant, such as a B. There were cases where Bely played with a consonant, say a sibilant S, where I could find no reasonable match or substitute from a phonetic or lexical point of view, so I selected an unrelated consonant, say a guttural G, which I might have found convenient at that point for lexical reasons. There were times when I was unable to match Bely sound for sound and simply was forced to surrender.

WORDS

Educated native speakers of Russian often have difficulty reading *The Moscow Eccentric*. In large part this is because of Bely's inventive lexicon. Attentive native readers are contantly aware of the ocean of new and unusual language in which they are immersed. Primarily, this ocean consists of: neologisms and occasionalisms invented by Bely; foreign or foreign-based words from mathematics, science, and architecture; archaic language; vulgar and street expressions, and; names.

Bely invented literally hundreds of words for this novel. Using contemporary and archaic roots, dozens of available and widely-used suffixes, prefixes, infixes, and particles and the incredible flexibility inherent in Russian grammar and usage, Bely infused the novel with a richness never before seen in Russian literature. Some of Bely's words are so obvious in form and meaning for an educated reader that it is easy for them to read on with barely a nod, perhaps a smile. Other new words are so confusing that the reader has no choice but to stop and ponder the meaning.

Bely's creativity leaves a translator, and readers, in a quandary: how to make a non-native speaker feel the "newness" and, at times, the "discomfort" of the novel's newly minted creations. I used three primary methods. First, where possible, I have favored colorful, unusual, even outlandish, language at the expense of anything dry or simple. Second, wherever Bely's creations must be translated by more than one word in English (the vast majority of cases) I have run the words together typographically. This format signals the reader that Bely is at play and, hopefully, slows the reader down just a bit, creating some of the "discomfort" that Bely clearly intended. Finally, a third way that I attempt to reproduce a bit of this "newness" and "discomfort" is by using, with explanatory notes, a handful of archaic English words. While a translation of *The Moscow Eccentric* stuffed full of Old English would satisy no one, I felt a light salting of uncomfortably old words would help provide a sense of the technique used in the original.

Aside from minting words, Bely's richest source of material, including arachaic and vulgar words and phrases, was a dictionary, *The Explanatory Dictionary of the Living Great Russian Language* compiled in 1863 by V.I. Dal. Known to experts in the field simply as "Dal," the dictionary is used even today as one of the best sources for regional, vulgar, archaic, and commonly used words and phrases whose meanings or sources threatened to be lost with time. Bely uses the dictionary indiscriminately, selecting the words he likes and using them without regard to a character's regional background, education, or place in life.

All three parts of Russian names – the first name, patronymic, and surname – were a rich source or wordplay for Bely – Gogol's influence here is unmistakable. Often, I found it impossible to reproduce the effect. For example, the novel's main character, Ivan Ivanovich Korobkin has an odd-sounding family name that is based on the word for "box." In many ways he is shown as a man in a "box," defined by social, professional, and family boundaries that limit and confound him. Korobkin, when at home, largely confines himself to his office, or, as he calls it, his "sweat box." Transforming his name to "Boxtin" or something similar would have done little for readers, but would have abrogated a sound choice made dozens of times by Bely throughout the text. With one exception, marked with a note, the names are the same as in the original.

LIGHT, SHADOW AND COLOR

Bely plays with light, shadow, and color throughout the book not only as a scene setter but also as a marker for mood and motivation. Some of the novel's most entertaining sections include the play of shadows on walls, the interplay of internal and external lighting, and the glow, from both near and far, of downtown streetlights and advertising. As readers become familiar with Bely's palette, they will start to see patterns in the choices he makes for characters and action.

GETTING STARTED
BELY'S SUGGESTIONS ON HOW TO READ THIS BOOK

Bely suspected that his experimental prose would face an uphill battle for acceptance. He had two primary bits of advice for readers.

First, he insisted, *read it aloud*. Bely was profoundly interested in the sonic elements of human existence, including not only conversation but rhetoric, poetry, and music. Bely insisted, in fact, that to be fully understood, his prose had to be read aloud.

Bely's second main bit of advice for readers was to *read it twice or more*. Not cover to cover, but read words, phrases, sentences or paragraphs, then read them again. Think about the wording. Puzzle over the images and sounds and all the other essential elements. He thought it natural that readers would cover the same paragraph two or more times until they fully parsed the sounds, the rhythm, and understood his meaning.

You might think of reading Bely's prose like a high school English class introducing Shakespeare's plays. It's the rare high schooler who breezes through: most struggle. Strange vocabulary. Unusual syntax. Order imposed by an underlying rhythm that can be oddly distracting (if you let it) yet seems to strengthen the message in ways hard to articulate. The mix of rhythm and meaning create sense of powerful underlying currents even though you can't quite parse them. Relax into the sound and enjoy the show!

INSTEAD OF A PREFACE

Finishing the front matter of the first volume of my novel... I should offer some words of clarification. The theme of modernity will not appear until the second volume... [*The Moscow Eccentric*] portrays the *mores* of bygone Moscow; through Professor Korobkin, a world-class mathematician, I illustrate science's helpless position in bourgeois society. Mandro represents the "Iron Heel" (those who would enslave humanity); the first volume of my novel describes the struggle of science, free in its essence, with capitalism; at the same time it shows the decay of pre-revolutionary society. In this sense, the first and second parts of the novel (*The Moscow Eccentric* and *Moscow Under Threat* [forthcoming]) are satirical caricature; this explains much in their structure and style.

The Author
Moscow. 1925.

CHAPTER 1

THE PROFESSOR'S DAY

Dedicated to the memory of a peasant from Archangelsk,
Mikhail Lomonosov[1]

> The abyss yawned – full of stars.
>
> M. Lomonosov[2]

1

Yes sir, yes sir, yes sir!

The stinging flies swarmed every August; their bellies were broader; they'd hatch, and as soon as their wings went to work they would fly with no sound; they were wiley: oh no, they'd not land on your skin, as a rule, but your clothes and crawl over quite slowly: then ow!

---

1. Bely's dedication of the novel to Mikhail Lomonosov, an early giant of Russian literature and science, has been explained in a number of ways. J.D. Elsworth, for example, cited Bely's interest in anthroposophy (*Andrey Bely: A Critical Study of the Novels*, Cambridge: Cambridge University Press, 1983, p. 197). I prefer the simplest explanation that, to me, fits the facts. This is an experimental novel, an epic poem in prose format based on a rhythmic backbone. Lomonosov was largely responsible for the adoption in Russian literature of German meter and prosydy.
2. The epigraph's images appear throughout the novel. The quotation is from Mikhail Lomonosov's ode, *An Evening Meditation on God's Majesty as Witnessed by the Great Northern Lights* (1743).

Yes, Ivan Ivanovich Korobkin[3] waged war on those flies; while they warred on his nose; so, as soon as he got into bed and protected himself from his head to his toes with a blanket (brick apples on black), just the tip of his haphazard[4] nose and a wisp of his beard sticking out, a small way from his nose on the pillow a fly would be waiting; and watching Ivan Ivanovich; and, Ivan Ivanovich, the fly; and the question was who would trick whom?[5]

On that morning the yellowest pollen[6] was wafting its way in the windows; Ivan Ivanych opened his eyes on the divan (he slept on the divan), and spotted a fly; he deliberately stuck out his nose just a bit from the sheets: toward the fly; then the fly saw his nose; so it flitted and, *plop*, it had landed; he scooped up the fly in his palm as he bounded from bed, out of breath, his nose bent to his fist; after catching the fly with his left hand, his trembling right yanked the stinger; then broke off its head; but the headless fly crawled; while Ivan Ivanych resembled a yellow-legged goat[7] in pajama pants bending to watch it move.

Donning a robe, grey with washedoutandyellowed lapels, and securing his gut with its belt, he then shlepped to the window in slippers and slung it wide open, surrendered himself to serene contemplation of Snuffsneezer Alley, his home now for twenty-five years.

---

3. The novel's first names and patronymics should be pronounced consistent with casual Russian usage which, not coincidentally, is matched by Bely's meter. Ivan Ivanovich, for example, loses three syllables and becomes, roughly, "Van Vanych," with the second syllable receiving the most emphasis. Pay attention – he plays with these names all through the novel.
4. Bely describes Korobkin's nose as *tyaplyapy*, a somehat uncommon word that means haphazard or slapdash. The word occurs throughout the text as a marker for Korobkin and matters related to his actions and mindset.
5. Bely puts a comic twist on "*kto-kovo*" (who-whom), a Russian political stock phrase for situations where one's loss is another's gain. Chernyshevsky and Lenin are among the phrase's best known users.
6. Note here and throughout Bely's use of yellow and other colors.
7. While Bely's aim is comedic, readers should know that the epithet "goat" is considerably stronger in Russian than English, so the humor is not too far from insulting.

Like an old man, the house on the opposite side of the fence stood there gradually yellowing, speckled with flies and hacking out smoke through a sooty old pipe of a chimney; its notes never matched the (raw sounding) harmonica that played of an evening out back in the alley; on the door, a small card, the name: Gribikov; there, in those walls, he had scraped-by for thirty-some years, slowly flattening, much like the leaf of a linden long pressed in between paper sheets at an herbalist's;[8] lax, vegetative, sclerotic: he had yellowing skin, even yellowing bones, and a wart near his eye like a raisin; concerning this resident Van Vanych recalled nothing else; no, one more thing: that the resident played with the wart with his finger half-crooked; in this gesture alone he stood out; on most mornings, in coffee-brown, worn-out old pants with suspend-ers and beaten-up shoes he'd slog to a pit in the yard with a bucket of nightsoil; most days he would sit in the window and drink while he reckoned accounts;[9] in the evenings he'd sit on a bench by the fence; where he'd sprinkleandrollhistobacco on scraps from the newspaper, coughing on hands that were crippled by rheumatism; later he'd sit in the window, relax in his nightcap and robe; then near ten, for some air, he'd make sure to return to the pit with the bucket.

The famous and busy professor's days started with thinking of Gribikov, thereby avoiding all thought of him 'til his next window-side session.

He remembered!

He'd dreamt a real doozy that night; he was sticking his head out a window, and wearing the very same robe while he toyed with the belt 'round his belly, and looked all about good old Snuffsneezer Al-ley; with nothing amiss: but the room was not at the same place as its

---

8. Linden tea is still commonly used in France and elsewehere as a soporific.
9. Describing Gribikov's activities, Bely references a folk rhyme about a finch, a popular euphe-mism for drinking that arose, in part, from the green and yellow uniforms of some bibulous law students. Gribikov's skin is described as a yellowing plant.

latitude-longitude; it was an eyeball; Professor Korobkin could look out the window, its pupil, and see all of Snuffsneezer Alley; it was paved not with cobbles but math and was missing the yellow house, dammit, and window, the one right there opposite his; then that window swung open and Gribikov sprang out, a cuckoo; he coughed on the alley; the "cough" caused the cobbles and houses and sidewalks to bubble and burst into atoms[10] of dust that went blasting through space; then Ivan Ivanych, now a dust mote himself, was back on his bed, in a ball, and was facing the fly on the spot out of which he'd been bounced.

After he'd thought through the dream, a most angry, loud buzzing commenced (a huge fly); he decided to de-fly the room; he recalled he'd been roused late that night by a telegram sent to congratulate him for election – for *you* sir – as an Academy member, correspond-ing; Professor Korobkin sat chomping his lips while he clutched at his robe's yellow belt; for a London Academy member, accepting election as a "*pshespolny*"[11] member of the Czech Academy (he did not under-stand the term "*pshespolny*"; it could be honorary or simply acting), was far from a given; Nikita Vasilyevich Zadopyatov[12] had recently gotten their nod, with the status of "acting"; he knew Zadopyatov's writing was plain, dammit all, chicken scratch; he, Ivan Ivanych Korobkin, a Doctor at Oxford, much later in life now elected "*pshespolny*" in Prague; oh, no way he'd put that on his tombstone: so, no, no, he'd decline.

He claimed science as his birthright; which no one disputed; they said he was science's sharpest, most sensitive instrument...

---

10. The word "atom" does indeed appear in Bely's original text.
11. Korobkin fails to understand the Czech word for "non-resident."
12. This name is an extended play on words. *Zad*, in Russian, in its literal sense means the back end of anything. As slang, it can be translated as rear end, backside, or many of the other words used for the body part in question. Though not as crude as some other potential choices, it would be frowned on in polite society. As we'll learn later, his wife bullies him, and *pyat* refers to her heel and the kicks she threatens.

Wrapped in his dark-grey old robe, he shlepped to the mirror; and pondered his tobacco-shade, eastern-set eyes; and his skullboned reflection with cheeks just like knobs[13] and a haphazard nose; with a crowning slight tuft of his hair up on end; and his hair was quite brown; then he smoothed out his beard and examined his profile; he could have stayed grey and unhappy, but no; brown hair worked well with the ladies. Between us I'll note that he colored his hair.

Then he skipped out while silently drumming his fingers.

His office was small with two windows: its wallpaper bore a repeating design that resembled a small yellow man with a black undertone; *and* when the pattern was seen from afar it appeared that the man on the paper was chasing himself; two bookshelves of yellow-grained oak, both quite dusty, were stuffed with thick yellow and darkleather tomes; a nice yellow-brown desk was topped with black cloth and was buried in books and some bunches of paper, all covered with scribbled and crossed-out equations; for comfort the desk had been turned to the window; a blackpawed chair, its claws splayed; two identical chairs: by the window, a brown curtain hung gathering dust next to one, while the other was next to a pedestal proudly displaying a small bust of Leibniz, who seemed to be speaking his famous assertion: our world is the best of all possible;[14] freehand, a carpenter carved on the column's flutes fauns with acanthus leaves clenched in their grins; on his desk, quite a load: with a silvery *presse papier* and two bronze condul[15] holders with

---

13. Describing Korobkin's cheeks and face, Bely uses a word root for "knob" (*pepyosh*) with a sound that will appear again and again throughout the book in (literally and figuratively) related words. With this uncommon and striking description early in the story Bely sets the stage for Korobkin's role.

14. Gottfried Wilhelm von Leibniz (1646-176), a German mathematician and philosopher known, in part, for his principle of optimism, which posited that our universe is the best one that God could have created.

15. An old variant of candle; Joseph T. Shipley, *Dictionary of Early English*, Littlefield, Adams & Co., 1968, p. 169.

light green patina; the floor, lightly polished, was under a black rug chewed-up by the moths.

The professor's attention then turned to some half-muffled noise from the hallway, a curved little corridor covered in crepe; and so scuffling a bit, he crept over to eavesdrop: a fracas: and, yes sir, the maid's voice:

"Well, you..."

"What a sight, that's the truth!" At that, Darya exploded.

"And you justarunt... ooh, my bosom, I'll go to my lady."

"Oh honey!..."

"Well, you!"

The voice – out with it – was his Mitya's![16] He threw the door open to stop the disgrace; but the fracas was finished; Korobkin's eyes blinked.

"Oh, now, dammit: yes sir... The young boy was already near grown... Ay-yi-yi, well we must have some words, I'll take action... Perhaps I should..."

Here, he got lost in the thoughts of his youth and the heat of his blood at that age; when languor assaulted his rational discipline leaving him mindless and sluggish; he too was convinced way back then, to his shame, that he'd happily shelve his Lagrangian[17] functions to see a bare leg; and so he hid his eyes in his functions in shame; bare-legged Fyokla, his family's maid, was involved with a man of heroic proportions, a bare-knuckle brawler; Ivan Ivanych stood up in support of the rights of all women; but didn't dare think of them; he was distractedandrandy in

---

16. Dmitri Ivanovich Korobkin, teenaged son of Professor Ivan Ivanovich Korobkin, who is himself the son of Dr. Ivan Nikanorovich Korobkin; Mitya is a diminutive form of the name Dmitri; Mitya's mother is Vasilisa Sergeyevna Korobkina *née* Kekaryeva; their daughter is Nadezhda Ivanovna Korobkina, called Nadya.

17. Joseph-Louis Lagrange (1736-1813), a French mathematician whose primary work was on functions.

graduate school, up until Vasilisa Sergeyevna,[18] champion of all kinds of progress, appeared; then they gave him a place on the faculty.

The door opened, and scraping the floor with his paws oh so loudly, the wetnosed and flapeareddog Tommie, a pointer, with yellow chest, brown fur, and quite a hard head with a knot on the back, flew straight into the office:

"Report if you please, sir!"

Tom lowered his wet nose and black lips and drooled on the rug; next, he covered his nose with his ears; the thick skin on his cheeks pulled far back, as he flashed sharp white fangs and he lifted all three of his whiskers: a most frightening muzzle! The hound dog was clearly attempting to laugh.

"Get the hell out, Tom... Where's the switch?"

At the words "Where's the switch?" the dog sprang to his paws while he bitterly squinted his blood-rimmed eyes, lowering his tail as he scooted right out; and behind him, parading the yellow-green hall, the disheveled professor with eastern-set eyes was reciting a short poem of his own:

Dreaming of chewing and chasing,
Tom is both noble and dumb,
Yellowed air stinks so he hastens,
Tucks his nose under his bum.

---

18. Vasilisa Sergeyevna Korobkova, his spouse. Her relatively unusual first name, her personality, behavior, and physical attributes, combined with the author's frequent mention of exotic animals, all suggest that Bely may be playing here with reference to a basilisk, a mythical lizard that could kill with its breath or a glance.

Here, at the start of this tragedy, I should include some small explanation concerning this famous professor.

Beginning, as they say, "*ab ovo*."[19]

Ivan Nikanorych Korobkin, a decorous doctor of military science, in the reign of His Majesty Nicholas I,[20] was transferred, for some undefined cause, to the wilds of the Caucasus; he had a son who was born in a fortress constructed to fend off the Chechens; Ivan's earliest memories: the roar of a cannon, the screaming of women: *Lezgins*[21] had attacked; with the senselessness[22] terrifying; fear became flesh: and it stayed his whole life.

The doctor's large family consisted of children: his Nikanor, Pafnutiya, Lev, Alexander, Ivan, Silantiya, Ada, Varvara, Natalya, and Marya. Ivan, a small nipper, turned ten, and was sent off to school by his father, who tied him tight onto a saddle; Ivan crossed the Caucasus; post office carriages rolled him to Moscow to the head of the First Moscow Gymnasium; he was first in his class and was proud; and as proof of success he had mind-numbing rows of top grades, so the teachers, whom students would flatter for even just D's, always savagely teased the young boy; this senselessness[23] lasted right into his fifth year, when Vanya received a dispatch from the Caucasus saying Ivan Nikanorych had died; they proposed that the boy should thence pay his own way; and thereaf-

---

19. Bely pokes fun at educated yet pretentious city dwellers and their uneducated country cousins with the Latin expression, "*ab ovo*," which means literally "from the egg" or, figuratively, "the beginning." Here, it comes across at first as a comical foreign flourish. However, Bely includes a second level of humor here because the pronunciation of "*ab ovo*" is very close to "*ob yevo*," "about him," a grammatical mistake common in the countryside. Thanks to Olga Kuzmina for bringing up this bit of Bely's brilliance.

20. Nicolas I, who reigned from 1825 to 1855, was known for his conservatism in politics and religion and ruled Russia (and Poland and Finland) in the run-up to the disastrous Crimean War.

21. The Lezgins are native to the Caucusus, rooted in southern Dagestan and Azerbaijan.

22. One of the novel's dominant themes is Korobkin's fear of *nevyatnitsa*, the ineffable, otherwise translated here to mean senselessness, disorder, and chaos.

23. I translate the traditional Russian grading system of 1 to 5 (worst to best) into the roughly equivalent F to A scale familiar in the United States.

ter young Vanya Korobkin had lived in the kitchen by leave of the cook (in a corner behind a clogged drain, and screened off by a curtain); by auditing all the school's courses he tutored his classmates and others his age for exams; it was these boys who beat him; and, senselessly, life went on. Life was despair; understandably, Vanya concluded that life's senseless nature could only be fought with the clarity found in ideas that had proofs. That's how science's ranks were expanded by one.

2

Houses, more houses, small houses, smaller houses, and even wee houses: a five-story, newly rebuilt, cream-toned house dressed with garland accents; a house, blue and cute, built of wood; further down: a grey-green colored house made of stone, its pediment statued, quite sloppily jutting; sagging, a cornice bowedclose to a column, the faded roof threatened collapse; all the windows were blinded by shutters; the house was surrounded by whispering maples; a tree with red paws hung above a stout, cast-iron fence.

A roughhewn and half-wrecked wood fence stretched along; through its gaps peeked bare patches of balded, bare soil; a huge and annoyed and quite bothersome fly loudly buzzed its fly music; in pipeweeds;[24] abandoned, a lot laythereempty; piled bricks (a new build in the books); and again that roughwooden, broke fence and a nice little house; and the owner was painting it yellow: it paled as it dried; and inside its gates was a noisome front yard that had yellowing grass; a white house with a mess in its entrance; and pillows were propped in the windows.

---

24. Bely juxtaposes fly "music" and pipe weeds. The Russian word for the weed here, *dudochnik*, can also mean fife or flute, or refer to a phallus. Bely is playing here (and not for the last time) with the sounds of the word "prostitute" when he writes *ros dudochnik; pusto...* (pipeweeds grew; a long vacant...).

Next to some trash, a stray dog, two-toned fur, its taildown, skulked away, in its dagger-sharp teeth an old yellowish bone; the dog jealously watched a fly: a real son of a fly;[25] out of the balding, worn lot, where bashedbits of smashed bottles flashedbrilliantasdiamonds, a huge fustilugs[26] hobbled, her heel in a bandage, to heave-ho some offal; a tarbarrell, wet, damp and stained and still oozing and stinking stood empty; the air bore the smells of dry hay[27] and manure, and of something quite sharp.

At first glance, this was Snuffsneezer Alley, dear citizen! Thus it was, thus it remains; no, the yellow, small house was dismantled for firewood.

Opposite, brick-brown, a house made of stone, Number 6; an addition, a second floor, boasted three windows, all smudged; and a frieze with carved garlands that grew from modillions; Hermetical[28] capitals supported the frieze; and framed the three windows;[29] blue taffeta drapes hid, shamefacedly, whatever went on there; the garden flashed green, in the rear was an entrance (the nameplate: Professor Korobkin).

The door opened and out down the alley walked, shuffling, a teenager, slouched, dressed in dark pants and dark coat; a growth roughened his cheeks most unpleasantly; forehead, half covered with unruly hair, he looked a real clopdpate;[30] his eyes barely peeked out from under his

---

25. This is a play on words. In Russian, "son of a bitch" is *sukin syn*. The expression *mukhin syn*, or "son of a fly," is a phrase with a crude yet playful tone that indicates the dog's distress.

26. A large dirty woman; Joseph T. Shipley, Dictionary of Early English, Littlefield, Adams, & Co., 1968, p. 287.

27. Another play on "son of a bitch." Dry hay, *sukhim senom*, is a rough anagram for *sukin sin*.

28. Decorated with symbols related to Hermes, ancient Greek god of commerce, profit, and also magic, astrology, and alchemy. Bely, fascinated with the occult and ancient mysteries, may also be referring here to a man named Hermes Trismegistus, who is credited with various works on mysticism and magic.

29. There is no way to arrange symmetrically five capitals dividing three windows. Bely hints at a fundamental disorder in the house.

30. Blockheaded, stupid; Joseph T. Shipley, Dictionary of Early English, Littlefield, Adams & Co., 1968, p. 155.

brow; he was sickly, his face had a yellowish tinge with some grey, and red pimples; held under his right arm were two smallish books; in his left was a smart canvas cap.

A young woman, a particular kind, skirt hiked-up and showing off stockings, her blouse nicely ironed, umbrella in hand as she dragonflied under a redfeathered hat and a veil.

A bell tower pealedgossip; a catafalque waited; someone was being interred.

That was Moscow!

Scattered all over were churches from various eras,[31] medium, tall, and some small, with gold leaf and plain; out from under a layer of windblown, thick grime peeked the green, red, flat, low, and high roofs of houses, large houses, small houses, some dressed with glazed tile, others stuccoed, or simply in tattered materials, types long forgotten, reposed under trees, some rebuilt, some with columns, some not, and some balconied, faced with acanthus,[32] caryatids supported each cornice and balcony; triangle gables on houses, large houses, small houses on Wildhowling, Snuffsneezer, and First, Second, Third, and Fifth, and Fourth, Sixth and Seventh Rottentooth Alleys.

The streets there were formed by collisions of houses and mezzanines, wings, and their fences; brick-brown, dark-sand, and pistachio, white, green, crimson, olive, and cream; in fine feather, a ribbon of signs hung there sparkling; a pretzel here; boots of gold there; and continuous

---

31. The original text has what at first glance appears to be a typo in one of the section's defining words, равных (*ravnykh*), which means "equal" or "the same." For the translation разных (*raznykh*) was used, translated here as "different." Moscow was known as a city of churches, and it is veritably coated in its older sections with churches and related buildings, courtyards, cemeteries and gardens; many other such facilities were razed after 1917 and replaced with unrelated structures. Bely is playing with the reader by implying the exact opposite.

32. Native to the Mediterranean, the long, narrow, and pointed acanthus leaf is one of the most commonly modeled plants for decorative architectural features. Examples of its use stretch back to Ancient Greece.

                    Andrei Bely

noise from trafficking wagons and carts, empty barrels boom-booming, and the swishing of sweepers; lots four and seventeen ended the street.[33]

Down there people were crowded together, a multileggedhuman,[34] a creature that flashed as it moved and it fidgeted, sneezed, and lamented, it squealed, and it snorted, and shuffled along, consisting of timid, small folk, who squirmed through front gates and the doors to their musty, stale lives: shod in boots, or flat shoes, or with heels, greyish-green; they were topped with frayed caps, or just kerchiefs or scarves, or wore hats; they hurried from market to market; their lives frayed their bodies; while one loaded sacks on his shoulders, a second lugged burlap, one carried a crate, and another heaved loads; as if fairies flew, dust got in runny red noses and in very large schnozzes, into mouths of all shapes spouting themselfishness,[35] and loosing tall tales in thin air; they were speckled with dog hair and dandruff, and covered with spit and foul-smelling smoke left by rotten tobaccos, and barely were able to speak; they would leave by themselves; or they'd walk off in pairs or in threes, from the left to the right and the right to the left,[36] sliding and skipping, and slipping and scrabbling.

There were thousands of people, shaggy and raggy and squinty and chubby, some curly, some grizzly or gnarly, and they struggled along on their feet; or they rode.[37]

---

33. The word translated here as "sweeper" is *yashcher*, literally referring to a pangolin, a mammal native to tropical forests whose size, shape, tongue, diet, and foraging habits are reminiscent of anteaters. Bely frequently refers to exotic animals.; The significance of the numbers 4 and 17, if any, is unclear.
34. Bely invents a word, "*chelovechnik*," for the crowd viewed as a whole, virtually a living being. The root of his new word is "*chelovek*" or person. It recurs throughout the work.
35. Thanks to Olga Kuzmina for suggesting theselfishness..
36. This phrase, repeated throughout the book, is perhaps a reference to the political "right" and "left." Bely might also be implying here that independent decisions, understood correctly, are based on some fundamental underlying order. Or maybe he is just playing.
37. This paragraph is a great example of how difficult it can be to recreate some of the sonic effects available to Bely in Russian. Here, because Russian is an inflected language where each of the adjectives has a genitive plural ending of "*ykh*," Bely is able to reinforce the text's rhythm with

3

A brunet with nice sideburns, a healthy physique, and smooth gestures sat waiting in traffic that shuffled down Vanka: he sported a grey English hat, its brim bent, which nicely set off a fine tailored grey suit, a pique vest, and a watch on a chain; it appeared that he'd leapt off a train, an express out of Nice, bound for Vanka; but spite filled his squint and his forehead was furrowed, while riding he clasped a thick cane; and his gloveless free hand lay across a black briefcase that bobbed on his knee; when he spotted a young man, he lifted his eyebrows while baring his teeth, with the knob of his cane the man banged on the driver to:

"Stop."

Like a tiger, he sprang, and surprisingly gracefully tossing his briefcase and cane and his gloves to the youth he said:

"Mitya dear boy!"

"Oh yes, greetings!"

"I don't need your greetings, it's *you* that I need."

And then, after removing his hat, he proceeded to wipe off his searing hot brow, with two strikingly silver locks slicing the black of his hair.

"Yes, it's *you* whom I need, sir, dear Mitya," and stuck out his chin.

"My Lizasha is having a party tomorrow, her birthday; she thought of you: 'Mitya Korobkin should come'... You'd be welcome."

But Mitya Korobkin, Ivan Ivanych's[38] son, stood there blushing profusely; browsopping; his face looked obscene, like a fist with a nose that was played by the tip of a thumb poking out midst four fingers.[39]

---

alliterative rhyme and thereby give the sense of variation within an anonymous crowd.

38. Bely goes back and forth between two forms of the patronynmic, the "middle" name that for Russians indicates one's father's first name. Ivanych and Vanych are shortened forms of Ivanovich (son of Ivan) often used for convenience in casual conversation and here for rhythmic purposes as well.

39. The obscene hand gesture described here is the *kukish*, the tip of a thumb stuck out through the middle fingers of a clenched fist. The gesture is used in various literal and figurative ways throughout the book.

"Well, I, Eduard Eduardovich, I..." then he mumbled.

"So, *what* is the problem?"

"Well, mama..."

"Your mama and *what*?"

"A long story... I can't leave the house..."

"Oh, good Lord show us mercy," he lifted his brow, a bit posed, and with subtle hand gestures he mimed: "Well, and then..."

"Shall we sit? And so, *what* are you saying! How *are* you!..." And Mitya blushed.

Here, Eduard Eduardovich wriggled a shoulder and grimaced acerbically, "I am just taking advantage of running across you, I've passed on the message: that's it..."

Then he whistled unpleasantly climbing back into the cab while he shouted most crudely: "Get the hell out of here!" They squealed out of a rut and pulled into the noise of the dangerous street.

Eduard Eduardovich Mandro,[40] a powerful businessman, lived on Petrovka; a tall, brand new, cream-colored building, its matching front doors set with azure tiles, ovals of intertwined lilies encircled an androgynous bust on a decorative gable; the home was well known for its rugs, and its staircase with steam heat built-in, and its elevator, silent and swift, its smooth honeytonedoak paneled front doors, from which could be seen their parquet and their mirrors; a sign with the name "von-Mandro" was newer and larger than others'; his daughter was named Lizaveta, Lizasha; she had a refined sense of humor, dis-

---

40. The name von-Mandro may come from the Dal dictionary, which contains the word "mandra" (мандра), which refers to a person with low morals. The novel is littered with exotic animal references, including monkeys and gorillas: mandrills, the largest of the monkeys, are close relatives of the baboons. The name may also be a veiled reference to a work by Byron, who in 1861 published Manfred: A dramatic poem, which he referred to as a "metaphysical drama." He wrote it not long after he faced charges of an incestuous affair with his half-sister. Von-Mandro may be an anagram of Manfred, especially if the "V" is reduced to an "F" as is typical in Russian pronunciation.

"I am just taking advantage of running across you."

played independence; Lizasha loved standing and chirping amid the parquet and the mirrors and chairs, in a brown little dress (at the Arsenev School, the girls' uniform), flirting with boys: Vedenyapins, the school, where Lizasha and Mitya had gotten acquainted one evening; and Mitya's whole class had then promptly all fallen in love with her.

Mitya was stupid and homely; and always a slob; how could anyone like him? But Mitya had pandered to all and got noticed; he went to Mandro's; Eduard Eduardovich treated him well: the schoolboy began to spend time with some friends of Lizasha from school, or he'd sit there alone with Lizasha in azure-toned twilight; Eduard Eduardovich encouraged them; what's so unusual about that? At Mandro's, all the guests felt at home after all; they were not there off the street, and were all from respectable families; and yes, Eduard Eduardovich very much liked that his home was kept orderly, clean; in black tie and white gloves, a servant stood welcoming guests; a respectable lady most fashionably dressed poured the tea; and no wines were set out; but why worry? The old days are gone; and Lizasha went out: to the theater and concerts, a "circle" they called "Free Aesthetics";[41] Eduard Eduardovich often was found, accidentally, attending *jour fixe*[42] (he was always in quite a big rush), he would stop in and stay half an hour, and quite wonderfully mingling, he'd grab onto the arm of a girl or a guy in a show of equality: "My young friends!" And then he would vanish, not wanting to get in the way.

One thing puzzled young Mitya: Eduard Eduardovich always had questions concerning Ivan Ivanych's work, seems it strongly excited his interest; but he had not met the old man; could manners require these

---

41. Bely is probably alluding here, loosely in a chronological sense, to the Society of Free Aesthetics, a group headed by the poet Valery Bryusov. Many of Moscow's symbolists and other members of the *intelligentsia* and high society met at the group during the years 1906 and 1907.
42. A French term borrowed by Russian Francophones to refer to a recurring event, usually weekly.

questions? And Mitya had sometimes thought: interest in him at Mandro's could be fed just by news that concerned old Ivan Ivanych.

"Please give my respects to your father: I honor his name and his work."

Later, Mitya was certain: Mandro was concerned with his father's achievements: just recently Mitya had been *tête à tête* with Lizasha; they sat in a corner in azure-toned twilight, just minding their business when voices were raised out in Mandro's home office; it seemed that a German was visiting, probably an agent of powerful interests; bits of their chat flew to Mitya:

"*Sagen sie* you... I... Coloss, geniu... *Herr* Professor Korobkin.. *mit seiner entdekung... Wir verden... Das ist, I, eine tat.....* For him *zugunftigen krieg*, introduced *sie...*[43]

Mitya was taken aback that Mandro had been speaking that way of Ivan Ivanych with someone just visiting Moscow, a foreigner; he also recalled: that Mandro had once come to the guest room, a red-headed, sweaty old German in tow with a wart by his nose, and a cigar with a stifling stink; as he tapped on his elbow, von-Mandro had leaned in and he'd whispered, while glancing at Mitya:

"*Das ist, ja, sein sonne...*"[44]

It seemed that the traveller had wanted to see the celebrity's son; Eduard Eduardovich worked in a field quite removed from the sciences; he was in business and often took risks. That thought flashed through the boy's mind; he suddenly found himself wanting to see the Mandros; with Lizasha in mind he had recently taken to wearing a flowery *eau de Cologne*; but the *eau de Cologne* was used up; and so therefore, he thought, he should scrounge up some money by selling some books.

---

43. A mixture of Russian and German: "What are you saying, yes... Colossal, genius... Professor Korobkin... With his discovery... We will... Yes, it's business... In the coming war, do you know..."

44. "That's his son alright."

4

Folks passed: an urchin burstout of a gate; a blind drunk barely bumbled along; and a skirt skittered by; a huge yellowmugged child with a scabby old sore; and two women who meeklypassed ducked in a doorway; a yellowbeard loomed but the women just shooed him away; and the people passed by there in twos and in threes; in small clumps; disillusioned, deluded, discarded, a spring in their step, or in families; black, brown grey and dun.[45]

Pripepyoshin[46] Place curved off the street then abandoned its houses, first rising then falling to end at a square: in the crush of a market; the crowd also turned and moved down off the rise: on the corner; right next to the door of the roachified shop, a pomaded haircutter was running a dirty old comb through a woman's *chignon*;[47] there were shoe shiners too doingbusiness; some shouting:

> *To impish Liza*
> *from Muir-Mirrielees-a's*[48]
> *department of ribbons and notions,*
> *our warmest emotions!*

So Mitya Korobkin had turned with the throng through an alley; approaching the rise, the boy mopped off his brow; then he rushed to the start of the bustling square, a broken-down bitofaboulevard bursting with bodies.

---

45. Describing people, Bely uses words for colors commonly ascribed to horses.
46. This street name, nonsensical, marks another occurance of the psh-sound that will be used again and again to symbolize the ills afflicting Moscow and Russia.
47. French hairstylists became wildly popular for a time in Moscow in the nineteenth century, at first among the wealthy elite and later much more broadly.
48. Muir & Mirrielees was a trading firm founded by two Scots who did business in Russia from 1857 to 1922, operating an eponymous, flagship department store in central Moscow.

Arrayed on the square, a bunch of deep basses did battle to peddle men's jackets and shirts, also boots, shoes and blouses, from carts with the smell of old tar, and at booths, little booths that had red, and some lemon, and black and some orange-blue fabrics, and calicos, striped, and batiste, they had woven materials, all shapes, and all types, quite creative, on counters or simply on boards or on trays with both green-grey and clay-colored piles, all displayed in an organized way on the ground; and so Mitya meandered; a crush of warm bodies; a pig was led in; you could hear:

"I've got leather..."

Some full-throated voices:

"A moment for..."

"You with the grabbyhands..."

"Hey, wait your turn..."

"Would you care, my dear lady, for bodysoap?"

"No..."

"And a bitmore, of that one right there in front..."

"I'll..."

"That's a kopek that I, bythesweatofmybrow..."

A dealer had dusty long rows of used atlases, textbooks and books and old histories, works by Sergei Mikhailovich Solovyov,[49] they were worn and stacked, bound in large bundles; then Mitya, while glancing around, showed his books: one was yellow, one brown.

"Oh hmm, what sir?... A textbook by Spencer?[50] *Foundation of Biology?* second edition," the heavy-set bookseller scratched right behind his left ear; after reading the title like eyeing an enemy, he coughedout:

"A trifle, sir..."

---

49. Sergei Mikhailovich Solovyov (1820-1879), a historian and a professor and rector at Moscow University, and a member of Petersburg's Imperial Academy of Sciences.

50. Herbert Spencer (1820-1903) one of the Victorian Era's most celebrated polymaths; made contributions in biology, anthropology, sociology, and political theory.

"New, it's brand new."

"It's just one of a set..."

"Take a look, what a binding!"

"What sense can there be..."

And then after he tossed down the yellow book, grabbing his glasses, the bookseller totally bunched-up his face in a tightballofwrinkles; examined the brown one:

"Hmm... Rosenberg... *History of Physics*... An older edition... How much are you asking?"

"How much will you pay?"

"I don't need it," he threw down the Spencer, "for *History of Physics*... a... ruble and fifty."

Unleashing *machismo*, men swung both their elbows and fists: a rough woman sprayed spit; a conservative cap[51] stood there rocking and awkward, one leg stiff: but clearly an excellent trader:

"Nice cloth here."

A man stopped, and he sprinkled tobbacky[52] on paper, and rolled and then licked it:

"How much?"

"I'm not haggling."

"Enough of your nonsense old soldier."

He left.

---

51. Bely, like Nikolai Gogol, who influenced him as much as any writer, delights in synecdoche: here, the cap represents a merchant.
52. Bely uses the Ukrainian "*tyutyun*" here instead of the more common *tabak*, for tobacco.

In tobacco and coffee-toned pants, and a much too large coat, with a dried-up old face that had something a yellow shade eating its way right along, an old man from the neighborhood passed; with no beard or mustache, a real eunuch;[53] a cap on his head, he was holding a rolled paper cone of red berries; and draggingoneleg; with a raisinized wart right down under his nose; he caught sight of Mitya, and quickly his face changed expression; he, casually, quietly, eavesdropping, pushed past the people; and rolled a fresh cigarette.

Snickering rat-faced his mug:[54]

"My dear Mitya, forgive me oh Lord, Ivanych, respectfully, greetings!" But Mitya was frightened: he blushed like a thief who'd been pinched; then he paled, and he pressed on a pimple, peeped…

"Gribikov!"[55]

Gribikov, exhaling smoke through a chuckle:

"Regarding those books, tell me, what?"

He pronounced the word "what" as if knowing the "where" and the "why"?

"Yes … I… see…" and then Mitya's hands twitched and he gnawed at a nail: "I came here… just to sell…

"Not to drink, sir?"

He thought for a smidgen:

He'll torture it out of me!

Mitya responded quite cuttingly:

"No!"

---

53. As an insult, Bely uses the word *skopets*, which refers to a member of a sect, the *kastraty*, that believed there was only one truly effective means of combatting the weakness of male flesh, castration. They were outlawed in both tsarist Russia and the Soviet Union.

54. This sentence presents a fine example of Bely's many playful inventions. He turns the noun "*krys*" or "rat" into a verb, "*raskrysyatilos*," that suggests the transformation of Gribikov's face when he laughs.

55. Caught unaware, nervous, Mitya rudely calls an elder male by his last name. Gribikov, with the look and habits of a street creature, could not have commanded great respect.

He had sold just two books; but old Gribikov got in his face:

"All your father's have similar bindings."

Then seeing that Mitya had paled, probed his wart with a finger, and peered at it probably hoping he'd spot something:

"Fine little books sir..." He sniffed that same finger.

"We use the same binder: your father and I."

"They quite recently finished some just like the ones that you had, sir, it's not just the paper I'm thinking about, it's the bindings sir; sitting all day at the window, I notice... oh, what's the address now, the binder's address?"

"It's on Lesser Lubyanka."

"In Leontyev Alley I'd say..."

What the devil!

"Nice weather," then Gribikov coughed in his hand...

But the boy had a runny, cold nose and kept silent.

"Semyonov's Day's gone and now Onion Day too;[56] but the weather is fine: walk to Snuffsneezer?"

"Yes."

"Well then let's go together." A lady, her hat flushwithfeathers:

"What's this?"

A tent flap flew open while slowly revealing a mercer.[57]

"That's *tvast*."[58]

"I've not heard of such fabric."

"Quite fashionable."

"Price?"

"Hm... ...teen."

---

56. Semyonov's Day, September 14, marked the arrival of fall and the beginning of a new year. September 20, Onion Day, was traditionally the end of the onion harvest.

57. Dealer in textiles; Joseph T. Shipley, *Dictionary of Early English*, Littlefield, Adams & Co., 1968, p. 422.

58. *Tvast*, a fabric.

"What!?" To her back as she left he said:

"Gawkers!"

And people passed through and passed by: one was cross-eyed and furry-legged, pant leg rolled up, with a box; and a drooler half-dressed, and a priest, and a guy with grey hair.

"Ball Ballovich! I'm selling Ball Ballovich!"

Then a beardless old panguts,[59] a cigar in his mouth and a melon tucked under his arm, stopped and stood:

"So how much?"

And between them walked cheerful young women in kerchiefs, bright colors and patterns, with tri-colored blouses: light blue, with some yellow and red; there were war rats[60] "protecting" the dealers: "Hand over the dough"; and the vagrants, in tatters, half-dressed, pushed and squeezed through the crowds; underfoot, the huge throng ground the dirt: and a windwhirl raised dustswirls.

Up over the market the air was not air if you looked from afar but a yellowish vapor.

5

Buxom young Darya had run down the hall in an apron; while holding a samovar (sleeves rolled), and brushing her skirt (it was yellow, with accents in lily) against the hall's berry-toned paper; she opened the door with her foot as she heard:

"*À propos*[61] I will say: he is posing here, really, an apothegm... True, Zadopyatov..."

---

59. A fat man; Joseph T. Shipley, *Dictionary of Early English*, Littlefield, Adams & Co., 1968, p. 486.
60. Veterans with disabilities loitering on commercial premises, often bent on "protection" or other nefarious activities, were known as "store rats."
61. Bely plays here and throughout the book with foreign words that start with the letter "A." This is one of several ways Bely signals to readers that Vasilisa Sergeyevna is neither as educated or as intelligent as she would like to appear.

"Again Zadopyatov," responded a voice.

"Zadopyatov: again, I'll repeat 'Zadopyatov'; and even a tenth time, because he is...."

Darya then set the fresh samovar down on the table.

Patterned, fine linen held trays and some tea cups, a pansy design.[62]

Vasilisa Sergeyevna's *Garnier* mixed with the scent of her lavender (made the old way, with vinegar)[63]; thanks to her *peignoir* with a bright orange broach pinned down under her throat, she stood out from the silver-grey wallpaper lilies; a clock chimed beneath a glass hemisphere perched on a pedestal; caged, a canary was chirping and hopping above the leafedpaws of a palm.

Near a shiny glazed stove.

Vasilisa Sergeyevna spoke, melodramatic, dry eyes:

"Zadopyatov responded concerning the party."

She started to read as she turned to the balcony door, where the square of the overgrown garden was fanned by tree branches:

> *Dear reader, I hear what you say,*
> *You'll speak from the heart when you stand*
> *And raise up a toast on the day*
> *My work anniversary's planned.*
> *Drink deep, my dear reader, drink slow*
> *Of the suffering in that libation:*
> *And witness, go forth and then sow*
> *In the shared fields of our writing*

---

62. The literal reference here is to "Annie's eyes", or pansies; however, the "eye" symbol is important throughout the book, not least because Anna Pavlovna Zadopyatova, wife of a family friend, has good reason to keep an eye on Vasilisa Sergeyevna.

63. *Garnier*, a French cosmetics company, founded as *Laboratoires Garnier* in 1904; Lavender vinegar, often made at home, has a variety of uses, including as a bath scent.

She read breathlessly, melodramatically, withered and wan, as if fed only locusts; her lips trembled nervously (cranberry-shade); a dark hair in a birthmark above her top lip; when reciting "go forth and then sow" she half-waved her lorgnette at the trees.

Then the curtains blew in from the pale window frame; in the panes a branch waved with a trembling blacklily leaf:

"What kind of verse can that be? Oh its rhymes are too weak; Dobrolyubov, a copy."[64]

The voice then approached.

"The idea? Oh it's popular, yes, not... some kind... of weak meter... like earlier."

"It's adonic: it alternates dactyls and choir..."

But instead of the dactyls and choir, with the wind, in blew Tommie the hound; right behind him, a breeze that was Nadya, in stripes with a greyberry skirt and nice stockings.

"Oh Lord, please forgive me, do not rush in here like that, *laissez aller allure*.[65] And I'll say... do not shout, my acoustic sensitivity does not...

Vasilisa Sergeyevna angrily snatched at the teapot, her bracelet, enamel, was flashing; she touched-up her hair with a mock-tortoise comb.

"Oh, *maman*, use your Russian; or you'll soon be confusing your words, like for sheets and for *enveloppe*."[66]

---

64. Alexander Mikhailovich Dobrolyubov (1876-1945), a Russian symbolist poet known more for his decadent lifestyle than his verse.

65. Vasilisa Sergeyevna's poor French: she complains about Nadya rushing in like a horse.

66. Vasilisa Sergeyevna apparently, confuses an archaic Russian word for envelope, *kuvert*, with the French word for blanket, *couverture*. Further confusing matters, trying to help her mother with a reminder, Nadya mistranslates *couverture* as sheet.

Nadya sat flipping her curls while she batted her lashes; she lookbored a painting; a landscape: a forest and streams, and some toothyred peaks.

Just like Negroes, black stools lined the walls on their gleaming black legs keeping watch near a massive buffet; its carved walnut puss bore a smile.

Vasilisa Sergeyevna's eyes oft suggested the melodrama never would end; that when years had gone by Vasilisa Sergeyevna's words and her eyes would not change; in her eyes there was drama; in her words was the strength of ideas.

"So, yes, nature must suffer amortification,"[67] galping,[68] she cut herself off: "Get the hell out of here! Tom, you're come spreading your fleas down there under my skirts."

The professor's wife nervously straightened her greyviolet hem.

Vasilisa Sergeyevna itemized incidents marking her life (in regards to this, *nota bene*: Vasilisa Sergeyevna thought "professorial" living was centered on fashions and styles found in Moscow): Dorothea Yermilovna wanted the post of director to go to her spouse, the geologist; she owned two estates but she wanted more money; and Vera Lvovna was studying the basics of fibroids with help from a gynecological intern on staff. Dvutetyuk, with a displaced left kidney and rotting-out spleen, who'd taken four buckets when given an enema (even then nothing), is aiming to steal archaeologist Pustopopov's fine wife, Stepanida Matveyevna, who... just imagine, would stoop. Dvutetyuk has a library worth many thousands, he's wealthy, the hump; if that pisspot succeeds in his thievery her husband will die; Stepanida Matveyevna is a bit old, but no fool; she'll return to her man; and whatever you might say he

---

67. This mangled word, perhaps a conflation of amortization and mortification suggests again that Vasilisa Sergeyevna's erudition is more appearance than substance.

68. Galp, thought to be a combination of gaping and yelling; Joseph T. Shipley, Dictionary of Early English, Littlefield, Adams & Co., 1968, p. 292.

does wear a sash that he won at Radynsk; so in sum, unending kerfuffle: a whole garland of flashing impressions defying beliefs that had trapped a young, principled graduate student in marriage, and when a professor to endure the ineffable, now in the form of a heavy-set woman.

"*À propos:* what a show! As you've heard, my dear Nadya, Elena Petrovna ran off to Lidonov, the acting director of endocrinology."

6

"We," a voice thundered behind a closed door, "are right angles: two complementary angles when summed are the equal of two right angles.

In his gown, tromping the yellow parquet, a strand of his hair loose, Professor Korobkin continued:

"The sum of these angles is botched, oh yes sir, by a failure here, dammit, to marry two complements!" With his huge head descending down into his collar (the collar kept riding on up to his head: he was missing a neck), he adjusted his words.

"Just solve for the cosine, you'll see what I mean; you were lacking, sir, rational clarity, wedding these angles."[69] The word tied him in knots while he stared at the word.

"Yes, yes, rational clarity my small young friend, it's the work of millenia, assuming your brain is equipped with those cells."

He remembered: at 35 he still had no beard or mustache, wore glasses, a frock coat and vest buttoned tightly above a trim ribcage; he made do by slinginhisthinkin on tangents; he'd battled the bedbugs, in vain, and debated the rotten-toothed docent; the smell of the garbage came in through the window; when choked by the smell they would air them-

---

69. Bely's pun here involves *brak*, a Russian word with two entirely different and unrelated meanings, marriage and shoddy work. Looking back, the play commences with geometry at the start of the section where he suggests that one angle (person) can make up for differences in its complement (partner, spouse).

selves out with some basic geometry; his views took on form; the irrational stink of the trash and the odor of rotten old eggs, by their vileness, suggested the logic at work in an abstracted cosmos, with greatest exertion transposed from the outhouse to existential criteria used by Lagrange and by Leibniz.

And somewhere between the trash dump and their work a professor's new worldview was forged.

He was thinking about this while squeezing the back of the chair with his arm; with a pen knife in hand; then he bumped; and the knife slipped and fell; and the chair started creaking, the tablecloth slid; the professor dove headfirst down under the table and stretched for the knife with a groan: so he picked up the knife, as he tossed it he sighed:

"Comprehension of rationality didn't come easily." Grabbing his glasses, he huffed on the lenses, and yawned:

"Well, yes sir, yes sir, yes sir!"

"You always resort to abstractions," his wife said indifferently, turning her eyes toward his Tommie and stopping her nose with a handkerchief:

"Dammit get out, oh you horrid old hound dog: foo, foo what a smell!"

The dog skulked from beneath Nadya's skirt; and he threw the man's wife a quite terrified glance as he hurried along; the professor just soothed the sad dog:

"It's not you, little brother, it's Nadya."

The doorbell. Pyotr Leonidovich Kuverdayev,[70] dancing a madrigal, silently greeted them. Dressed in dark blue, he adjusted his tie, a bright crimson; the aphorisms already played in his eyes when he peeked in

---

70. Bely plays here, in Kuverdayev's name, with the old Russian word for envelope, *kuvert*, a word that Vasilisa Sergeyevna, in the previous section, had trouble remembering and that neither Nadya or her mother could use properly. Perhaps, it also suggests that he is someone whose exterior presents few clues to his thoughts.

at Nadya, there looking askance at a clucking and yellow-clawed cock coming in from the garden to peck for some crumbs;[71] Vasilisa Sergeyevna pointed to Nadya:

"Just you look, *mais quel blafard!*[72] Why? From her poetry... Earlier, I went to see her: and listened a bit; while she read; then I took it and looked, it's apostrophe."

Pyotr Leonidovich breathed and then spoke: an *arpeggio*:

"You're an *author* Nadezhda Ivanovna?"

Nadya was cute as a doll: like an aquatint:

"No."

"And why not?"

She kept quiet while scattering crumbs for the cock; while a ring on her finger reflected the sun through the greenery, sparkling with lilybright light.

Kuverdayev was courting her: gave her a poem, an acrostic, that used some alliterative tricks; alliteration, in truth, can give depth to one's thoughts, or to put it more plainly: Kuverdayev was nearly engaged.

Kuverdayev had given up graduate studies and somehow had danced his way into a job, he became an inspector; he got himself in with the head of the district; who got him a job at a school; he taught rhetoric at Fischer's Gymnasium; the young female students all fell right in love; he played on their fantasies, speaking of nature, in dithyrambs, breathlessly gazing afar with his unseeing, overexpressive eyes; but if someone dared make a mistake he would shriek, give poor grades, and threaten to keep them behind after school for an hour.

And, of course, Nadya noticed; so while he was pouring on charm and embracing her waist as if dancing a polka she recalled how he an-

---

71. Note here that, since the time of the ancient Greeks, a rooster has been a symbolic courting present from an older male to a younger male lover. Kuverdayev and the rooster enter simultaneously.
72. She's so pale!

grily hissed at the girls; with displeasure, and even with fear, she noted his visits on Sundays for dinner; he'd enter, all dandied and costumed to flirt; and was decadently drenched with perfume; he would give himself up to discussions of books, or tell stories: Benvenuto Cellini,[73] artists and medalists, yes! Vasilisa Sergeyevna watched, quite enthralled:

"Persnickety people: so capricious."

The scent of the ladies was fanned through the atmosphere.

7

"Well then, into the sitting room..."

So they went.

There were bronzes, and bright chandeliers; they had armchairs upholstered in satin, soft lily with highlights in green, and a divan stood gleaming, its woodwork well polished; a mirror and decorative frame with carved bunches of grapes could be glimpsed through the gloom; on the wallpaper, whimsical lilyshapes sprinkled with berries with dark crimson shading and foliage: aquatint prints told their tales, the *Bastille*, as well as the fight in the *Convent*, *Saint Justin* as he looked at a dove; then they sat at a table; and leafed through old albums.

While covering theme after theme, Kuverdayev had skipped on from question to question like you click castanets; and poor Nadya was pale as a lily; Professor Korobkin was knackered; a tuft of his brown beard stuck up; and his nose kind of dripped.

"By the way, old Vasily Gavrilovich got a..."

"?..."

"...new post in the ministry – yes, yes!"

---

73. Benvenuto Cellini (1500-1557), an Italian soldier, writer, musician, artist, and craftsman. He was accused multiple times of criminal acts with young boys; eventually, he was arrested for sodomy, tried, convicted, and sentenced to prison for 4 years. Later, the sentence was commuted to house arrest.

Vasily Gavrilovich Blagolepov, a rector 'til recently, was now a trustee; but, when young, he'd been forcibly dragged by Ivan Ivanych out into society: sickly, a consumptive young man... he had started to mentor him 18 years earlier, right here, in that chair; oh what chicken crap! He, an old teacher, forgotten by petty officials; his pupil though...

Turning reproachfully toward Kuverdayev; and pushing his glasses up onto his nose with two fingers against the two lenses:

"Dear man... don't you know... well the lackeys are running the place: Blagolepov? A ninny!"

He slapped a palm down on his knee as he quipped:

"I think anyone could; oh you too; in ten years, you could be a trustee."

Then his armchair complained, the soft tablecloth slipped to the floor:

"You'd burst into song old man: there, right in front of me, wound a long line of his type: Blagolepovs, every last one, sir," he yelled, only not with his face but a purplish old puss, "So, I pulled them along: just how many I placed, old man – don't even ask – and I gave them all some sort of preferential, dammit..." he failed to find words for his thoughts, and then after stretching five fingers, he made a tight fist with the edge of the tablecloth wrapped-up inside it.

"Cattle like them, it would seem, in... in..." looking for words, he said, "figuratively speaking, it's time, it might seem: put the ministry back in good order... you're... done! I say no: they'd continue the nonsense. Results? We'd have muddle and rot and more questionable moments, I say," he was sweaty, his messy hair waving.

"At one time, I wrote papers for them: Anov, Delyanov, Liyanov, and, dammit, for lousy... the whole of the Scholars' Committee; the Georgievsky Council: they promised; well, what came of that? All my letters collected dust under their carpets: yes, sir!"

Then he leapt up, intending to put his fat nose up against Kuverdayev's, he tossed his eyeglasses up onto his forehead; quite red-browed he walked:

"We had a moment, I'd say: our life tookform; we gave up utopias, finished with revolutions, stopped catastrophic... well... Russia grew stronger... And it would have been possible, I think, little by little to build out a system of schools and achieve universal, yes, education. My writing about a new state university in Saratov attracted attention," he looked up, but no one was listening. "Petty officials and Germans, sir, sat and did nothing. And some well known young prince had arrived with the Germans sir; but, I say that's not the issue!... The Tsar Peacemaker,[74] rationally speaking; right there on the throne and just simply a sad sack,[75] I'm telling you... And the governor-general, dammit, was shipped off to prison: to hell with that pederast (better, they blew him to bits).[76] The Blagolepovs, well what did they do? They reshuffled the pederasts; surely you still can recall Langovoy? Spun like a top!"

And he sat in the wide-legged chair as he panted; dark shadows completed a circle then lowered revealing some scenes from his past.

---

74. Alexander III, known as the Tsar Peacemaker, reigned from 1881-1894.

75. In Russian, "simply a sad sack," is *prosto tyutka*, a clear play on prostitute.

76. Bely is likely referring here to the murder of Moscow's Governor General, Prince Sergei Alexandrovich by anarchists in 1905.

8

He'd been humbled by life since his boyhood; it grabbed on his ear through the hand of a teacher; who tossed him on down to the cook off in back of a curtain; his life could be seen in his louse bites and smelled in the oniony steam near the stove.

He had no close relations or friends!

Zadopyatov, a classmate, was friendly; but later his ego inflated; he greyed and became the one writer who penned introductions to Ibsen (called Ibsen a roaring Norwegian lion, a wonderful mane of grey circling his head),[77] Zadopyatov, considered a torch bearer, writing on Russian societal issues, had marked all the usual milestones, won fame when he wrote *An Apostle of Love and Humanitarianism*, later came speaking engagements in Petersburg, Moscow, and Nizhny, Kazan, and Samara, Saratov and Yekaterinodar, and he published – though rarely, in truth – his own poems.

> *I, tortured with grief, won't take part*
> *In pouring and foaming and clinking,*
> *But will stand up and place in your heart*
> *A codex that sums up my thinking.*
> *If a crude civic foe must be fought*
> *Much harder than natural quartzes*
> *May my codex appear in your thoughts*[78]

---

77. Bely refers to playwright Henrik Ibsen's works throughout the book, most frequently *The Master Builder*. First performed in Berlin in 1893, it is regarded as one of Ibsen's most symbolic and mystical plays. Solness, the master builder, is approaching the end of his career. He longs, however, for youth and the courage to build towers. His ambiguous relationship with Hilde, a much younger woman whom he had first met years before when she was just a girl, is at the heart of the action. Her reckless, almost supernatural character inspires Solness.

78. The weak rhythms and poor rhymes are found in the original, simply indicating a weak effort by Zadopyatov.

A regretful old man's final words. He both led and now symbolized "the" Zadopyatov school; wrote as a critic while hiding behind the two pseudonyms "*Sower*" and "*Petrel*," opining: "*Nikita Vasilyevich stands like a lion, a wonderful mane of grey circling his head*," in both language and style: "Zadopyatovist" thought; an aside: his old colleague and childhood friend, Professor Korobkin, he'd once inappropriately called, "an old turkey and bore."

Out behind that worn curtain they fought the ineffable; there, Zadopyatov pronounced: "All intellectual history is split into eras: the first, Heraclitus the Obscure[79] to Aristotle the Bright: and the second, Aristotle to Kant, also Smiles;[80] and with Smiles came the start of the third."

When Korobkin read Smiles's *Thrift*; its lucidity shone; so he categorized lice in the bathhouse, red roaches, and odors from leeks, and the cook; he drew borders 'round things, he derived rules and principles, formulae; thus, in this way, he established a tolerable life: his baccalaureate thesis, "On integrals," his master's exam, and his targeted studies abroad (the Sorbonne and at Oxford), and talks with the young Poincaré, the mathematician, who gave him his first taste of Paris's boulevards' nightlife ("*Allon*, Korobkin, *le Boulevard, c'est si gai*,")[81] and the work for his masters degree: "On invariants" his doctoral dissertation too: "On the classification of series by general form"; a sensation in Paris and London, his book *Independent Variance* won him his spot as professor; only then did he purchase a ticket to see the play *Humpbacked Horse*[82]; his modest resources forbid entertainment; it all went on books and mathematical *festschrift* and *contrandeau*...

---

79. Heraclitus of Ephesus (c. 535 – c. 475 BCE), a pre-Socratic Greek philosopher famous for the epigram, "No man ever steps in the same river twice."
80. Samuel Smiles (1812-1904), a Scottish writer whose first book, *Self-Help* (1859) made him a celebrity by arguing that poverty was largely a result of irresponsible choices by the poor. *Thrift* (1875) foresaw a larger role for government intervention in the case of market failure.
81. "Let's go, Korobkin, to the boulevard. It's fun there."
82. This reference plays on Korobkin's peculiar body, especially his humped shoulder; a fairy tale in

So these were the achievements, the product of efforts that finally trampled the senselessness: the cook and the room out on Lesser Bronnaya Street (with a view of the trash for a landscape), the curtain had torn; and his books were all scattered around one whole wing of their home facing Snuffsneezer, where now for 25 years he'd sat and conceptualized papers and sought immortality: yes, his "rational clarity" won; the ineffable looked out the window across the way from that yellowish house.

He still feared any senselessness; if he suspected it anywhere, no matter where, he immediately tore out its stinger: he decapitated it, ground it up, shredded it, or swinging the biggest and heaviest cobblestone bashed it to bits: in the basement, however, still sat the ineffable, a prisoner, there, dammit, and always just waiting and toying with some kind of balls; so he lived ever fearful of cracking the door just a bit; or the cook with the oniony breath might start coughing; a cockroach might crawl down the berry-grey wallpaper.

He was frightened of insects.

His worldview was based on two points. For point one: the whole universe trends toward empiricism, clarity, reason; point two: mathematicians (Poincaré, Issi-Nissi, Pshordonner, Shbesh, Klein, Mittag-Leler, and Karl Vyer-Straus) had already arrived there; along the same road, behind them, the main mass of humanity moved, he supported and longed for universal education: society's ills – here alone he had questions.

He wrote to the Scholars' Committee. His letters got coated with dust in their archives; then he got distracted by thoughts of his future,

verse, *The Humpbacked Horse* sometimes known in English as *The Magic Horse* or *The Little Magic Horse*, was written by Petr Pavlovich Yershov (1815-1869) and has been adapted for ballet, film, and other media. A translation has been published by Russian Life Books.

and, assisted by Jacob's ladder,[83] he climbed to a triangle, drawn on its inside, an eye, a place where he could integrate everything, sharing with Leibniz the thought: that our world is the best of all possible worlds.

Therefore, he hated all hints of the word: revolution; he thought the ineffable served as its trigger.

While comfortably daydreaming, he sat on the throne of the Lord God of Hosts in the center of the "Eye": in the pupil!

And during the reign of the Tsar Peacemaker, he'd ruled the whole universe; under Tsar Nicholas,[84] tremors had rocked the parquet in his wing of the house; the professor supported rational criteria; he brandished a pencil: "Clarity, clarity!" So, he demanded a total review of Tolstoy's education curriculum. The Scholars' Committee kept silent. At first he was ready to kill all "the japs": post Tsushima[85] he realized: a nation where people had rationally chosen progressive ideas, dammit, had every right just to wallop us; then, the 1905 revolution[86] had fallen apart; since that time he had been all but mute; when the retrograde label "cadet" grew more common, his eyes, which were rapidly blinking in back of his glasses, had pupils that visibly rolled 'round in panicked, round hoops. [87]

He retreated to integrals, thereby ignoring the senselessness, waiting there nudging his elbow already; in... yes: Vasilisa Sergeyevna took up the banner of pessimism, following, thus, Zadopyatov; and Mitya, the

---

83. Described in *Genesis*, Jacob's ladder is a staircase to heaven that the patriarch Jacob saw in a dream while on the run from his brother Esau.

84. Nicholas II acceded to the throne in late 1894; his official coronation was not until 1896.

85. A war with Japan, fought in 1905, was a resounding defeat for Russia and a sign for many that the old system needed to be changed.

86. A string of uprisings known as the 1905 Revolution, occurred across Russia throughout that year.

87. The Constitutional Democratic Party advocated liberal policies in the closing years of the Russian Empire Its primary support came from professionals and the intelligentsia. Members of the party were called "cadets" as shorthand.

devil, was pawing up Darya; the government's actions and rules... he was horrified trying to think it all through.

He decided against Jacob's ladder, he'd remained in the eye for a while, in his armchair, supported by *catheti*[88] (optimism and evolution) a hypotenuse (clarity) linking them, forming a triangle, just like the ark as it coursed on the flood; the one thing that was left was releasing the doves out the window, with olive branches,[89] his papers; the latest was titled: "On common divisors."

He awoke.

Kuverdayev? The garden: most probably, strolling with Nadya; apparently, he had been left all alone: and everyday life stood before him, too heavy, a burden: insensible.

Nasty, a stink had engulfed the apartment: some shouts: "foo, foo." Angry, and wearing a mousegrey-shade dress (she had changed just for lunch) Vasilisa Sergeyevna sniffed out the source: and she stood right there cursing out Tom; the professor jumped up like a ball that was thrown at a target, and rebounded back when he heard that the source of the problem was found, the dog, Tommie; he'd brought to his corner to chew a most foul-smelling rag from the street; and as they were removing the foul-smelling rag the dog pawed it while turning and pressing it into his drool-covered jowl:

"Grr-ruff-ruff!" While his bloodshot eye sized them up. Pleased, the professor adjusted his specs with two fingers, delaying the rag's swift removal.

"I agree that it stinks; but how was our Tommie to know it was bad?

Vasilisa Sergeyevna squeamishly lifted the hem of her mousegrey-shade dress and demanded:

---

88. Catheti (singular, cathetus) are the two sides of a right triangle that form the right angle. The hypotenuse is the side of a right triangle opposite the right angle.
89. A reference to Noah's ark and the flood in the *Book of Genesis*.

"You nasty dog, give it!"

The hound dog relented and layed down and curled round like a pretzel and hid his nose under his tail while he bitterly howled.

Next, Professor Korobkin appeared with a huge bone in hand (he had probably run for it). Waving the bone as if he was conducting the howls from the dog, he recited some improvised lines (he excelled at improvisation):

> *Truth may be two-sided,*
> *But things have one "it":*
> *This one's a canid,*
> *That one's a kit.*
>
> *Moonlight starts dogs barkin',*
> *That's a well-known fact;*
> *Fate will always hearken,*
> *to the Zodiac.*
>
> *Loyal and devoted,*
> *Tom please take this bone,*
> *Have yourself a chew, but,*
> *Leave the cat alone!*

Such was the start of his nice little Sunday; we too met, this fine day, the Distinguished Professor, an Oxford University doctor.

The bell rang.

So they shooed out the dog; it might be a trustee, that Vasily Gavrilovich; Darya pushed open the door; it was Kiyerko.

"Kiyerko, hi there."

"I'm pleased sir," and so the professor shook hands; quite sincerely: and plainly quite happy; the visitor, squinting his left eye and blinking his right, not with lashes, but reddish swift butterflies; still, like a needle, his little grey pupil went darting along and right through: Vasilisa Sergeyevna, then the professor; the professor, again Vasilisa Sergeyevna.

Average height, thickset, a red trim cut beard, a bit bald: a straight nose, a small curve of a mouth; a red suit;[90] and the way that he slapped his right hand in Korobkin's suggested he visited daily; as if they were close; just like equals.

"So, where have you been?" They repaired to his office.

Where Kiyerko crossed his arms over his vest; and adjusted his patterned suspenders, right there at the ends of the vest, with his fingers, both index and middle:

"Well, sir, well you: how are you?"

Rubbing his bald spot and fixing the edge of the table with one of his eyes, he heard voices:

"Who might that be?"

"Kuverdayev..."

"A beaver, a silver-pelt, by no means the common," he spread out his elbows and flapped just a bit, "how is, well you, Nadezhda Ivanovna?" Swiftly his pupil tracked up from the edge of the desk to Korobkin; from Korobkin down back to the edge of the desk; pirouettes just like this one enabled Kiyerko to spot things that people endeavored to hide.

Then he grabbed the professor: as he was preparing to go; that was Kiyerko:

"Beaver's my favorite, rustic I am; so I wander around; you might say I'm a rambler!"

---

90. Lest Kiyerko's political inclinations escape the reader's attention, Bely put him in a red suit with a red beard and red eyelashes.

He shuffled a bit, absentmindedly; stood there and fingered the edge of his vest, and then turning his shoulder a bit and adjusting the edge of his coat he eyed a huge roach.

"This whole generation acts like they're peasants!" Korobkin adjusted his glasses and looked at him, clearly with pleasure, and even with gusto, like waiting to try a nice dish.

"Yes, that's right, peasants," his left lid aflutter; its pupil then traced out a triangle: roach – the professor's eye – yellow tile – roach.

As he lowered his right hand he pointed his left and he mimed an attack on Korobkin, his finger extended, resembling a rapier move known as a *"prima,"* it seemed he'd exclaimed, in reproach, with no way to withdraw the remark: *"J'accuse!"*[91]

"You're a peasant, like me; a nice lunch with fine trimmings, well, you: things are not as they seem: and we share the same problems."

Roach – the professor's eye – yellow tile – roach:

"Just like horse collars, yes, we're on the shelf, we sit idle. However," he addedemphatically, "collars hang up on a hook: 'til they're buckled."

The visit transformed: it was quiet, relaxed, entertaining; but awful, a bit: and quite interesting. Noticing Tommie, who'd opened the door with his muzzle, he crouched, snapped his fingers:

"A hound, yes, humongous, *Canis domesticus,* hi; there's a saying," he turned on his heel, "'if you love me, you'll love my dog too: and so, hounddog, your paw!'"

He grabbed the dog's ear and he stretched it down over its nose, which was salty, wet, canine:

"A pointer, a purebred; but I see a flaw, yes a flaw: oh my, brother," he crookedly offered Korobkin a smile, who warmed when he saw the

---

91. A comic reference to a serious matter, the so-called Dreyfus Affair in France (1894), when an officer, Louis Dreyfus, was accused of crimes against the state, but it later became apparent that it was an anti-semitic campaign. Attacking the proceedings, writer Emile Zola published a front-page open letter in a popular newspaper under the title *J'accuse* ("I Accuse").

attention he paid to his dog, "I'm an animal too, but approaching perfection; while you, for now, no."

Then he "caught it": the owner and hound had quite similar lines in the nose and the jaw.

Kiyerko paid great attention to trivia: he noticed small details; and later he'd put them together as parts of a whole; his conclusions struck most as completely spot-on; and compelling; his memory worked like the purse of a miser: where various bits were forever at hand, half-completed descriptions, small details: one might call it trash; with it Kiyerko built unassailable arguments: often, his predictions seemed perfect, true iron-clad fact; but before every deadline he dawdled: he fussed with the curtains, had bouts of complaining; and paced with a hint of a waltz in his step.

And he seemingly finished just one-tenth of everything possible: he used various pseudonyms in letters to *Chess Review*: they were "Kiyerko," "Sir" also "Puck"; although most folks used "Kiyerko," that was his favorite.

"Call me, well, "Kiyerko": really, my name is too long; tell me who the hell knows it: 'Tsetserko-PuKiyerko.'"

He finished one-tenth and left all the rest of the tenths, as he said, on the divan at home, in a 3-story white house nearby on a huge lot; its first floor was filled with the poor, but the second was nicer. And Kiyerko lived there; from there he had come to play chess maybe 25 years (he remembered Korobkin when he was a bachelor).

"An intelligent scoundrel, Tsetserko-PuKiyerko: too bad he's so lazy."

At times there were people who tried to grab on to the tenth that life gave him, considering Kiyerko only a boon for themselves: but somehow it never turned out like they thought. Korobkin took note: if he got just an inkling of Kiyerko, Kiyerko soon rang the doorbell, and smoothly appearing relaxed, and as if they had spoken just earlier.

Kiyerko was not in the way at Korobkin's; he seemed to observe all the household's traditions: played chess with Korobkin; he worked on duets with Nadezhda (he lugged his violincello along); and he sparred Vasilisa Sergeyevna, labeling *Russian Thought* [92] trash and *European Courier* too: with the cook, he made pickles; or puffing his pipe while he twitched his right shoulder and nose, with a finger pushed under his vest he would poke all around underneath his own armpit, and then he would dig out some pellets: a gag, and pure "Kiyerko."

But sometimes he'd suddenly vanish; and not show his nose for a while; then appear once again, and quite often: the professor's wife even considered the man a real source.

"That Tsetserko, I say, *à propais*, is he published in *Iskra?*" [93]

"Oh Vassochka…" chuckled Korobkin. [94] But once he inquired:

"Do you, Kiyerko, really…"

But Kiyerko tapped at his pipe (when he puffed, he sent tiny clouds flying), and answered the, damn him, question quite cryptically.

"Meetings, and assemblies," puff, puff, "are forbidden by law…"

Then he blinked his left eye; and he turned up his beard and his pipe at the ceiling:

"A spider web: time to get cleaning in here." And he steered the entire conversation to what? To a spider web!

Yes, the professor was happy to speak with Kiyerko; just that same morning he'd thought:

---

92. *Russian Thought* was a literary and political journal published in Moscow from 1880-1918; *European Courier* was a liberal magazine published in Russia from 1865 to 1918.

93. Bely has Vasilis Sergeyevna mispronounce one of her common expressions, emphasizing again her intellectual pretension; *Iskra* was Lenin's party newspaper.

94. The chuckle can be understood as nervous cover for her statement, really an accusation given the day's politics. Bely exaggerates the notoriety and power of Iskra (and Lenin).

"PuKiyerko should visit; we'd sit and play chess."

He arrived.

So they sat: and they set up the board:

"Well, you, fine... Take a look at your queen... Just like always, what's new?... Blagosvetlov!"[95]

"Taking your pawn."

"Hey, waiting for the ice to break? Your move." His pupil, not unlike a cricket, jumped briskly, from object to object; he got it back under control:

"So, what if," and the professor slid forward a piece, "but no: all will remain as it was."

"They, well, need him," he said while advancing a knight, "they've swept all the junk in a pile, but a bastard like that has protection, that's the way, the tradition... It stinks like it's rotten: no, I, you know, I am an orderly, I keep the place clean, I... you're moving the queen?"

"Well you, Kiyerko, you are a socialist."

"That's what you say; you're 'conservative'? No, you know what?" and he nodded his nose, took his pipe, and he knocked it out, sneezed, then he coughed and he drew on the stem: puff, puff, as thin smoke streams shot out.

"Clearly, the queen."

"You're an anarchist: really a wrecker: you're muddling their heads with your math... And, well: they would have destroyed you; you'd figured it out, the whole thing; it's entirely natural; and they'd have said patriotism plus all the rest; were the 'japs' a true threat? You became a

---

95. Kiyerko seems to be joking here in the elliptical way common among friends. He may be referring to G.E. Blagosvetlov, the owner and publisher of *Russian Thought* who accepted ownership of the journal for free from a friend who had tired of unending disputes with writers and censors. Frequent polemics with other publications often included barbed questions about the price of the acquisition and, suggestively, the worth of the journal. In this case, Kiyerko is needling Korobkin, who is about to give away his queen on the chessboard.

conservative; this, let me note, is insulting, a thumb and four fingers stuck right in your face: 'cause you live for your math…" and he furiously stoked-up his pipe while he chomped it, his fingers tucked in his suspenders, and he turned up his nose.

"Well then, I'll take your queen."

"What the devil."

"Our liberals, sir, are full-grown conservatives; yes, the right light makes things look like their opposite; wolves look like sheep, and then sheep look like wolves," puff-puff, smoke flew in clouds.

Then he wiggled his shoulder a bit and walked past as he blinked his left eyelid.

"Compare for me please two plain fractions; let's start with numerators "two" and, say, "three.""

"I would work out the least common denominator!" shouted Korobkin.

"Then?"

"Multiply the numerators."

"We use the same method," said Kiyerko, bending and pointing a finger.

"The least common denominator is the equalization of all economic relationships; multiplication, is the growth of our wealth: well… to multiply wealth we first find the least common denominator: our fronts are united."[96]

The professor, not listening, waved his palm over the board, now quite empty.

"Well, dammit, a stalemate: not check or a checkmate."

---

96. Bely is playing here a bit through Kiyerko, drawing on the Bolshevik idea of a united front of workers and peasants in the struggle against capitalism. Suggesting an alliance between mathematicians and revolutionaries, Kiyerko is courting the professor's good will.

A relaxed and smooth atmosphere reigned: but it grew both amusing, and scary, a bit.

Well that's Kiyerko.

10[97]

Mitya and Gribikov struggled away from the throatydebates of the market, approached the Arbat as they pushed their way through the manyleggedhuman; the whole place was terribly littered, lit-up by the unblinking eye of a street lamp's reflector.

Next, the Arbat, unavoidable.

Gribikov hardly took time for a sneeze before pouncing:

"Have many such books?"

The boy turned not a face, but a fist (since his face had the look of a fist, with his nose sticking out like the tip of a thumb when making the rudest of gestures).

"So what's it to you?" And he sulked:

"Well, if you are just giving away all these scholarly works, may I say…"

"That you'll sell…"

"It would seem, sir, the old man isn't giving you money at all?" countered Gribikov spitefully. "Nowadays, even a rat needs some money," he added.

"Not much, as you see…"

"What?"

"He doesn't give…"

"Pushyoldbusybody," thought Mitya, if only he'd leave…

"Well it seems clear to me that your place should be rented-out, horde-ed:[98] instead there's just him, and your mama, and you, and

---

97. The numbering in the original skips from section 8 to section 10, with no section 9.
98. With a home, university position, and foregone rental income, Korobkin seems wealthy to Gribikov.

"Nowadays, even a rat needs some money."

Nadezhda Ivanovna, meaning, it seems, that he lives on a fourth of what's possible, and he simply begrudges you money."

There, Gribikov caustically nodded.

"Farewell." With that Mitya escaped. But just barely.

Gribikov instantly spun; passed heehawinghawkers, considered the question (and not with his mind but his gut, and it noticed and knew about everything), aiming his steps to the dustbowl, returned to that very same booth:

"So hey, bud, can you show me the book there by Spencer, the one that the rich little pup brought, I'll pay, but not much."

"A ruble and 25."

They talked, and they haggled, and they waggled their tongues:

"So, brings them here, does he?"

"He comes by: he's brought maybe 40 in all, but he steals them I think."

"Oh the parents, the parents! The father lives grandly, a general; and I've known for some time that on Sundays the boy has been leaving the house with small bundles; a shame."

"And so that's what they're like; learn to read, start to rob; and the father robs too; oh, I know them."

Gribikov slipped off the street with the copy of Spencer; and entered unpeopled, dark alleys; at night they were peopled; all day they stood empty.

A house, on the corner, a rather large house; a small, dark-featured man rushed around in a pince-nez; with sharp looking eyes and a striped hat; and Gribikov knew him: a gent from Nikolsky;[99] "they" came for

---

99. Bely may be referring here to ghostwriters who worked for theatrical production companies writing material for the stage, often by adapting and rewriting foreign works to the point of unrecognizability. Familiar as he was with the Mocow literary scene, Bely was surely at least acquainted with the practice, which is described in *Moscow & Muscovites*, by Vladimir Gilyarovsky, translated by Brendan Kiernan, Russian Information Services 2013, p. 313.

Mr. Ivanov; "Mr." Rachinsky yelled with a cigarette propped in his lips: "Isaiah, rejoice,"[100] so they raced to the door; then Mr. Ivanov, a scribbler, invited him in; where they'd smoke right 'til dawn; which was fine, they were average guys. And old Gribikov knew all the houses and rooms and apartments in seven-odd Rottentooth Alleys and Snuff-sneezer; here for example, this building: why empty? A prince named Kitaisky had died when he choked on a bone nearly 25 years past; the dead prince appears here at night: and he chokes; and he chokes every night; there's no proof of these chokings. His wife lives abroad with their daughter, a princess who cannot get married; she's enlisted, an army; an army that really exists; the army for scammers' salvation.[101]

11

Gribikov walked through the yard past bald patches with bits of old bottles and went by the white house; he stood there and blabbed with a crone in cheap slippers; the crone pointed out a pale gentleman:

"'Uncle Kolya says this, and her 'Uncle Kolya' says that, simply everything's 'Uncle' and 'Uncle.' If *he* is an uncle, let him *act* like an 'uncle,' but she calls him 'Kolya': I heard it, I did…"

"Well, he's Nikolai Ilych from Kaloshin…"

"Together they purr little tunes."

And the lady that they were discussing was bundled in muslin; in summer she suffered from hay fever; colds in the fall; all across and above the small house clumps of clouds growing whiter had blown in; their shadows were fixedlikeinmarble; they sang:

---

100. Like Christ the Savior, prophesied by Isaiah, this man was expected; hence, the slang phrase.
101. Bely is referring here to the Salvation Army, which operated in Russia from 1913 to 1923, when it was dissolved for its alleged "anti-Soviet" character.

Forgive me, heavenly creature,
For disturbing your peace.[102]

A man sat on the stoop, quite a bigmouth, a boozer, red eyes and red freckles; and lazier than lazy, he eyeballed his filthy old boot; at that, Gribikov's words were all business:

"Time for the scrap heap!"

He fingered his wart and he stared at his finger as if he might see something.

"Again with the bruises, your mug?" And he sniffed at his finger.

And, scratching himself, the man opened his mouth and displayed bad teeth spewing bad breath and bad booze:

"We opened a bottle, 'cause life is a mess."

A pig's snout poked his knee.

"Hey, Romanych, you're all coveredwithsnot," Gribikov ratsmirked, "and look at your face: it's so purple, an eggplant."

"That's nothing, the 'beer'!"

Then they opened the beaten-up door to a room with the reek of old urine; they went to the kitchen; a woman was cleaning her face with warm steam, no cosmetics from France used in that place; fat cockroaches scurried and whiskeredalong up above an old drain; something nasty and oily had seeped there. The house was all peopled-up, roachified, smoky and noisy; its windows were soaped and the floors strewn with filth, in the hall was a rug with all kinds of dried stains.

The door's rusty lock squeaked; in the room a stale stiflingstink, it was damp, had a filthy old bed with a beat-up, thin blanket, a dirty old dresser, daguerreotypes, moths: a man slumped on a crude trunk and

---

102. The quotation derives from A.S. Pushkin's *Queen of Spades*, a short story about gambling, greed, and human nature. In 1890, the work was turned into an opera by Tchaikovsky, and these lines are sung by the main character, Hermann, to Liza, his love.

grieved; and then Gribikov, after he sniffed at his finger, rejoined a discussion that probably started much earlier but never concluded.

"Romanych, just *think*: oh, why live in this mess?" But Romanych just waved with a yellow-haired arm.

"I will die here: I've nowhere to go."

"Well just yesterday you said you would: took the dough!"[103]

"So, I took it, I drank it; and for you, not a 'whiff,' and I'd do it again."

"That's what you think, well... Mr. Mandro gave you..."

"What?... It's a gift, if he wants this old louse nest so badly…"

"To you, it's a louse nest, so why must you stay here? To you it's a louse nest, to him, it's the Promised Land." Gribikov didn't just glare at him, no, the man crapped on the guy with his eyes, "tell me why are you renting a room when you'll live maybe five years and die: in a clinic."

"I could still get married."

"Mr. Mandro has proposed that I give you a hundred to put his new guy in your place: a haphazard affair; will you naysay Mandro? In the end, he's Mandro," and a grimacing Gribikov hissed in his ear: "can't you *smell* things are nasty, and he'll make it worse, it will stink; and he'll go to the cops, get you pinched and sent home with no patchport."[104]

Then, savage Romanych letloosewithsomeyelling:

"I'd smash him to splinters with just my bare fist; we're aware of Mandro, von-Mandro. I'll deal with Mandro by myself; and what's with the grousing; I saw his guy yesterday: dragged himself down here; just filthy, a dwarf, with his face all infected, no nose...[105] And so why pick

---

103. The reference here is to *aleksandreyka*, a fabric. The word is used in this context either as slang for cash or for an item (the fabric) that would have been easy to sell at the market.
104. Gribikov mispronounces passport, but the larger point is that Romanych's passport does not have a Moscow residence stamp. He has what is known as a "wolf's" passport, which was a common practice in those days, and still is, for people who want the benefits of life in the capital but do not have the money or connections needed to get proper paperwork.
105. The dwarf's name is Ludwig Avgustovich Kavalkas, and he is a longtime criminal associate of

on me?" His head dropped to the table, and he covered his face with his fists, shook with sobs.

"You accepted the cash," uncontrollably trembling, Gribikov hissed just like butter when dropped on a griddle; a yellow fog covered the group: "He will force you to lick a hot griddle, endure boiling oil; he, my good friends, is not like other men: he will not..."

Gribikov paused, then he spoke in a quiet and even sweet voice so the walls could hear too:

"Well who cares if he hasn't a nose, he's a person and sick, and so what of it, brother! Mandro is just trying to help find a home for him. I say God bless him."

Suddenly, piercing the wall, which apparently did have an ear, yipped a woman:

"Romanych, you better stand firm, or he'll ruin you; the room has been paid for, and who's gonna drive you out? I'll tell you, Sila Moseyich,[106] it's very unfitting at your age, just scaring the man: push a drunk to his ruin.[107]

And then, after it spoke, the wall stopped, or more accurately, people behind it shut-up, and then Gribikov coughed:

"You'll get yours, hag!"

He left and he sat on a bench and smokeduptheair all around him, expecting the sky togrowlight and the gloom to disperse and the clouds to clear up, that the burst disk then hooded on high, that was scream-ing-out heat would become an extinguished, and cooled, rose-toned sun, and unblinking would glide off and into the rustling trees.

Thin and curly red smoke from the chimney was grabbed and blown off by a breeze; and the panes of a red-eyed small house stared out at

---

Mandro's. He appears here with no introduction, but the reader should take note.

106. She is speaking to Gribikov, so here we learn his first name and patronymic, which are clearly Jewish.

107. The woman's speech is uneducated.

the twilight, were later cloaked off by a wrinkled old blanket of darkness: the coloration, during the day, a most strikingly beautiful pattern of spots, in the evening slowly toned down; it was night there outside of the windows: they partied like savages, yellow-eyed flames; an old crone dressed in chintz and a dark yellow blouse, with long needles was knitting with care a grey sock from the fates of the people; at that hour, in back, a ridiculous concert, a mixture, non-sensical singing and left-handed fiddling; everything finished in fistfights, the women stood whining; and a nose bloodydripping; a scream that attracted a glance out a window by someone quite frightened.

Gribikov silently stared at the night, half-expecting to spot assignations of one type or another; perhaps see a crone, an old woman, in a worn-out and yellowish blouse and a faded old hat, scraps of cotton; toward evening she'd seem to expand to a massive old woman, there knitting her fateful and thousand-thread sock. That woman was Moscow.

12

"*À propos*, I will say: the Likhoveshchanskys and Kudakovs, both from old money, served apples and sandwiches made with dried-out old cheese; what's his name, Tyuk..."

"Dvutetyuk, it's not tyuk..."

"Dvutetyuk..."

"Not ashamed?" the professor asked turning, "dear friend... all these trivial people."

Vasilisa Sergeyevna, rigid with anger, said:

"Life is that way: and it's you that flies off to empiricism, not seeing that Nadya does not even have a presentable visiting dress."

"Oh my friend," the professor tossed down his knife, "that's a trifle; consider an algebra problem, a letter is written above any number," he turned and he pointed his nose at a fly; Vasilisa Sergeyevna said:

"'We're not numbers,' declares Zadopyatov...," and then she declaimed:

> *You think glances are oh so revealing,*
> *Here is something your numbers can't parse*
> *Noble, burning inside me a feeling*
> *That is bursting to flame in my heart...*

"Well, I've sewn Zadopyatov a book cover."

"Again Zadopyatov!"

"Well, go right ahead: you could sew him a girdle!"[108] Hundred-foot-stomping his way down the corridor. Mitya arrived:

Were you called-on today?

"I recited… a question on grammar…"

"Well, really, so how did you do?"

Mitya well knew that his father could not acquiesce to a B, he would shout at a C, and a D'd just flatten him; Mitya turned red and he frowned and he gnawed at the nubs of his nails.

"I… got… an A…"

"Things are clear: there's no need now to tear at your clothes! You're a *slob*!" Through grey twilight, where yellow-brown bindings stood out on the brownish-grey shelves, the professor went into his office, his face like a dog's; and in there, on his desk, much like ash blown by wind, was a pile, a huge number of all types of papers, long papers, short papers, wee papers, all scribbled and crossed-out, rewritten; he looked at a cyst (on a finger, his right hand), ran his eyes through the papers (to cross out again the once crossed-out analysis crammed in the margin… and so on); a fidget, he tapped both his feet.

---

108. Korobkin does not seem to resent Zadopyatov, but does not miss the chance to make a weak joke.

Then he rummaged around on the top of the shelf with a veined hand; he sought an edition of Ben that he needed; the first tome was, dammit, was gone from the face of the damn earth. Just lately he'd noted one fact: that was, book after book had been vanishing; books about math went untouched; although someone was touching the rest.

All the veins in his forehead felt tight, with sweat soaking the mop on his head, the professor cracked open the door to the shelf, and assaulted the books, set to moving and putting them back willy-nilly, and did it again, tossed them back on the shelf: yes, yes. Ben was gone; that was real cause for concern: in its pages he'd buried some sheets; calculations, and most, most essential (his drawer in the desk had been stuffed, chock full):

"Basically, dammit!

Then he wallowed around like a hippo and sighed while he wandered from bookshelf to bookshelf; and walked 'twixt the arms of the chair and a table; he dug up a pair of his glasses down under some papers; thank God, he exhaled when he spotted his other pair... there on his nose.

In the window already, a berry-red dawn; but a red sky at dawn was a sign there'd be rain.

So he started to look at some integrals.

Down in the jumble matured a mathematical discovery, an idea in mechanics; defying predictions: its use in due time would upend all the sciences, accelerate maximum speed to... the speed of a damn ray of light.

His hand, violet veins standing out, held the stub of a pencil and shook: he leaned into the table; gone yellow with obstinance; throwing his elbows across, and then scrabbling his legs on the chair, with a quick hand he scribbled parentheses, modules, and other math symbols along with "P," "Z," and "F."

The author of thick books and articles grasped by just ten men of science from Berlin, Paris, New York, Stockholm, Buenos Aires and London, united by shared mathematical *"compte rendus,"*[109] but divided by languages, oceans, beliefs, and their lifestyles and tastes: the same word started each of his articles, "Suppose…"; next a formula, three-pages long, and then a decipherable *"and* suppose *that,"* then a formula (three pages) up to the words "with the condition that," and a formula (three pages too) that included a lapidary "then, if" that summoned a series of models, differentials and integrals crowned by an eloquent but universally impenetrable: "thus," at the bottom a signature: I.I. Korobkin; if one were to read all the words in the piece, and exclude the equations that can't be expressed in plain language, the only words left would be: Suppose…. Suppose… Then… Thus… with the silence of formulae, weighty and ready to smash all to pieces the engines of steamships and trains, and to launch in the oceans and skies fleets of ships and whole squadrons of planes with innovative new motors, the sight of which would make the generals in all other countries drop dead.

His most recent four works were of similar import; but Korobkin downplayed them; only ten scientists grasped the most recent, which barely alluded to things soon to come; and Ivan Ivanyich's works were translated in all of the West; in the Far East; small groups of professors discussed all his papers; ideas; Issi-Nissi, a Nagasaki professor already was planning a journey to Moscow; to speak in the flesh with Ivan Ivanych, to declare for all humans their… and, well, so on and so forth… He straightened up, scratching his waist ("tell me please, that the flea-bitten Tom-dog sat here on this chair"); then he pondered some formulae; after he dug all around in his books and a pile of papers, and splatteredsomedrops of blue ink; he arrived at the formula; "N minus

---

109. article, report.

one, divided by two… In parentheses, squared… Plus… N minus two, divided by two, squared… Plus… And so forth… Plus, minus… square root…" he refilled his pen.

While his facewasallwrinkled from laughter he grabbed his thick leg, which was crossed at the knee quite triumphantly, looking as if he had climbed 200 obstacles; his shirt tails stuck out because of his hump; and they crackled with starch when he pressed his chin into the starch; he had pinched a small tuft of his beard with two fingers; and jammed it up into his nose.

From the corner, the usual evening shadows descended; the moon up, its lilybeams slicing the bottlegreen glow of the twilight; the shadows established the borders; between all the houses: the pathos of distance.

Slowly he straightened while clasping his hands at the small of his back; as this pulled in his stomach; his head slid back onto his neck as if drawn to his spine.

"I wish Tsetserko-PuKiyerko would come by: I'd sure like to play chess."

The canary had toyed with a ball in its cage the whole evening; the air in the rooms had gone thick with the absence of people; and shadows arose from the corners on lily-wings; back in the corner, and cruel, a creatureofdarkness foretold a collapse with a threatening finger.

And clung to the windowpane: Moscow.

13

He walked with a light fromthedark.

The weak rays of the condul shone into the gloom and off to the sides of the room and completing a circle, they dropped, cut apart; and there, peering from under the potted palms, Nadya was sliced by a ribbon of moonlight.

"My friend, may I enter?"

His small brown eyes peeked in: at Nadya, the bronzes, the doily on top of the chair and an antimacassar.

"Oh Papa," said Nadya, her face like a song, as she looked.

"Just one minute," he said, slightly raising his glasses.

As always his visit began with the words "I'm not bothering you," "just for a minute," "it's nothing"; she knew that it never was "nothing," he felt an internal imperative: he came to sit for a moment and share a few disjointed words.

He quietly groanedasmallseriesofgroans as he looked at some grapes, they'd been carved and then lacquered; he played with a pencil stub; used it to scratch at the back of his ear; when the Snuffsneezer house, No. 6, had stood out in a forest of integrals; he'd gone walking: to Nadya.

"Oh, Papa, you know that you never annoy me." He slapped on his knee with the palm of his hand: while he sharpened his thoughts like a pencil.

"Oh… What did you say?"

"Oh it's nothing."

She knew there was much of the "what" that he'd "say" so she waited. And finally, after a time, his thoughts setjustlikeconcrete:

"Kuverdayev…"

"Well, I should have known!" And she smiled.

"So what can you tell me, dear daughter, about him?"

He stood like an oakrock (quite awkward): and always for her he'd been "Papa."

"I'll say Kuverdayev's deceitful, ill-tempered."

Then straight-legged he walked to the wall, where the lily-grey wallpaper's berry-red accents baited him: berry-red accents: and, musing, he took out his pencil and circled a berry.

"But how can it be you don't see it yourself?" Then he battered a berry with words.

"How could you... Well, he is an actor of sorts... and then, after all, he seems happy with *some*thing," and he wiped off his palms:

"So then, basically..."

Playing the bumpkin and lowering one shoulder, he lay back on the divan, looked up, as if innocent: wide-nosed, bespectacled.

"Papa, so that's how you are: a bit crafty," Nadya cooedlikeadove.

"Oh what can you be saying!"

"Well, you're pleased yourself that I'm talking about him this way."

Then she loosed, in the mirror, her braid, thicknsoft chestnut.

"Why act?!"

And her eyes saw right into his soul:

"Are you satisfied?"

Betraying his ruse with a smile, he relaxed.

"And so, basically..."

He held his tongue, took out matches, a box: and he laid them down parallel, angled, and squared; as he searched for the words, could not find them; his mind left and wandered; it flowed 'til it reached his subconscious.

Light rain; it raindropped then droppedout and quickly.

He rose and he clomped as he paced:

"Yes, yes, do you know..."

He was surprised when he looked out the window: stray light from a windowside lamp at the neighbors' cast shadows from devilgone this-tles.[110]

"You know, I just don't understand this... Just where is this leading?" A violet shape stuck to the window.

"Now nothing is clear." Then he stomped all around: and sat down once again.

He was thinking of Mitya; now just getting worse as he watched, such a slob, in a moth-eaten jacket, his wrists sticking out, with a faceful of feathery whiskers: his lazy mug leering while Darya washed floors with her skirt hiked: he just stood there and panted, all flushed and ignoring harsh whispers each morning: "I'll go to my lady."

"There's Darya, you know, but he somehow... gets A's..."

"Gets A's?"[111]

"I mean Mitya."

He drummed with his fingers: tra-tata, tra-tata, tarara-tata.

"Yes, sir," tarara-tata.

Whispering aspens like thieves could be heard in the garden.

"But basically, he's a young man, and so it's understandable..."

"But all in all, in the end..."

"And concerning what I saw with Darya..." well, no: he said not a word; after all Nadya, well yes, if you please, as a lady..." And so, af-ter tossing around disconnected ideas (Kuverdayev, metaphysics, and Mitya) he lifted the condulstub.

"Sleep, sleep, my daughter."

He smooched her good night.

---

110. Devilgone, *chertogon*, is the popular name for a weed common throughout Russia, *Eryngium planum*, also widely known as bluehead. Folk wisdom holds that a vase of devilgone shelved over a door will prevent the passage of unkind or unfriendly people.

111. Nadya is surprised at the word *pyat* (five) as a grade (A) for Mitya. She may confuse it with the word for foot/heel as mentioned earlier for the name Zadopyatov.

Fromthelight he returned to the dilating darkness; out into a thicket of questions.

And Nadya sat under the palms; while she quietly gazed at the beaded night light, where a moon of chalcedony[112] shone its first quarter, appearing translucent, its setting dark violet.

And time, like a terrified rabbit, ran off for the door.

In a flash, by the first light of morning, the frost had licked everything: loudly sleet clinked all around, then it clankedoff; rain flooded, reflooded the leafcover; while cloudcover strode through the sky; and whole puddles were cried; the earth drunkenly drank down decay.

Begrudgingly, morning glowedweakly.

Ivan Ivanych, still wrapped in a grey robe, with washedoutandyellowed lapels, his belly secured by its belt; at the window he gawked at the puddles the sky had just spit.

The horizon was covered with clouds tinted blue; and red chimneys sketched pencil-line smoke; and... and...

"What could that be?"

At the house, on the far side, now fadedtoyellow, aired out by the window where Gribikov usually sat; there enjoying a drink, a man crouched, then he stuck out his head with black hair, and while stroking his sideburns with both hands, directed his eyes at Korobkins'; as

---

112. Chalcedony, a variety of quartz, often greyish or milky, can be semi-transparent or translucent; many semi-precious gemstones, such as agate, are varieties of chalcedony; This is likely another, somewhat veiled reference to one of Kuverdayev's favorite topics, Benvenuto Cellini, a medieval Italian artist accused of sodomizing boys. It is said that Cellini crafted a chalcedony masterwork and gave it to the Pope, who in gratitude absolved him of his sins.

he pulled his head back, he bumped into the frame; then a slam: then, as usual, nothing.

A racket commenced: tools and lumber, the squeal of wood splitting.

The impersonal, urban cacophony cacked.

14

The door opened; it spit the professor out sideways; he stooped, one black paw was most awkwardly squeezing an open umbrella, a brown leather case in the other, and wearing a black hat; his brown beard hung down in his collar.

"Deplorable wind!"

A hunched spine; a nose, crumpled and propping up glasses haphazardly; cobbles of hard stone were rounding and rumbling: a blue-nosed cab driver used reins on his horse; and goading the driver, a woman was wearing a lily coat topped with a bluefeathered hat, and was holding a very nice purse and a box tied with ribbons; and that's when he knew: Vasilisa Sergeyevna.

"She, truth be told, is delivering the cover she's sewn Zadopyatov."

The humanthing swarmed; and out there was a corner; and here was the hub-bub of carriages; a taxi flew past; and a general, chaffeured; and some vases, nice crystal, a shop window display.

So he started to run for the tram; where he jammed himself into the crush: Mokhovaya bound; so then he jumped and he crossed in the path of a carriage, went into the yard, and then raced with a group of some happy-faced students:

"Professor Korobkin!"

"Where?"

"There!"

Out of breath, he ran into the doorway's grey damp; the old doorman walked him to the coat room. "Like always, sir, everything's filled!"

He immediately saw: Zadopyatov there flowing along down the hallway; surrounded by students.

"That's fine… or a girdle," unbidden, he thought.

Zadopyatov's locks, white, like a peacock's fan fell on his collar and shoulders, a soft wave that broke on his cheeks, lined by wrinkly thick jowls; his nose dripped in his silver groomed beard which was topped by a dirty and yellow-stained mustache; a curl hung down, hiding his wrinkled, small brow.

And his eye, what an eye, was swollen, and watery, bulging, its eyelid was puffy, and wet with his tears; his coat stretched, a balloon, that barely just covered his gut and the place from which bulged, monumentally, something upon which, basically speaking, people sit down (where his handkerchief hung).

Zadopyatov, when seated, was taller than everyone, really a giant; when standing he wasn't, his legs were too short.

With some ceremony, taking small steps, Zadopyatov flowed-off and froze-out the student who clung to his side, and then, squinting one eye, made a rousing remark:

"We have no constitution."

He dryly stuck out swollen fingers while pursing his lips with a look that said:

"Really, I don't know: can I shake your hand, and avoid getting smeared with a mess?"

With cadets to one side, he just stood there and pulled on his lip with an insincere, bitter-sweet grimace; but when a cadet stood before him, he quickly became a respectable dear, and most charming, his hair curly, bouffant, one huge swollen eyeball protruding: his fingers all puffed-up but waving.

"I know you… It was you, Milyukov, Dolgoruky… with them, in the days of the Petrunkeviches…"

Tightly encircled, he stood; and they asked him to sign "Zadopya-tov," his book; so then loosing his pince-nez, he'd opened the cover, inscribed a few words (about sowing fields, everything honorable), fold-ing his brow up in meaty lined shelves.

He'd long been a Field Marshall: the critics' artillery, a known heli-ometer measuring "weather" but constantly skewed;[113] and he'd often arrested opinions in scholarly journals;[114] and planted careers behind bars; although now they had torn themselves out with the aim of up-rooting this rotting but somehow still living old oak; though his roots were still holding, he was fiddling quite ominously in search of the criti-cal line as he dared to assume he could work like a simple harmonica; harmonize goals, while establishing society's rhythms, and running its word parade. Here, Ivan Ivanych recalled a mean-spirited verse:

Ladies, lights, a few folks clapping,
Scholars waited, water too,
Students stuffed-in, overlapping…
Some beard standing in full view.

With his bald spot safely hidden,
Five years more to celebrate
Zadopyatov starts oration
Water bearer, billed as great.[115]

---

113. A heliometer is a telescope that measures angular distances, such as those between stars. In this case the "weather" refers to political trends.

114. Bely refers here to "thick" journals, indicating the high page count, not the mental acuity of their readers. This word is short-hand for hefty but widely-read literary journals.

115. This is a reference to the myth of the Trojan boy Ganymede, said to be the most beautiful hu-man, raped by Zeus, taken prisoner, and made cup-bearer to the gods on Olympus. Ganymede tired of his duties and poured out the gods' wine, causing floods on earth, and ending his time on Olympus. Zeus gave him eternal life, transforming him into a constellation today known as Aquarius. References to this myth recur throughout the novel.

Twenty-five years, squinting eyelid
Thick grey lashes, wore a suit
Ruined him was all they did
Made him a true tailored coot

Swollen ego and unstable
Like bubbles blown from soap
His stupid bulging eye disabled
Turned and slanted, staring up

His conclusion, fainting, shouting
In our greedy, debauched land,
Zadopyatov, you're astounding,
You have spirit, you're our man

Someone chimed in standing near:
"Somehow all the logic's sound:
'Cause, 'zad' in old Slavonic's 'rear':
And his is huge and round.

Zadopyatov bumped into Ivan Ivanych right outside the professors' buffet.

"Hi," Zadopyatov assumed a harmonious look as he noddedhisbeardasawelcome:

"My hemorrhoids simply are torture."

At his height, Ivan Ivanych would say Zadopyatov's bad eye had the look of a fish's if served on its side on an egg white.

"Did you hear?"

"What?"

"Blagolepov is being appointed."

"And what of it, sir?"

"Oh, we'll see the results," and his eye, one of Moscow's attractions, much like the tsar-cannon, or even the tsar-bell,[116] was set in a thicket of lashes; he stood with a pained look, his bodyslumpeddown, he was limp: it was hemorrhoid torture!

That said, Ivan Ivanych thought:

"Fool."[117]

And, unsettled, he shuffled his feet just a bit:

"You should visit, Nikita Vasilyevich, sometime: come see us..."

For his part, it seemed to Nikita Vasilyevich that:

"Yes, eh-eh-eh, his brain has gone soft."

The thought softened his attitude:

"Maybe I somehow..."

They parted.

Students then mobbed Zadopyatov; he nodded his head and his stiff swollen fingers adjusted his pince-nez, then traced in the air an entrancing parabola: with this parabola, he tried but he failed to hook onto and hoist up a Ganymede-student, like Zeus as an eagle incarnate.

The professors' buffet was clouded with smoke: his brow green,[118] a colleague tried pushing Ivan Ivanych off into a corner; the lunch break was ending: and elephant-footed and snake-haired old men herded past to the lecture hall. Putting his papers away in a folder, Professor Korobkin flew out of the room and he sped down the hall; a young student, an aide, pushed by boys hairunkempt in unbuttoned grey coats, then approached the professor to stop him and show him

---

116. Tsar cannon and the tsar bell bear the moniker "tsar" because of their large size. They are both popular tourist attractions, even today, for first-time visitors to Moscow.

117. The word used here by Bely, *durak*, is a good example of the general rule that many epithets, in Russian, carry much heavier weight than their English counterparts. The thought is strong enough, for a moment, to throw Korobkin, usually emotionally blind, off his stride.

118. Green-browed: too much nicotine.

his place; so the limping, and awkwardpawed man with dirty hands followed behind.

A mathematical audience awaited him.

15

There!

He saw chairs piled with bodies, in grey and white jackets and shirts; and they filled all the windowsills too; his department; they lined all the walls and the halls; a small table was set on a teetering platform; and clusters of people were seated in groups; with a blackboard, a small bit of chalk; a wet rag.

The professor stoodawkwardly pawing his clothing as hundreds of eyeballs devoured him; then, conscious of stares, he adjusted his posture, appeared a bit younger, his cheeks got some color, and he squared-up his shoulders while pushing his glasses up using one hand, his head swiveled, and he was prepared to commence.

Some smattered applause.

He leaned both of his hands on the table, his shoulder blades turned to the blackboard, his tassel free, dangling, he ran up a step, maybe two, and he smiled as he flashed roguish eyes and he poked out a finger.

"Sirs," he began, approaching the tabletop, "I must request, and most humbly, that you not voice agreement or," miming surprise, his eyes turned to the sky, "disagreement...

I speak to you, as a professor, and not a... a... basically... actor; for this is no stage, but, the, well, Mathematics Department's meeting room; this is no theater, it *is* a cathedral of science, where I, basically, work, yes sir, as a natural condenser of mathematical thought.[119]

---

119. Bely is referring here to an electronic component that later became known as a capacitor, which is used in a variety of ways to manage the flow of electricity in a circuit.

Here he paused at a sprinkle of clapping; he stopped; and ceased all reaction.

"Ahem... The scientific-mathematical method encompasses," spreading his arms, "it encompasses all parts of life; so that," winking, "this method, basically, gives us a standard for everyday thinking," a flash off the lens of his glasses.

"So, sirs, a scientific approach to the world," as he flipped his eyeglasses up onto his forehead, "depends, yes, sir, rationally speaking, on data," pause...

"Psychophysical and biological data become, through analysis, biochemical and physical-chemical principles."

"Now, let's examine," he clenched all his fingers while forming a fist, "our sensation," he fanned-out his fingers, "a physical-chemical experience that is explicable purely in physical terms."

"So that physics," he turned to the right, "also chemistry," he turned to the left, "are both general processes."

"Hm... in all chemistry, any one process," he lifted his brows, "qualitatively, is a material process," he cleared his throat loudly, "chemistry," clearing his throat more convincingly, "was" and he mimed a discovery, "up until now," his face showed great surprise, "was... a... basically... science of qualities." With this important discovery, placing his hand on his palm, he walked toward the students.

"But physics," he boomed," is a science of quantities."

Stressing this concept, his finger flew.

"So," his eyes summoned the room to attention, "our dealings with physical chemistry are, yes sirs, serious," quietly he carried-on: "they are such, which, kha," he coughed, "and however..." he lost his way.

Puzzled, he stepped back: and chose a path straight on to math.

He advanced down the stage like a conqueror, puffing his chest.

Introducing the course he just waved his way through, but it took half an hour, then after grabbing the chalk he got right down to work: at the blackboard; his head was relaxed on his spine and his collar rode up on the back of his head; so, when turning his back to the students, he showed not his head but his collar; he held one short arm to his back, in his rapid and crude hand his letters inclined to the right and the left (that was easier) and rapidly wrote out the formulae.

"This modulus,[120] basically, is just a number: the kind," and he turned his head, "which can be multiplied by any logarithm at base one, hmm, to generate logs of a different base."

Then, he ran a small piece of the chalk down the board.

The distinguished professor became, at his lectures, well, truly, a type of a miller: where flocks of young students, like sparrows, with much happy chirping pecked formula after formula; integral after integral.

Sprinkled with chalkdust and weary he pushed his way through flocks of students and left the department; and hurried to reach the professors' buffet.

"You, it's clear: well go ahead and enroll, yes, with Kosha."

"The Swedish Mathematician, Sophus Lie, pointed this out."[121]

"So, award him a stipend?..."

"Well, what can I do here; go see the departmental secretary."

He was stopped while approaching the professors' buffet: in front waiting, an educated German, a man representing a business, who raised a most complex mechanical question.

"*Vell, vut you tinkin'*, professor?"

---

120. A number by which logarithms at one base can be multiplied to yield logarithms at another base.
121. Sophus Lie (1842-1899), a Norwegian mathematician whose primary work was in geometry and differential equations.

"Well you sir ought *not* speak with me... you should see, yes sir, Nikolai Yegorich, or, logically, go to Zhukovsky... he's the mechanic here, basically, not me."

But one thing was odd: his discovery concerning applied mathematics and mechanics directly addressed the point raised by the German; the professor looked over the interesting German and noticed a wart and he smelled a cigar, a strong one; Korobkin remarked that he might soon return to the question and would write in detail on the matter in March's *Mathematical Courier* (no sooner); the German politely took notes.

"Do you know of a yellowish journal, *Mathematical Courier*... Yes, well: I edit it..."

Quite absent mindedly jabbing him, jotting in pencil, he wrote out some formulae right on the German's red jacket.

Mokhovaya Street; drivers, and passengers' backs, and just tram after tram.

The professor stopped walking: from under the stripes on his hat he jutted suspiciously, angrily, dull-eyed, at some new idea; in his mind, a small whirl of a formula hung: and some formulae rang in his head, which allowed him to scribble them down; then, a black square just appeared right in front of his nose[122] and obstructed his view of the columned Manezh.[123]

---

122. This may be a wink and a reference to Konstantin Malevich's painting, *Black Square* (1915), one of the most powerful and well known works of the Suprematist art movement.

123. The *Manezh*, across the street from the original site of Moscow University and one of central Moscow's best known buildings, was built originally as a manège, or exercise ground for horses and parade ground for soldiers. Later, the building took on a wide variety of uses, including as an art exhibition hall as well as a temporary holding pen for demonstrators arrested downtown.

The same square appeared near the sidewalk, presenting itself in a way he found tempting:

"I'd sure like to scribble some numbers on that!"

The professor was tempted; a small piece of chalk in his pocket, he almost knocked over a passer-by, and almost tripped over a bollard, then quickly and rashly jumped down off the sidewalk: he stood near the square; with the chalk in his hand he wrote out a long ribbon of formulae; most interesting!

Solved.

More compelling, he thought, than "Fermat's last theorem" (that formula really exists: he had even once written about it a bit).[124]

"So sir, so sir, so sir; divide this, and carry that." He had succeeded, yes, basically, overturned everything, strikingly simple: and simply discovered. I'd just like to fix a parenthesis: just one.

However the square with the faulty parenthesis, dammit, had moved; so Professor Korobkin turned 'round, one galosh probed a puddle, to round the parenthesis: but the black square, ay, ay, ay was moving off, rushing; the scribbled-down formula with the discovery skedaddled off toward the ineffable; all of the rational clarity sketched in one plane was torn from beneath his own nose, but this left a new space, a dimension all crowded with images having no link to "Fermat" or the sketched-out discovery; the discovery was now something else: a mind that was starting to guess that the square was a carriage's squared-off rear panel.

The carriage was gone.

His discovery struck him no less than the recently parked but departed black panel and carriage: was someone attempting to get him? You think you are on an uncharted, small island in waters unknown to

---

124. A conjecture in number theory scribbled in the margin of a paper by Pierre de Fermat in 1637. The idea, long unproven, became known as Fermat's Last Theorem and achieved a degree of notoriety unusual for relatively obscure mathematical ideas.

you: whoops! The whale dives and you surface in, dammit, the Indian Ocean (your island, a fish); and so, anything static can also be, dammit, dynamic, accelerating: bodies already in motion experience acceleration as falling.

So, squeezing and lifting the chalk in one hand the professor accelerated up Mokhovaya, his hat fell, his coat tails flew wide; he was squared, then the square tried accelerating; skedaddled; in rushed the ineffable: both the square and the professor were set in a hollowed-out sphere of the universe, faster, and faster, and faster! But suddenly, moving, accelerating in out of nowhere, two shafts and the head of a horse: how it whacked him!

A body deprived of support falls: Korobkin fell too on the stones with a trickle of blood on his face.

There they crowdedaround him: and took him away.

CHAPTER TWO

"MANDRO'S HOUSE"

1

It poured.

All the sing-songy tree whistling stopped; but one leaf had hun-gon; drips of moldering mold and everythingsoaked; the days short-ened, with dimming black dimness; the edges all started to ice; the wind turnedtothenorth and blew frost; all the grime in the street turned-toiceinthenight; the damp days were harshened by cold; and the rain turned to snow.

And they said to each other:

"Hey, look!"

"Here comes snow!"

"It's not rain!"

Thus, October turned into November, and icy and drippy No-vember mists hung in the mornings; and colds were a threat: and sore throats.

Eduard Eduardovich noticed: that things in his home had cooled down; seemed the tension had gotten to everything; hot water out; the door knob, that too had turned cold.

He was performing his daily ablutions in front of his bedroom's wall mirror.

Imagine: that he, Eduard Eduardovich von-Mandro, as the managing director of "Mandro," a fine company, known as a social lion, waited to greet in his bedroom just whom?

Yes, a dwarf!

An entirely and simply disgusting male dwarf: by his height just a child, perhaps twelve; by appearance, a moldy old man (though, most likely, near 30); and clearly a total degenerate; couldn't find slimeballs like him if you tried; just, perhaps, in a nightmare. Such types are depicted in paintings by Bruegel the Elder.

The dwarf had a flabby and wrinkledupface like a lemon, chewed-up, a bit yellow, no mustache, a dirty thin beard, a small bit had been eaten away on his lip, his nose wasn't there, so he wore a black cow leather patch that covered the cavity; sharply, its triangle shape cut between his two eyes; his eyethings were gone; in their place he had yellow-red, puss-bags, no lashes, cynically smiling; the dwarf often winked with a cynical smile.

On the arms of the paw-legged chair, which he'd barely succeeded in climbing, defiantly slamming his elbows, he collapsed and he crossed his legs; drummed with the fingers of small hands; his ears were quite large; they'd grown out in divergent directions; his hair had been cut in a bowl; wore a tie, torn and dirty, the color of blood, and his brick-colored coat was all stained, and there seemed to be blood on the cube-patterned fabric that covered his chair; no, yuck; someone had definitely smeared a dead louse!

He just looked like he stunk.

So while raising one brow at the dwarf, his face flooded with loathing, he buffed-up his rosy nails; tossed:

"I am saying..."

But standing his ground, the dwarf pointed to where his own nose had been.[125]

"Nose."

"What?"

"My nose?"

Then he recrossed his legs as he tapped with a finger.

"I'll say it again, the bill must be paid for my nose."

"For your services yes; but the nose?" And then, whimpering:

"I have no nose: and you can't give it back." And at that von-Mandro felt just horribly sick.

"Oh that's nonsense!"

And tossing aside a brush crafted from elephant ivory, looked at him, coffin-eyes fixed on his face:

"50 thousand rubles: 100 thousand marks!"

"That's not much."

"Paid by check, from a bank in Berlin: does that suit you?"

But seeing the dwarf was defiant he flashed a fake smile:

"And you know, it's not difficult work... plus it's only 'til summer. By then you're abroad."

"You'd pay someone else more..."

"But your life would be set for ten years; and I'll pay for your doctors, your food; and..."

The dwarf bared his teeth: his teeth always were bared (well, his lips were both gone):

"And don't you forget that if rumors start up, or there's even a peep..."

125.Among the symptoms of syphilis is the wasting of flesh often including facial features.The dwarf's missing nose may also be another of Bely's bows toward Gogol, whose short story "The Nose" is a classic of the surreal and grotesque.

"I'll say it again, the bill must be paid for my nose."

Eduard Eduardovich stopped him by wrinkling his brow to suggest that the meeting was over.

"Agreed."

And then grunting, he tugged himself onto the floor; he approached, on his swaying bowed legs, went right up to Mandro: to his waist; and he tilted his yellow-red eye at the thickly-grown sideburns.

"You want boys, like before?"[126]

But Mandro just kept silent.

He stretched out a hand for a crystal decanter of, sloshing, a lily-toned liquid for grooming mens' sideburns.

Then, after applying the liquid, and hearing piano scales, wearing a warm hat and beaver-shade tunic, and comfortable beaver-shade shoes, took the dwarf and went into the guest room.

Lizasha was playing.

Morose, just plain bored, he examined the things in the room: the curved lines of the pieces were facing apart, which both showed off the size of the room while reducing the furnishings' profiles – to mini-profiles: and then, crossing the parlor he stood by the window; and with a small mirror fastidiously plucked a grey hair.

And the armchairs, a circle of leonine paws painted gold, drew attention, both playful and graceful, and covered with red-speckled, pistachio-tone, smooth satin, telling each other how sad it was being neglected. Von-Mandro stayed there sitting, reclining, but after he'd checked the chair's gold-pointed wings with a garland that twined all the way to the arm.

Standing between this duet of nice chairs was a goldleaf-festooned but chipped oval-shaped table, that held some nice albums and trays, fine examples of china, and ashtrays: chalcedony, veined; and the

---

126. Perhaps sleepy or drunk, or simply from spite, the dwarf confuses Mandro's request with services he had performed in the past, elsewhere.

background was filled with a screen, green and boasting a golden-winged, golden-billed bird.

Up above, from the ceiling's *faux* garland encircling the room, hung a green Chinese lantern.[127]

"You'd best leave..."

"Yes, I'm going, I'm going."

"I ask that you never come back: I'll be getting reports on your needs."

Very unusual: next, von-Mandro took his impolite guest not down through the main hall, but the dining room, thence down a hall to the door, embarrassed and sneaking along; he glanced all around; and he locked the door too; he was clearly ashamed to be seen by the servants: what would they say? Mandro, von-Mandro, of "Mandro" his own company, seen with that dwarf.

He returned to the guest room.

Indifferently marking the sound of piano scales, Eduard Eduardovich broke in, in baritone: it was as if a harmonium had started to play;[128] from behind all the sound peered grave beaver-toned eyes; but this look was pure artifice; plumbing the depths of the mirror, vanishing inside and excising all rational thought from his memory; just like a statue of marble.

Mandro had real skill, an *artiste* at finance.

Sometimes it seemed that he flew like an eagle, in gyres, to see the entire horizon of businesses covering Europe and even America; he was the equal of Rockefeller, was said to deserve highest honors in business in Russia; one dope, who was missing the point, said he

---

127. The color of a Chinese lantern is chosen to symbolize the needs and wants of the owner: green has been said to symbolize life, growth, and spring.

128. A harmonium, sometimes known as a pump organ, is smaller than a pipe organ and enjoyed its greatest popularity in the nineteenth century both in homes and churches. In imperial Russia, it was especially popular with German immigrants.

simply ran scams: but he actually *was* in the darkest of circles among international agents.

At home, in a bathrobe, he wandered the house: and yawned lazily. Sideburns oiled, each single hair neatly groomed, he walked up to the mirror; turned side to side, batted his lashes, adjusted his tie; 'cause he searched for a setting for all of his acts: he'd noted he contrasted well with the green in the wallpaper; here, where he stood, his exquisite and narrow-nosed profile would show in the mirror; he brushed his own hair, and, supporting his elbow: the top of a cabinet, placed there to help.

He furnished his gestures.

The company bore his last name; there was gossip that it was no more than a front: did Mandro need such things when the strength of his will and refinement would lead to success and protect his good name?

But he spoiled it.

And shuddering over the thought was his mane, blue-black, twinned locks of silver, like horns that were set to the right and the left, both quite artfully combed up and over, and his sable-black sideburns, and a satiny spot on his chin (a nice dimple); his brows came together and rose in a gesture just over his nose, reminiscent of hands with joined palms raised; between them were wrinkles, three, a trident up-raised and then cutting up over his brow; showed his silent distress.

As if singing *"Miserere."*[129]

---

129. *Miserere* (*Miserere mei Deus*, Latin for *"Have mercy on me, O God"*) is a musical version of Psalm 51, written by Italian composer Gregorio Allegri. In the 1630s, during the reign of Pope Urban VIII, it was written for use in Holy Week services in the Sistine Chapel. At some point it became forbidden to transcribe the song's music, and mystery grew up around the piece. Legend has it that the embargo was lifted after Mozart, at age 14, attended the services and some time later transcribed the music from memory.

It was said he was gaming the market, for which he was given, by someone, a cut; that this weakened the Russian stocks sold in Vienna and London; in one case, they said, he had practically ruined a firm where he served on the board of directors.

Just rumors!

In other affairs his audacious approach and unusual risk-taking earned him high honors.

"A pity!"

"Eduard Eduardovich could be a symbol of pride; and a powerful force in the Russian economy..."

"But he is not one of us," they said, stepping away, and He did not chase them.[130]

And smiling to all with his white teeth, he seemed a reserved, disorganized, gentle and amiable man; but his mirror image had threatened to torch them: in gestures, Mandro surpassed the fine arts which, it seemed, he'd perfected; and looking at him, one just wanted to say:

"Right out of that damned Stanislavsky."[131]

Mandro's family pedigree wasn't that clear; it was said he was Danish, but others had argued at length that was bunk: Eduard Eduardovich had been adopted; his father was Greek, the most common sort, born in Odessa, quite near Malakak; von-Mandro himself always claimed to be Russian, his great-grandfather lived up in Edinburgh, where he was said to belong to the Scots Masons, and rose to the highest rank, died heaped with honors; supporting this claim he showed-off a ring; it was really Masonic he swore.

---

130. "He" is capitalized in the original.
131. Bely uses one word "*Stanislavshchina*," translated here by a sentence. The *–shchina* suffix is appended to all or part of nouns, often names, to indicate a period of time in which something or someone was influential or powerful and carries negative connotations, such as Stalin-*shchina*. Here, of course, Bely turns it to comic effect.

An ornate, rococo fireplace, black jaws blocked off by a decorative screen like a muzzle; a porcelain clock on the mantle, not ticking; and nearby he'd placed, with his own hands, a *flageolet*.[132]

2

Then the scales were cut short: and some steps could be heard in the hallway; they slapped like a smack in the face as they echoed; the door swung: a middle-aged servant, who stood at the threshold, announced:

"Solomon Samuilovich..."

Eduard Eduardovich said:

"Come in, please."

And he closed a white cuff with a massive cuff link.

From the door he caught sight of Lizasha: in a brown dress and apron, getting up from the bench at the keyboard, once mother of pearl, but gone white; and her moist eyes shot sparks that were aimed at her father, attempting to lure him; he was walking quite briskly with footsteps that slapped like a smack in the face.

And Lizasha Mandro stood there, curtsied, and seemed quite per-plexed: she parted her small and cute mouth.

Solomon Samuilovich walked through the cold room right past her.

Instead of fine paper, the walls had been surfaced with stone, pale and fawn, and were polished and shiny; some carved bas-reliefs 'twixt the stones were inset in the walls; they depicted a line of old men[133] all with laurels; they'd lowered the wreaths on their palms to their heads. The men stooped, rococo curls cascading; twelve figures were there on the wall, there were six on the right, and six more on the left, and all

---

132. A small, end-blown flute with four holes in front and two in the back. This refers back to the flute mentioned in the opening pages of the novel and will be repeated hereafter.
133. Compare these to the small figures on the wallpaper in Korobkin's office.

twelve raised their heads; and were fixing their visitors strangely with stares from their eyeholes.

The windows had mirrored glass panes; they were screened off with floor-length fawn curtains with edges of lace just like spider webs.

An enormous, fine chandelier hung, with its crystals all swaying on high like the back of a rocker; the room had an oddly carved ceiling, six cupids, cheeks puffed and set 'round a small circle.

Solomon Samuilovich quickly scanned everything, went to the sitting room; noticing squinted eyes darting to check in the mirror each tiny hair in his sideburns and eagle-like, vulturous nose.

Von-Mandro shook his hand with a powerful motion.

"Solomon Samuilovich."

His juicy-red lips looked made-up.[134]

"Well, so how's the proposal?"

They talked up a storm. And Mandro stood there pursing his lips, while his fingers (his thumb and his index) came softly together as if he were pealing some tape from his lip.

"Well, tell me..."

Lifting his hand from his lips, he then rubbed his two fingers together a bit (only here he abandoned aesthetics); this was strange: while a wrinkled-up brow hid his eyes; and his sticky red lips were relaxed and the topic was changed to impressions of Paris.

"You know," Solomon Samuilovich wiggled a finger, "it may be high time, for our stocks in Siberian sunflower oil..."

"Huh?"

"You know the barometer fell: just preceding the hurricane."

"I do not think..."

"But then I know for sure."

---

134. Referrring to Mandro's lips, which he describes as "sochno-alye" while noting that they appear to have lipstick, Bely appears to be suggesting (if not playing with) the sound of the word "sexual."

Solomon Samuilovich hurriedly tried to establish that war was inevitable.

"I had a chat in Berlin..."

"Met with Rathenau?"[135]

"Yes." And I showed to a certain fine someone among our top men in mechanics that little old document, you know the one.

Von-Mandro's full keyboard of teeth set to playing:

"Yes?"

Then a devilish snicker contorted his lips:

"Got terms equal to Krupp's."[136]

His long arm made the friendliest gesture (he had long-arms).[137]

3

Once more, Lizasha was at the piano, well-tuned, long since faded; while her fingers ran down through the keys they conversed with her heart; as they fought her heart quickened:

"No, no!"

With her narrow nose, round-face, a small parted mouth, and a girlish physique, she stood up and left: pale, petite, narrow-waisted; Lizasha's demeanor left people confused: there was innocence; eyes, half-toned: now they were emerald, now they were agate: if you looked in her eyes they shot sparks.

She said horrible things; and she did some most horrible things.

To her girlfriends and Mitya she'd say:

"I love freaks." She also said:

"You are my freak, and I love you."

---

135. Walter Rathenau (1867-1922) a German industrialist and statesman who served as foreign minister for Germany's Weimar Republic.
136. Krupp, the well-known German family of industrialists.
137. Moscow is said to have been founded by Yuri Dolgoruky, or, literally, "Yuri Longarm." Bely repeats this motif throughout the novel, identifying Mandro with the city's founder.

But at the same time she had innocent eyes.

"I am not all alone: there are, after all, many of us." And Lizasha took medicinal chalk.

And at night she'd sit up in her bed with her legs crossed and think:

"Oh how, excellent, excellent, excellent!"

She got up around noon; and she'd turned up her nose at her studies; became a recluse, though some evenings attended the theater and concerts, and visited frivolous friends, and she flirted with schoolboys in blue with pale piping (from Kreiman Gymnasium). Everyone mentioned the ambience, and Lizasha, an eccentric young lady!

During the day she sat watching the clock: in a year the clock struck a full year's worth; and time, like a blacksmith, can shackle your hands; but she parted the lace of the curtains and fingered the iciness; cold and uncomfortable; and cobblestones clattered as carriages cut off sharp edges; but soon they'd be covered with snow: and the sleighs on their runners would shuffle and bump right along; it was daylight, a dandelion, puffed white at night, caught a chill from a breeze so it shriveled: a frozen small ball, to be tossed like a ball, but no.

What do you mean by that "no"?

No, no, no: and off into the guest room.

Here, scattered, were trios, duets, and quartets of especially arranged and then rearranged chairs, next to divans, or not, and at tables (or not) a most exquisitely assembled arrangement arising from furniture anarchy, failing to crowd out the cold of the space laid with blue-gray soft carpet, a carpet that everywhere (divans and chairs, and the mirrors and screens) smelled of smoke; there were shelves and some pedestals, collections of china, the finest designs in blue-violet, and lily-rose shades and some figurines.

Meowing: the cat.

So Lizasha went into the sitting room, practically scaring Madame Voulezvous, the head servant and housekeeper; who always had wanted to care for Lizasha (the young girl's own mother had died, which Lizasha remembered just vaguely); you might say Madame Voulezvous had succeeded; but she was not loved by Lizasha; Madame Voulezvous was upset and she wept.[138]

And for years she wore only two colors: pistachio and grey: and she wandered around with a swollen left cheek (the result of a flux); in a dither; a craze, mixed with tragedies; helping the cat, and the maid; and she felt like the lives of Lizasha, Mandro and Merditsevich trapped her, a bird net, in every small bit of her life; she was quite a good friend of Madame Evikhkaiten's; and praised a man, Shturtsvag, to everyone (once, she had met him); she clearly had trouble with everyone, got some sharp-elbowed replies; she spoke Russian quite beautifully; she was a Russian: her husband had left her.

"Lizzie. I finally guessed…"[139]

"Well?"

"I think Fedka, just outside of Moscow, caught it and brought it here, but let it go accidentally."

"All this is what? A mere trifle."

Maybe four days before, while cleaning, Madame Voulezvous, in a wardrobe, behind a shelf, found a small bat; but more accurately, found a decayed little body; this triggered her temper, she yelled of "migration" and asked where the bat could have lived.

"I've smelled it a while, a good long while: you smelled it?"

"Oh yes, even I…"

"And it stinks!… Well that's it: this is Fedka's affair."

---

138. Translated literally from the French her name would be "Mrs. Wouldyoulike?" The basic facts of her private life, job responsibilities, and personality make it entirely appropriate.

139. Lizzie: no one else uses this nickname for Lizasha. It is the type of false note that defines her relationship with the girl.

So Lizasha walked out to the sitting room.

It had grey walls and glittering fabrics, with divans, a table; the divans had pillows, all colorfully sewn, with chameleons and peacocks on brocade; a lamp with a shining stone hung from the ceiling; a table had burnished bronze boxes and knickknacks (some onyx); a cage held a parrot that never stopped squawking:

"Atheists."

Strange: for Lizasha believed. Then behind a screen voices were heard, and Lizasha's nose stuck through a fold of the drapes.

"Oh yes, yes, an industrialist," Mandro smoothed his sideburns.

"And what of the files?" Solomon Samuilovich wiggled his fingers.

"The book?"

"They will get it." Solomon Samuilovich wiggled a finger.

She sat in a corner, between a few pillows; sunk into the divan; she dug herself into the pillows: her red fur cloak lay there; and sometimes for hours she'd sit thinking, while fanning her skirt on the divan, legs tucked underneath, crossed; with moist eyes she'd sit quietly, lips slightly parted, her fingers would pull at her dress's black collar, the other hand, manicured, pale but dull-skinned with a light touch of yellow, like elephant ivory, always cold, ice. She smoked cigarettes (she was a girl but she smoked).

And rolled up in a ball.

And it was as if she had stored so much cold in her body that thawing her out in a hothouse, her tiny thin frame would remain cold as ice for some years; and she sat, a real snugglebug, wrapped in a robe trimmed with sable and fingering knick-knacks of onyx; her large distant eyes never blinked, her mouth open; she drowned in those eyes, yes her own: and small whirlpools appeared in her eyes as she drowned while unborn. Yes, a nymph!

"I'm going to feed all my shadows."

These nymph games with herself and with others had led to a meeting: with Doctor Dass, a top neuropathologist, who came to examine her:

"Don't be surprised. The young lady is having a nervous attack: pseudo-hallucinations, yes, sir!"

She squinted at him with the eyes of a nymph.

She responded to everything distantly somehow; she passed through her life from a distance, as if she was wandering far away fields picking flowers of azure that cast all their shadows toward Moscow; and one of these shadows was given the name of Lizasha Mandro.

"I'm going to feed all my shadows," she told Mitya, and time and again.

Yes, that girl was quite strange!

Her relations were strange with her father too.

Anyone could tell you: rabid hero worship; she called him her "little god."[140] And she got reciprocity; calling her oddly: his Sister Alyona;[141] at times he was totally tender, entirely unexpectedly tender; he seemed a close comforting friend; and he asked, on occasion what he should be doing in one thing or other; and listened to her:

"You have no self-control."

"You're defined by your business."

---

140. "*Bogushka*," or "little god," is the diminutive form of "*bog*," or "god," and is Lizasha's pet name for her father. The word is used here in lower case, like the original.

141. This name is from a Russian folk tale, *Sister Alyonushka, Brother Ivanushka*, the story of orphaned siblings who leave home, battle evil, and eventually triumph. Alyonushka spends a good part of the story at the bottom of a river, helpless because of a rock tied around her neck by a witch.

"You're out of your mind," was a frequent remark.

And then suddenly, no reason, he was her fiercest tormentor; for weeks would not so much as look at her, froze her like ice; and Lizasha wandered around in a panic, afraid, she was trying to bump into him, and on purpose; she looked at him sweetly; but he grew more cruel and capricious; his brows came together, the ends raised not lowered and meeting up over his nose in a gesture reminiscent of hands raised up, joined at the palm; as if out of his forehead had come a performance of *Misere*.

It was as if he'd done something that tortured him; but, in this pain he sought pleasure: for him and Lizasha. Lizasha especially.

Thus, for Lizasha, existence kept switching from drama to joy: she'd had drama three days in a row.

In the window, Petrovka.

Everywhere puddles were freezing; it seemed instantaneous! And, if you looked, the thermometer stood way down past zero; the chimneys stood curling out smoke (and it smelled of the ash); there were blue-white and blue hides (not clouds) on high plodding across the cold sky: and beneath them the frozen street glowed, a metallic sheen; out of the dark grey and grey gloom white puffs soon would pop through; with snow-maidens everywhere, in gutters, on bushes, and boxes; the mud in the street splashed on maidens of snow.

In these fateful days, the earth's in a half-faint: held together by frost; and its half-dead heart says its farewells when departing from something quite dear.

4

Solomon Samuilovich Kavalever.

His forehead was narrow, his beard trim and grey; he was bald, the huge hump of his nose was always right there; and he played with his profits like others could play with their fingers; would only express quite well founded opinions; the man was a bright constellation of stars that they hid with a decorative screen called: "Mandro."

The whole office was wallpapered, dark blue and blue, in a very depressing deep tone, a bit blackish; the background appeared to recede: like the walls had all vanished; the chairs were quite sturdy and large with Moroccan tooled leather upholstery that shone in the night.

A divan, Moroccan tooled leather upholstery, shone there as well.

And the floor, which was covered by dark blue and blue rugs, was dark and depressing, with black at its edge; and it gave one the sense that the chairs hung suspended in night; right in front of the divan was thrown the white pelt of a polar bear, teeth snarling, its muzzle gone yellow; it seemed that the beast had been stuffed while it scowled.

Kavalever looked all of this over; by the time he was done a filigreed candelabra stood nearby on the table; Mandro showed up wearing a tux; in the tux he seemed younger; he wore black pants, pulled up, a black cummerbund and dark-lily socks with his shoes mirror-shined; he came out of the bedroom, a small scrap of paper in hand.

Von-Mandro's full keyboard of teeth set to playing:

"Look: a facsimile copy of things that Berlin's mathematicians are working on now."

He extended the paper, all rumpled, and spotted with bead-strings of formulae; here, Kavalever could see every hair on Mandro was combed with precision; he laid out the paper in front of him flat on the table, one hand on the other, and his right hand's fingers were curled 'round his left:

"So, you see, this scrap of paper is..."

"Yes..."

In his beaver-toned eyes flames played, very cold flames.

"How'd it wind-up in your hands?"

Eduard Eduardovich rippled a wrinkle: then smoothed his white forehead (a ball would've rolled on it); just for an instant it seemed all his facial expressions had died; he continued on, once resurrected, by pleasantly smiling:

"I like to collect fine old books... Once, entirely by accident one of the volumes I bought with the label "Korobkin" (I purchased it as an antique, or "*ex libris*") contained a small paper; and you know the rest of the document's tale..."

Eduard Eduardovich, satisfied, fingered the hairs of his sideburns.

"A common – well – tragedy here... well, yes... Children and fathers..."

"The son will be punished, it seems," Kavalever concluded around his huge hump of a honker.

"It's not *even* worth talking about: the son visits us here."

"Well, you know, if the old man hides such things in books in his library and the son..."

But, after seeing the gesture Mandro made, rephrased his thought:

"If books go missing, then documents too could just vanish. You know: disappear."

"No, they note each book leaving the house."

With a very smooth movement a hand and its fingers (his thumb and his index) came softly together as if he was pulling some tape from his lip.

And then moving one hand he pretended to rub the two fingers together.

"It all has been planned."

Here he stopped:

"Well it's time: and the hour has arrived: Solomon Samuilovich?"

"Varvarka Street."

"I'm on my way to Kuznetsky."

And after grabbing and clutching his briefcase, he waved a long arm (he was long-armed) invitingly; massive, a ruby ring sparkled.

He walked with his sideburns and grey-horns, quite stately, behind Kavalever's curved spine, through curtains that screened-off the entrance, then nearly bumped into... Lizasha, who bounced back toward the divan; and after she spotted her father, she blushed a rose-pink; and the set of her mouth made her look like an imp; and a light like the dawn lit her face like the Northern Light waking a wraith:

"Why are you here?"

Just the sight of him stunned her; her face shone, a star, but he failed to respond; her mood soured; he was focused on striking a pose that would match Kavalever's while walking beside him; his steps on the mirrored parquet, which reflected just everything, echoed and smacked like a slap in the face.

He was crowned at his age with grey horns.

The door opened wide; out he walked, in blue fox; there, a grey-maned and porcelain horse clomped its hooves; on the corner a white-tongued bright flame could be seen in the lamp; there were stains, wet and blue on the street; on the blue-grey front walkway, all glowing and smoking, a row of small lanterns with amber shades; torchflamesmallmen and their shadows.

Some blackclouds of smoke rose above the unwinding light-grey of the evening; in vain, they had battled the darkness: the grey was seduced, corrupted to nothing, to one, all to black.

Then a coachman adjusted his reins and he cut through a crowd; at a trot and as black as a crow they flashed by, blurred, a rose pillow; Mandro was off to Kuznetsky, dressed sharply, and smelling of blue fox.

5

Readers ask: what of Professor Korobkin, whom we left where he lay on the pavement unconscious and bloody.

He came to.

He was given first aid on the spot right near campus;[142] alas! They could see an arm fracture (right above the left elbow), a cut on his head that was cause for great worry: his head fully bandaged and left arm immobilized, he was sent right away to his brown little home: with a respectful attendant.

His spirits improved on the way:

"So, sir!"

"Basically!"

"Nothing, sir!"

Climbing down out of the carriage he managed to pinchoffaloaf of a joke. And at home, they all "oohed." But just Nadya cried; though, as it turned out, it wasn't a "nothing, sir," it was a "something, sir"; the pain in his arm grew quite sharp; and then drilling commenced in his skull, his ears echoed; so, sadly, he quietly moaned, the whole time he sat clutching his arm; Doctor Kapsky, a surgeon, put his arm in a cast, and then sent him to bed with an ice bag, of gutta-percha, on his head

---

142. Moscow University was originally located in Moscow's central downtown area near the Kremlin and Manezh. Most of the university's departments moved to their present location in the hills across the Moscow River in the 1950s.

(filled with ice); and they closed the brown drapes; and another attendant arrived from the clinic; emphatically: doctors forbid him to work,
read, or even to think.

He was in bed for 14 whole days.

All the newspapers blared; *Russian News* was upset at the whole situation; and letters, greetings, and sympathies poured in from colleagues
and groups. Zadopyatov had sent him a telegram.

> *"No, darkness has not overtaken me!"*[143]

Students had sent a poem: but it was… here:

> *Carriage swerved out, knocked him senseless.*
> *Right near school, as he walked through,*
> *A mathematician and quite famous*
> *On the street in plain view,*
> *One arm broken in two.*
>
> *Then torn by what happened*
> *all the students had outlashed:*
> *"We protest! We're unhappy!*
> *Famous people get bashed!"*
> *Get better fast.*

Out of bed at long last: no more ice: and the nurse was dismissed;
forced to rest one more week in a sweatbox: his yellow home office: he
slept there; relaxed; ate his meals; there was nought to be done: when
he read it was hard, calculations were banned: his pulse showed in a vein
on his temple; his head felt like a beer keg.

His leg fell asleep.

---

143. A Bible verse, *John*, chapter 1.

A cloth bandage was wound all around his whole head: and a bib was attached right down under his beard, it was tied at the back of his head with long straps; and he wanderedaroundfornoreason, all wrapped in his worn-out old bathrobe, his beard had been flattened and bound up from bottom to top, with his arm in a sling: a white stump slung suspended; it was like he was missing a hand; his free hand groped his head and he grabbed at the straps of his bib; smacked his lips; he examined the world through both nostrils; and his fingers, like claws, drummed out ditties, his leg kept on falling asleep (pins and needles).

He felt like a rabbit.

He didn't sleep nights; so he'd sit there observing the daylight replacing the dark; as a spiral of time led him out of the night; and the light probed the curtains; and sometimes the curtains, all black, looked like brown; and the bookshelves looked brown: or a violet; the wallpaper pattern, a figure, a small man who seemed to be running; when viewed from afar the small men there all seemed to be hopelessly chasing each other: and failing to catch-up.

He'd jump up.

Like an old, twin-horned bull in a worn-out house coat, with a beer-barrellgut, he racketedloudly, eyes wandering, one arm unharnessed and groping, the second one slung in a cast; he scouted the hall and the sitting room, counting innumerable berries that spotted the wallpaper; smacking his lips at the berries, he suffered, his eyes had noluster; he'd go to his room just to dirty the sheets, take the towels and stuff the commode; or lose his old textbook by Lange.

"Ffr-ffr"... he'd flip through a book; and make marks with his thumbnail.

He trapped lice; and chased moths; once he noticed his hair had grown out, that its brown did not match with his beard; all his roots had gone white; so he colored his hair with one hand; and it turned out a mess.

So he wandered around with his face stained by dye; and he looked just a bit like a dog.

6

While the professor was ill, truth be told, he had played on their nerves: Vasilisa Sergeyevna's, Darya's, and even his own: and he bothered them all to no end, free hand quaking; you'd hear him there moving and shifting the drawers, making noise: it was clear why he dug all around in his desk; but not why he searched the buffet or banged dishes, he examined most curiously everything visible, touching it, feeling his way all around like a child.

"You should go to your room," Vasilisa Sergeyevna often would say.

She kept pursing her lips, just as if she'd sniffed smelling salts. Staring right through his thick glasses, quite wild, he would stand and talk back: then go into his office to be by himself in his sweatbox. Things clarified: peace in his family life hung on his leaving the family, by lecturing, going to meetings; in essence he never had lived in his home; he just worked on his math; that is, he was entirely gone; math was now difficult: hitting his head, it turned out, vexed his wife and the servants, and showed how entirely not home he felt when at home: that's it: dammit!

Vasilisa Sergeyevna knew the professor was present at home through his absence alone; and his presence made everyone angry; her face would perform a sour drama; all morning and throughout the day, like a crane hen, she lounged in her apricot dress, with a border of fawn. And her dresses all hung on her just like they hungontheirhangers.

And her breasts were mere rags; and her legs were thin sticks, and if not for her corset, her gut would stick out like a swollen old watermelon; her brabble[144] was boring; he was sick of the agethatshowed under her powder; she bored Ivan Ivanych green; her strong lavender water was not to his liking; he knew that her mouth, a soft berry shade, vented bad breath; she chewed mints.[145]

Of a day out you might hear:

"The thermometer's way below zero... I bought moth balls..."

"Wonderful," faintly replied the professor.

"I say *à propos*: hypochondria's taken my health: Zyadopyatov's as well: that's because of *autocracy*, plus there's a stink from the stove..."

The professor would bark:

"Don't divorce me, understand!" And then Nadya would cry:

"Oh no, don't use that word!"

Mitya continued to trudge to Mandro's: Vasilisa Sergeyevna scolded:

"A bit of a plate licker there, aren't you?"

He grinned: and went anyway; once the professor, quite bored had asked Mitya to solve an equation: but Mitya produced a real mess.

"You are, brother, a dunce."

But the boy smacked his lips, blushed and left: for Mandro's.

---

144. Similar to babble but quarrelsome; Joseph T. Shipley, *Dictionary of Early English*, Littlefield, Adams & Co., 1968.
145. Vasilisa Sergeyevna's breath mints are a reference to Bely's play on the mythical basilisk.

The professor could only relax when with Nadya; who sometimes was out at a class. In the evening she often attended the theater; but when she was home, her voice tinkled all over the house: and her eyes shone like springtime; she played with her tops; and she ran like a quail; in the evenings she usually wore a red blouse with a nature design (a bird chirping), was wrapped in fur cozies, she'd run up the stairs and she'd read in the blue velvet room: stay 'til three.

Once she brought a blue flower: to Ivan Ivanych; with kindly expressions he looked at it saying:

"Ah, girl!"

He loved flowers: his nose was forever in flowers.

He dropped in a chair at a table already laid out. Vasilisa Sergeyevna started in:

"Nadya's white winter coat, I say we sell it, the coatguy, and buy her real fur; they say sable coats aren't that much."

Beneath its glass hemisphere on an alabaster table the clock chimed the hour.

"A nice sable coat puts a bite on your wallet, yes, basically: *half* a year's salary."

He pushed back his plate.

And, he threw down his napkin, "The soup and these meatballs are tasteless."

He rose and he shook the buffet as he passed on his way to his sweatbox to sit by himself: and to sneeze from the pollen.

Just outside the window, they shoveled wet snow.

7

The whole house filled with blue smoke when Kiyerko visited.

Loudly he clomped all around in warm boots, winter coat, and worn sheepskin hat likeahood, shouting helloes from a little ways off:

"Well, so?" "How are things? Going well?"

He twitched at the shoulder while rollinghiseyes, interrupting a spat; then he deftly embraced the professor by grabbing his sides with both hands:

"Hey, enough, that's enough: what a grump!" Then he took out his cherry-wood pipe:

"You're no stronger than mush, well… divorce, that's what *I* say!"

He kept one eye closed and the other one peered through the smoke; as he rubbed the new growth of his beard he revealed his head's bald spot.

With Kiyerko there: the professor stood waiting in front of the door: the professor's wife wearing an apricot dress with a collar, white fur, stood behind it (he saw her pale cheeks wet with tears).

"Wait," the professor had boiled over, arms open wide.

Vasilisa Sergeyevna blathered:

"This house isn't run by a beard."

"Nor by braids."

As she arched-up her lip her foul mouth spewed out poison:

"You toad!"

"Killer whale!" at that Kiyerko said to them:

"Stop!"

The professor, hair raised in two horns, in a robe, shuffled off to his office; his peepers were tumbling, his speech was justmumbling, his arm goodforfumbling; he bumped into Mitya:

"And *what* are you looking at?"

Kiyerko sat and he smoked a quick pipe near the dining room.

"Well, what a life, it's just no way to live."

Vasilisa Sergeyevna offered no answer: she cried.

"It just his way to justify himself."

Then Kiyerko's pupil glanced 'round, and he smoked one last bowl, then he pulled on his nose, knocked his pipe on the edge of the table, stood quickly: and bumped into Mitya.

"You're a lad, just a colt."

Then he added:

"You've grown, time to work: but a joker will get what a joker deserves."

Then said sharply:

"Stay out of the market; well, I don't believe it, not one word, but even now on the street all the talk is of books."

In his office, Korobkin had senselessly heapedthings in piles: all the shelves were a mess and beneath the shelves also.

So Kiyerko watched for a while.

Seemed the least they could do would be wipe off the pollen: the room was the yellowest yellow: and buy him more shelves, maybe three, with a lock and a key for his books: then at least they'd be tidy and much more secure.

The professor extended a hand and he pulled out a handkerchief. He was seized at that instant by doubt: and then, loudly, he sneezed.

"Dammit, a rooster has how many legs?" as he looked up at Kiyerko.

"Three, they say!"

"No, if you please," the professor seemed hurt, "I do know there are two."

Well then why did he ask?

His face suddenly wrinkled.

"My arm has been bothering me."

He patted the cast with his hand.

Then, when Kiyerko left, he dug through all his notes, and he pulled out three sheets from a pile, locked the door with the key, then he squatted and pulled the rug up by a corner, and lifted a piece of parquet (the one piece that he knew he could move): he concealed the sheets under the piece of parquet; on the papers were symbols; they laid out the sense of his life; so why didn't he lock his discovery securely in steel? It just didn't occur to him; he did not know, perhaps, that there are rooms in all banks that have boxes of steel you can rent.

There was much that he simply did not know: the corner the cook lent him always went with him.

At that time he suffered true sorrow.

His Tommie, the hound, was brought home, his gut swollen, paw smashed: he'd been crushed by a taxi; they blocked off a hall; and they wrapped him in blankets, they cleaned off his fur with a special solution, and bound him with rags; then, all bandaged, he silently shook as he squinted his red-rimmed, sad eyes: the professor remained on all fours for the evening:

"Well brother, it's tough?"

And he paced 'round the rug through the night: in the morning the hound dog was gone: and poor Nadya sobbed hearing them fight:

"You know, he should go out with the garbage!"

"Oh, what are you saying, oh, what are you saying," Korobkin seethed, steaming, "we must dig him a grave in the garden!"

So, that was done: Tommie was carried on out to be buried; Professor Korobkin, still inside the house, roared:

"Not a drum could be heard, nor a funeral note as we," choking, he sputtered on, "buried the dog..."[146]

The whole evening, he lectured them all:

"Well the Hindus, yes, basically, say that animals' souls reincarnate as humans; oh, yes... in their view, a dog, rationally gets reincarnated."

"Scammers all," Kiyerko hissed through his pipe.

But his Nadya believed:

"Well perhaps the poor dog will return to us someday: a boy. Yes, a bonechewer wants a long life."

8

In Moscow, the river slowed down to a stand-still.

The water had clouded, congealed just like fat, its flow weakened, was barelyjust moving the icechunks: it froze in one mass: and it shone like a block of pure ice.

Winters are fun! The closed windows of houses on Snuffsneezer Alley were coated with ice: clumps of snow like white cotton fell down, right on people; a Savage, the frost, crunched on fences and gates, and on rooftops, while playingwithpowder and goosing the girls as he painfully pinched at their piggies; and smoke wreathed the chimneys; the snowiest, messiest caps topped a splintery fence that had blued; snow was cleared off the roofs; and it cottonballed off of the five-story homes there on Snuffsneezer Alley: while under the cottonfall gathered the yellow and red sheepskin coats.

The deep freeze had arrived: one Cold Coldovich. Branches hung down all around a greyish-green home: on its gables, the napes of the

---

146. This was taken from *The Burial of Sir John Moore at Corunna* (1816) by Charles Wolfe. "Not a drum was heard, nor a funeral note, as his corpse to the rampart we hurried..." These words were put to music and used during Russia's wars in the Caucasus. The song later was popular in the Red Army.

necks of the statues wore drifts; and its doorknobs would stick to your skin; and the spot where the shoveled-out snow had been thrown was right next to a break in the fence; through the gap you could see, not the dirt, like in summer, no no: all the piles of snow from the shovelling thickened its white winter coat: and right near the gate, where the house had been fading to yellow, an icerink had formed, covered the street with its slipperyness, powdered a bit on the top.

A dog lived in the yard: a real wolfhound: he barked at two men (there to clear snow and ice).

"Go to hell, no good bowser!"

So, one of the workers, Romanych, with red hair and freckles, unwashed (how the grime lined his wrinkles), he lived off the yard: in a three-story house with its paint peeling off; and he shoveled the snow; and another, in leather with buttonsofleather, and square-jawed and square-faced with strong lines and hard eyes, removing the ice with a bar made of steel: Klopovichenko.

Wearing his sheepskin coat, Kiyerko came out ('cause he lived right nearby in a three-story house that was peeling); he patted his hat, stomped his boots.

"Hey there… You got a shovel for me? Well, you… I'll work with you." And then Kiyerko briskly cleared snow with a shovel: a snow shovelers' shoveler.

An awful wind whipped: and whole drifts roverotated; and up near the chimney, and thickly and roughly above the raw howling a voice could be heard; it was whining, then quiet, but audible through the white howl and the whirlwinds of snow; wild streams hurried above waves of snow; and it blew and it threw things out: wailing white howls.

That's what it's like when the wind's from the north.

By the coal chute, a mirror of ice, Klopovichenko chatted with Kiyerko, dumping some ice:

"There is no common ground! Give up on those dandies... come over... express your opinions on things; we're real workers: so share your opinions with us, not with them; we rush in for first call to get work for the day in worn jackets and clothing just patched for the winter, not like *them*, they show up, when they work, in nice shoes, not in boots: you might just as well shave a priest![147]

"Well, you! Well, you, alright!"

And then Kiyerko threw down his shovel and sat on a step while he took a quick pull on his pipe.

"Work your shift, work your shift at the factory: guard the politically ignorant; wrack your brain, you poor guy: you crawl past your own peasant fears[148] toward a class consciousness: but you might just as well shave a priest, take a book and just shove it in Kautsky's[149] teeth; know how many years I've lived with a class consciousness. Plus, I'm under suspicion... Take just the work: you could shrivel from heat from the furnace..."

"It's smoky down there, where you work."

"Yes, there's smoke," Romanych allowed.

The porter's voice boomed:

"That's enough, move some snow!"

So they grabbed for the shovels: had fun!

But the colordead frosts had arrived for the winter to stay; in the alleys folks ran in their furs (downright awkward) down past all the gates; hats, small hats, plain old ugly hats: noses were lilied and cranberried; moving around just a bit through the clear and wide snowscape; the sidewalk was chalk white (and only a thin path remained); the chalk

---

147. Describing a useless or ineffective action, this phrase appears frequently in coming pages.
148. Moscow's factories were filled with migrant peasants from the surrounding countryside and further.
149. Karl Johann Kautsky (1854-1938), a Czech-German philosopher and Marxist theoretician. He was an outspoken early critic of the Bolsheviks.

disappeared; the smooth spot grew darker; a fur-covered waif who had thrown off his gloves loudly dragged a sled over the ice in the cold; and their cranberries fruited bright red, but had not yet turned white: it's their ears, man, their ears!

All their ears felt like ice!

Gribikov stood not far off from the three, his hair red, with one hand on the arm of a poorly dressed crone while talking of church.

"Just you wait: and it soon will be Easter!"[150] Then the three listened to Gribikov.

"Just who is he really and where does he come from?" So Gribikov hissed:

"Just a lover of numbers, a counter: he multiplies numbers."[151]

"The son, you say steals from the father."

Then Kiyerko looked at him, frowning; Romanych shot spit right near Gribikov:

"He's just a chicken."[152]

"You might just as well shave a priest!"

Klopovichenko grabbed for the bar; while Gribikov lectured the badly dressed woman on teas:

"My dear, teas come in all sorts: black, red, and the better types, yellow.

At that, Klopovichenko tossed:

"An expert on tea!"

"Well at least I'm no thief," whispered Gribikov, "thieves, once discovered, get beaten." His words were unclear: he spoke poorly and couldn't put two words together; but he'd watch.

---

150. In the original, Gribikov refers to the Easter-season liturgy used in the Byzantine tradition of the Eastern Orthodox church, which is collected in a work known as the *Pentacostarion*.
151. Gribikov's use of the word for numbers (*tsifry*) in Russian plays with the sound of the word schizophrenic.
152. This is consistent with his plays on "son of a bitch" in section one of chapter one.

Then the porter declared:

"Well, you, oh yes, you'll be a giant, the others… oh well."

Klopovichenko grabbed at the bar:

"A horrible hour, a horrible day, a horrible life for us workers; well, it's useless, like shaving the beard off a priest."

A steely wind roared: and a foul ice storm howled; drifts encircled; and powder was blown off the tops of the drifts.

And when Gribikov passed: red-haired Romanych spit:

"Phew, you chained animal, you beast with no legs, grovelling trash eater, worm!"

At that, Gribikov fled: and Romanych just huffed.

"When we're done, he'll sniff everything: eachlittlething that he finds…"

Someone went through the gate in a coat made of bear-skin: and trod through the snow in red boots; and a woman in red went by; and the sleds bumped along: all the nags, their tack worn, had to struggle to get to the corner: and smelled of cold sweat; and the snow was not snow: it was frozen-stiff rays of the sunlight!

And crunch just as much as you'd like!

9

Kiyerko sat and played chess with Korobkin.

"Well, which do you want?"

"Oh, the black?" Then the doorbell.

Darya came in and she coughed in her hand:

"If you please, sir, a gentleman. Asking to see you: it's business, he says. You should know it's that Gribikov fellow…"

Kiyerko's face whitened:

"That's just what you get!"

So he trailed the professor out into the hall: the professor's nose dribbled: and Gribikov stood on the rug, he was waiting and clutching the yellow-bound tome and the little brown volume: he'd seen him and seen him but just through the window for twenty years; only just now in the flesh.

He was dressed in worn clothes; had, up close, both an old and surprisingly womanly face; but he seemed like an old man; was a chicken-leg[153] wearing the face of a worm; his pants showed their age; and his eyes were a shade of tobacco; God knows that his eyes were a vulture's: his nose was a beak, a smallmouth (with chewed lips) like a stripe: his thin chest a dry breadcrust: in a word a real staleguy; a glance clearly showed: all was fine: then it seemed there was some sort of flaw: like his nose was all gone (but he had one) or ear (there it was!) or his throat made of bronze (no, it's real!).

It was clear: he was worn, had been chewed by the years: by old age, as they say, souls get chewed (not each one).

He slowly prepared to speak up: but then suddenly hiccupped and coughed with a hack, his whole body was racked; and then like a small file made a cut with a barely detectable rasp:

"Well."

"Hm, basically: how may I help?" the professor asked, stumped. By then Mitya, all ears, had just barely edged out of the hallway and into the front room: his pimples oozed blood; and his face had gone pale, his jaw shook:

"For one moment, he'll praise me; and then he will shame me."

But despite it all, he wanted one final insolent act: jump right into the pool; and he'd lie: 'til he blacked out; his eyes flashed bravado.

---

153. Emphasis on the height rather than skinniness.

Pale cheeks came in sight: Vasilisa Sergeyevna stood there and listened. Kiyerko traced out a triangle darting his eyes: he traced Gribikov, Mitya, his father.

In dim yellowlight the professor was red-faced and looked quite a bit like a dog: his appearance was frightening; then, he saw Gribikov holding two books and announced:

"Those are mine, from my library, basically... How did they end up with you?"

"You should know that is why I am here, I just happened... to buy them, you see, from a dealer.

Here, Vasilisa Sergeyevna barked from a distance:

"*Mais je vous dis que la femme de chambre...*[154] Darya!..."

"Do not interfere," the professor ran toward her, shaking the brown book (the yellow he'd dropped).

And then Kiyerko, looking on craftily, followed Korobkin, eyes peeled, he ran up, with one hand and struck Gribikov; using his other, quite rudely, he turned him around; pushed him back to the door.

"Well you, leave the books... Yes, yes, yes, leave them both here. I'll explain... And I do know... Now, get!"

And he whispered:

"Keep mum about things you may know, my friend." Gribikov's peepers were pie plates.

He struggled to speak; and suddenly, like an old man who was fighting a cough and a cold he then clutched at his chest with a hand; and it shook as he flushed; and he waved a weak arm; he was suddenly ready to leave, he went straight to the door (his legs flew).

The door slammed.

---

154. But I told you that the maid...

And he crossed the street, cautiously, slowly, a eunuch, while thinking:

What happened?

Completely unable to comprehend facts: he could only just stare.

Not yet back in his spot in the window, he stood near the gate; but he didn't go through; he just pressed on his wart; then he lifted his finger and looked: and he sniffed it; he turned, then decided on something; and looked, most perplexed, at Korobkin's.

A fierce altercation ensued: Vasilisa Sergeyevna desperately battled with Kiyerko; right in the hall; Vasilisa Sergeyevna tried to articulate what she was thinking.

"It's Darya who's taking the books... You don't know... There were, well, antecedents: she stole from our kitchen, some sugar!"

Kiyerko argued, but most unconvincingly:

"Darya has nothing to do with it..."

Truth be told, he was entirely unable to say what he wanted: and *him* a real thinker.

"You don't know, well, you see: that a burglar's adroit. I know burglars: it's a burglar," he said, grabbing the window lock's latch.[155]

"*À propos*: he didn't take more, or some valuables?"

"Well, perhaps, well, they scared him; he did get his claws on two books, that's exactly what happened!" he said as he snapped his suspenders."

---

155. Bely cites a particular type of burglar, a "*fortochnik*," usually a small boy skinny and agile enough to squeeze through a narrow window, known as a "*fortochka*," used for ventilation.

"A window thief," runny-nosed Mitya, watched scornfully, stared straight at Kiyerko, begging. All covered in sweat: he was horrified thinking about his misdeeds. But the professor was aimlesslymoving, just pacing, from Kiyerko to Mitya, and Mitya to Kiyerko; visibly tortured by something; his eyes lost their shine; and his whole reddened mug lost its color; a bitterness set in his eyes.

"Vasilisa Sergeyevna, Darya had nothing to do with this!"

Hearing Kiyerko's assertions he blinked, he saw double; not two books but something like forty were missing: no burglar could jump out the window with forty.

"This fall, you know," Mitya grew bold, "near the window, I..."

Here the professor's eyes flashed and then rolled and grew angry. Then, aiming at Mitya, he spat out a stream of goo:

"Silence, just zip up your lips!"

He straightened his spine and went into his office: to nap for a while.

But the bell rang again.

What a mess!

So abitlikeanoldman he stuck his head out of the door: Gribikov: sticky and stuck!

"Well, so, you?" Kiyerko queried.

When Gribikov caught sight of Kiyerko; he lost his head: he'd hoped Kiyerko wouldn't come out to the door; he just stood stood there and looked but kept silent: then timidly:

"Let in your cat: it's out meowing down under our porch..."

When he finished: he left.

So they opened the door; but no cat and an icy draft hollered, infected with flu: "Close the door: the apartment's an icebox!"

✳

The professor walked through to his office.

He'd aged: bitterbrowed, humped; he slumped down in a yellow chair under a portrait of Leibniz, who'd proved to us all: all is well; two books gone: out from under old Leibniz; Korobkin's huge earlobes hung down like a rabbit's, beneath a small tuft on the top of his head; and then dull-eyed he stared at a forked condul holder, his glasses reflecting the light, while under the glasses he mourned with his eyes, as if waving away a most difficult matter; and multiple thousands of little men ran there before him, seemingly chasing each other.

He leaned from the chair to a shaft of dim yellowish gloom (where moths fluttered), and toyed with a worn yellow tassel behind the old curtains, his head wound in bandages, bottom to top; and his arm all wrapped up: a white stump in a sling; and with dull eyes he languished and stared at the grinning fauns.

"Space has been fractured!"

Then Kiyerko entered while quietly smiling in pity:

"How are you?"

"So-so: but my arm has been bothering me!"

Then he touched his cast, walked to the corner, and stood near the pedestal: Leibniz was proof that our world is the best of them all.

"Hey, it's fine. You'll get through it." And both kept their silence: 'til sundown.

Beginning that day, the professor stopped speaking with Mitya.

Thereafter, when leaving the house he would lock up his office; and take the key with him; at night he would hear good old Tommie, a scraper, in the front room just scratching his claws on the floor: all while chewing his bone; he'd go out in the hall with a condul.

But Tommie was gone!

The wind swung to the south; at that, everythingliquified, flowed; then they took off their winter coats; carriages started their grumbling; then it froze just a bit once again; in the evening the grey-rose and fisty stone cobbles were visible, all hardened and cold, the deep cold of the North.

10

A cutelittlesnowflake on top of a fisty stone cobble. A blizzard crouched down on the streets. And a whistling wind sounded; and swarms of snow raced; and November blew cabs off the streets for the sleighs to appear and it snowed cold white flakes; the flakes melded together; white floods drifted down.

Out of the alleys and streets, and along all the streets and the alleys they wandered; past profiles of buildings, and churches and fences; in twos and in threes; they came singly; their shadows were torn from their legs: then they greyed and they broadened, ran up and away, and then broke on the walls: turned to giants; and carriages rumbled; the trams squealed; green circles of light from the street lamps expanded; a star twinkled then burst and became a new sun, it was light from the beams of a heavy black car; the light shrunk to a point. And flew off in the dark.

In the distance they moved, overtaking each other; they came from Petrovka, Mokhovaya, the Arbat, Prechistenka and Sretenka Streets to a spot that was bright, where a lily mist melted because of the light, where the noise of the cabstands was topped by the gas pumps. The lights of Kuznetsky!![156]

---

156. One of the busiest streets of Moscow's old central downtown.

Waves of bowlers, fedoras, and hats and caps, fur hats, capes, shirts: all the way from the corner; "Avantso" sparkled;[157] and people were swarming and pushing and then slowly they stopped, stood there fiddling with hats; while they looked at the hands of the clock, and then clutching their cases while pushing and shoving, stepped aside for each other; one pale spot of a face then appeared; and this visage stood out; for its carmine lips gleamed and its earrings shone brightly; in bowlers, far easterners[158] thronged day and night; and they aimlessly watched: all and sundry; here bundles of bodies were pressed right up flat to the windows and crushed: and they robbed folks from 12 right 'til six, the whole day!

Square black cars were confined by the flow of the carriages, careful in crowds, but exploding with gasoline backfires; not moving, they stood, turned enormous round eyes on the cop's white baton and made way as they watched: they saw hookers and merchants and currency dealers, and strollers, respectable ladies and actresses, students. A street: no, a diamond! Each corner a bouquet of flowers.

Here, things turned blue from the mercury lights; over there, it grew rosy, lit up, it got brighter and warmer; from out here the streetlamps all glowed a dim green; in the second floor windows, just look: there's asoftlight, a yellow gonedark. Up there higher and higher, from whence flew the silver-plumed snow, and now fading in bloody red chaos and darkness, the cornice's edges just visible.

Under a yellow-cream border of twin-horned rams heads: light; behind all the windows was May: there were grass, purple flowers, and roses and leaves; just like Nice;[159] all the dandies rushed there to fill buttonholes; daisies, carnations, and quick; they'd run out, run across

---

157. A popular restaurant.
158. These are merchants and traders from Central Asia.
159. Nice, the French city, perhaps a reference to fashion or flowers.

the dark street, and they'd weave in between the black cubes of the carriages, carts, and landaus, to the crosswalk.

Beside them, a storefront had windows displaying sheer fabrics: and laces like spider webs.

Girls passed with boxes; a red-faced *lycée*-boy pushed through (he was suffering, clearly, from lovesickness): skinny legs! Waiting and watching, a woman: she turned; and her man had already arrived; so they walked off together; through circles of fabric a face had appeared; it was covered in cold cream; two eyesballs, entirely otherworldly, appraised an old soldier, who barely could drag his old saber; he was wearing worn sky-colored breeches; a woman: Zobikova, well known, and rich, stood there wearing a coat; if she took it off, she'd be in lace: made to tempt; a quite subtle scent rose from her just a small distance; that old soldier...

Clouds of a blizzard approached: and they sprinkled the city with powder.

And soon, the refrigerator revved as it castironed everything: flat roofs of metal sheet boomed in the cold; and the wind howled in chimneys; and whole flocks of snowflakes would screech in your eyes; and there outside the windows it all was one color; the color of mercury, blue, and white!

Rose!

Out of nothing a light burst to blinding; another, a third; then light poured on the street; it formed letters: "Cognac" in bright red; and then "Shustov's" in white; plop, again the dark, once more: no end, no beginning!

Advertisements at play.

There were five floors of rose colored, sugary ornaments, sickeningly slapped up together, like sweetly-iced cake; at the top it ran toward the night-shaded lily (oh no, make that dark lily); down off the top its sides glowed; and behind one large window shone crystal; and a second gave views way deep inside: of curtains and drapes; and an olive damask, a brocade, striped the walls; shelves and statues and furniture had various fabrics; and it was as if the most private of rooms in the cosmos was tossed on the street; a bright clerk, with his hair neatly parted and sleeked, his lips purpling, was standing and stretching a bit, his beard messy, and motionless, serving a lady, displaying some cloth; as the woman considered it, bending her head, you could see through her veil: yes, a blonde!

Automobiles sped.

And they seemed to be monstrous huge pugs that were snarling and baring their teeth with their headlights: and flying from where the lights flashed, from where the trams squealed in the distance, at times splashing violet, and purple at times.

White Kuznetsky!

11

But no!

Eduard Eduardovich served as her font of perfection; Lizasha, of course, had, occasionally, wandered in spirit; but was flooded with life: and she marked all these times in her father's life, using these moments to make her own path; but the path was a mess: she neared an abyss. She stared in.

Well, so what of his business; it was Solness who troubled her greatly, he built a most wonderful life (she enjoyed reading Ibsen); perhaps she saw Borkman;[160] and maybe, just... here the ineffable started; and it became clear that things were not right: just not consistent with Ibsen's ideas. And not even Borkman's!

---

160. Two of Ibsen's characters, Halvard Solness, from *Master Builder*, and John Gabriel Borkman from a play by the same name.

So, like a detective, she raced to explain all the gestures he *lived*; and she later was drowned in a world filled with nymphs; she would traipse through the house with a green sleepless face through stale air and her cigarette smoke.

She learned all of her father's pet gestures: while one of his gestures related to this; and another to that; Kavalever's arrival meant business abroad; and the phone: Merditsevich, Siberian affairs; and she knew what Madame Evikhkaiten's place meant; and where Madame Mindalyanskaya stood; and she envied her.

All was clear: what, why, who, where.

It seemed totally senseless why, smiling, the horrid dwarf came, with no nose, a decaying face; why, just a week back, a most unpleasant eunuch named Gribikov visited.

"'God,' who is this?"

"You are curious, sister."

He said nothing more. And that paper?

Lizasha was standing alone in her father's home office and turning it blue with her cigarette, smoothing a paper she'd found on the rug; the small paper was old and had yellowed; the hand unfamiliar, small, beaded, including "Fi" symbols and X's; crossed out; re-re...; well, just impossible to grasp; though she knew it was math; but no – why mathematics? She understood Kavalever's real role; and she knew Merditsevich's role and Madame Mindalyanskaya's: clear and quite simple! But here she ran onto a reef; and her "path" was torn up; the abyss loomed.

But she did not know just what type of abyss.

She could not comprehend why her "god" at one time had called her "Lizaveta Eduardovna" not "little sister Alyona"; remembering, she grew insulted: and flashed her eyes (like radium, the flash hurt the body itself not the soul).

The paper then slipped from her tiny chilled fingers; and later, a cigarette stuck in her cute lips, she sat for a smoke.

While just outside the windows, wind whistled: it blew at the window.

Madame Voulezvous's soft but searching voice loudly came from the next room.

"Oh, Lizasha, hey?"

Quickly she lifted her hand up above her small mouth as she tilted the cigarette's ember up.

"Yes?"

"What are you doing?" rang out from the hall. But Lizasha just narrowed her eyes at the curtain and thought:

So then, what's it to her?

"It's that Mitya Korobkin."

"Oh-oh? I'll be right there! "

Then she stuck the small scrap in her pocket and ran through the sitting room into the green of the guest room; the fawn room held Mitya.

He wore Vedenyapin's school uniform; but, more precisely, was not in his uniform: he wore a black but plain jacket and pants (on the weekends): a filthy red spot on his boot dripped and soiled the floor: and he looked at Lizasha and, mumbling, brow sweating and pimply and pie-eyed, he asked:

"Am I bothering you?"

Smiling, all fleshy gums, Mitya extended his jaw.

"Oh of course not, no bother."

"You're sure?"

"Believe me: and don't stand there just looking hysterical."

Lizasha exhaled curls of smoke.

"It's not comfortable here, let's go into the guest room." Her tiny, cute mouth, the rogue, twitched with a smile.

Conversations with her would upset him profoundly: she seemed like a fable that he'd never read.

She was turning the guest room to blue with her cigarette, miniature body all buried with pillows, (and knitting intelligent brows) she sat waiting to hear what he'd say; he was brimming to say the unsayable; but: his two lips were clipped shut.

Then he somehow was able to lick both his lips, and could click with his tongue: a wet noise came out slick: and his mouth filled right up with wet spit.

"Well you wanted to speak: that's it: you yourself said; I've heard all of your promises; you've fed me *these* lines for *some* time now."

"I've never been a good speaker, you know that."

"At least you could try."

"I'm afraid I won't find the right words, will be forced to make something up; you know I get tongue-tied; and something entirely mistaken comes out, and then I'm forced to lie – I can't find words that are right eous."[161]

Madame Voulezvous woke that day with a swollen, sore cheek.

"*Excusé* but I didn't know." "You're... not alone?"

But Lizasha just grimaced: her eyes flashed with anger.

"You know he's with me, Madame Voulezvous..."

"Would you like tea?"

"I wouldn't, would you?" she asked Mitya.

"I won't, so, uh, no, no thanks."

"That won't be needed Madame Voulezvous."

"*Excusé,*" said Madame Voulezvous from the back of the drapes in a very smooth voice as she moved down the hall and she jingled her keys;

---

161. Explaining why he speaks poorly, Mitya speaks poorly. Bely plays with the typography and wording to offer a bit of additional humor by adding an extra space that emphasizes Mitya's troubles.

but the keys soon went silent; Lizasha, who'd waited for something, jumped up; and stuck out her head: and she ran her eyes over the chairs in the guest room.

It was empty.

When she prowls you just can't hear the keys, and while walking away she intentionally jangles them, then she sneaks back and she eavesdrops...

"So, what did you want to say?"

Mitya had sealed his lips tight.

12

"Hey, hey!"

Fat-reared, a furious coachman; his cushion flashed red as he lifted and parted his hands while he cut through the crowd with a white-maned pure porcelain trotter; in front of the yellow and spiral-horned ram-headed border, the driver, with very deft reins, stopped the horse.

Eduard Eduardovich, wrapped in blue fox, jumped straight down and went through the lit entrance, a bronze plaque there announcing, "Mandro and Co."

He climbed 24 steps to the top; then he cracked the door open a bit, and went into a polished establishment known as a banker's front office; there, pale, shaved, and bald men bent over their desks in the light of green lamps, and divided by yellow oak counters from the rest of the office, they filled out bank forms; and they spiked them; and, near a cash drawer, and a sign that said "Checks," stood respectable customers.

Quickly he carried his sideburns through into a richly appointed, unoccupied office with views of Kuznetsky.

✳

A gentleman, middle-aged, neat, bowed down low to Mandro while extending a folder with papers; Mandro used a pince-nez and looked through the papers with swift and sure hands.

"So then. Anything else?"

"Yes, a personal matter."

"Oh. Please."

The doors opened; and Gribikov, yellow and pale, looked 'round, stuck in his nose and right shoulder.

Politely, he stayed by the door; in the light his small eyes were half-shut; Eduard Eduardovich gestured invitingly.

"Please, have a seat."

At that, Gribikov limped to a chair; but he stood near the chair, did not sit right away, then collapsed on the chair: like his tendons were sliced.

"What do you have to say?"

And then, Gribikov fingered his wart and examined his finger.

"I will take one liberty, note just one miniscule difficulty, sir," he said sniffing his finger, "there is no agreement at all."

"No more rooms?"

At that, Gribikov's pupil crawled up on Mandro.

"I've got *quite* a few tenants."

The pupil hid under its lid.

Mandro, most dissatisfied, strode to the window: he played with a sideburn; and jammed a hand into the pocket of tightly cut pants; then he pressed his brow onto the pane as he whistled, impressed by a sparkling spectacle outside the window: a show of bright colors.

A crooked-legged man; and behind him, a woman, her veil with black specks, and behind all the specks her eyes flashed; while the wind pulled the scarf.

Then Mandro turned to face the whole room.

He saw Gribikov sitting unmoved, face displaying indifference: he smirked.

"So, the hell with him: I don't need this."

Then he rolled his eyes, turning away once again: in the window, a lady in marten fur.

Gribikov felt beady eyes on his back.

"Here, if... I, well, another thing." Mandro turned:

"What?"

"If, um... it'll be fine."

"Speak more clearly."

"If he stays with me, well: your man."

"Is that possible?"

"I think that it's possible: but he, your man, has no nose, is quite sick, and he speaks like a foreigner; he's not one of ours, and he's here all alone, so just where could he go; and he *does* need some care; it's all there, that is, such as it is; so to tell you the truth, I've a two-room apartment; he'll live there with me if you'd like... That's all fine, bless him: later we'll settle the rent."

And he winked a small peeper.

13

Mitya's ideas did not fit any phrases: and he felt like his soul did not fit in his flesh; while describing his troubles he seemed to Lizasha quite funny by accident; foolish; his hands were like paddles; his face was severely misshapen, a grimace that doctors dubbed – this is the medical jargon – "Hippocrates's mask."

Then Lizasha grew cross:

"We've been here half an hour: not one word."

"There are times one can't speak, you know."

"Give it a try."

"I will try; but, Lizasha, just stop with your pushing."

But something just clicked in his mouth, it smacked, stuck; then it caught in his throat; and he wanted to cry.

"You know, at home, our family life's bad, I'd be better off leaving; my father is nice, you know; he's just not relaxed when with people: he lives for his math; he thinks that in forty years nothing has changed; we can't talk; and when something is troubling my soul he refuses to listen; he's simply some sort of, you know, he's a forma list."[162]

"Well, and your mother?"

"She reads all the time; she just read Solovyov's latest history; right from the start; she's had nothing to do with me; mother's a stranger."

Lizasha sat, thin, right in front of him, snuggle-bug-wrapped in a red brocade sable-trimmed robe; then she poured from a cup some small polished stones: onyx, black knick knacks…

"A stranger?"

"Completely a stranger at home; I forgot how to speak: so I'm silent: I know if I say what I think they'll reject it in any case: so, you know, I have to lie."

"You poor thing: you deceive them."

She nervously tossed one small knick knack from her palm in the air; and beneath her fanned skirt her legs folded, a pretzel.

"Yes, that's what I'm forced to do."

Mitya's raw cuticles clutched at the divan:

---

162. Bely leaves a space here, suggesting Mitya's misuse and/or misunderstanding of the word.

"And my father, you know: can't ask me anything sensible; I scare him: so he checks me, checks, how and what: like, well, 'Were you called on in class?' or it's, 'How are your grades?'... You won't hear a kind word, you know."

"You get…?"

She sprinkled the onyx stones onto the cloth.

"As I said, I get A's… I…"

"So, you, it seems, also lie here."

And she threw down a stone as he said:

"What else: even try telling the truth, they will yell; and you see, God knows what."

"Well, I sure don't envy you."

"How else could it be? And my friends, you know, spend their time learning things; one just read Buckley, and one Cherynshevsky…[163] I can't even peep about owning a book: you can sit all day long and just study; but owning a useful and much needed book…"[164]

"Poor thing!"

The tip of her knee peeked from under her skirt.

"And no entertainment: we don't go to the theater; well, I, you know, read a lot: over at Sennaya Street, at Ostrovsky's.[165] I don't go to school: and then later I say that I went."

Mitya just ogled her knee: she got worried.

"Well then, Mitya dear, you are both guiltless and guilty." She straightened her skirt.

"I read Ibsen, the play you suggested."

"*The Master Builder?*"

"Yes."

---

163. Buckley; Chernyshevsky: *What Is to Be Done?*
164. By useful, he means socially useful.
165. Ostrovsky opened a reading room in downtown Moscow with free public access.

"Oh, my dear monster freak," her darling voice chimed, "you're abandoned; just look: the whole game is the feathers, appearance is everything."

Lizasha leaned over: he heard her exhale.

"Let me straighten you up: there you go."

She leaned back with the cigarette held in her lips, her head bowed as she narrowed her eyes with the pleasure.

"I'm loyal, so that's why I help you; you're homeless."

Lips parted, she sat:

"You come here, like a dog: it's your habit."

She tossed a small lock of her hair to one side; and she said:

"It's my nymph that you visit, not me."

Her hand (it was frozen) had touched his.

"My nymph and I talk all about you."

Her eyes flashed at Mitya.

"Some stars shine together, the Pleiades;[166] remember the Pleiades? They are high in the sky in the summer; at night, when it's late: near my bedtime."

The atmosphere cleared at Mandro's; and at least they were speaking.

"A home with an atmosphere."

Keys rang again in the guest room; it seemed that Madame Voulez-vous's swollen cheek would be thrust in the room once again; but the keys moved away; then were gone.

"She's obnoxious."

Lizasha's head stuck through the drapes:

"Well, she's gone."

---

166. In Greek mythology, the Pleiades, nymphs, were the seven daughters of the sea-nymph Pleione and the titan Atlas. The star cluster Pleiades, with seven stars, may have first been important to the Greeks in navigation.

But the atmosphere dimmed: lost its luster.

They listened in silence; the wind swept the roof: and Lizasha just sat as she drowned in her eyes, in her own; an ashbit plopped into the ashtray: her eyes shone.

"What's next?"

His lips smacked.

"I will take the test over again: back in August I hid."

"Ay-yi-yi!"

"You, Lizasha, excuse me for speaking like this; but now I… you know, want to tell you now finally, I have been searching for words, this and that, but to speak with my father: you can see it yourself; and my mother, well, bless her... Nadezhda, my sister," he snorted, "Nadezhda..."[167]

His thoughts dulled: it was odd, he considered his sister quite close, but was awkward around her; his eyes lost their focus; and speech was a struggle: his jaw trembled, lips shlurpped, smacked, and chomped.

All for nothing!

14

A carriage arrived.

And its coachman, in fur, sprang down out of his perch, he held a small top hat, one handed, and opened the door with the other.

Blown down by the wind, a coat fell in his hands, and a curly-haired blonde in a transparent veil, lips luxurious, bosom – perfection, descended; she held her sheer skirt in the wind, but she showed the pedestrians imported stockings, *feil morte*, beneath her rose hem, its lace flowing.

---

167. In Russian, Nadezhda means "hope."

She entered the doorway right under the yellow rams-headed border by the bronze plaque that shone "Offices of Mandro and Co."

An announcement:

"Madame Mindalyanskaya wishes to see you."

Eduard Eduardovich started to lead him out; Gribikov, gripping his cap, limpedalong and ran into Madame Mindalyanskaya just as she entered the room.

She entered.

And off flew her cloak; folds of silk fell around her; a huge hat like a tray with long feathers that flopped; both her hair and her person were pleasingly plump; the air puffed as she passed: perfume, opopanax.[168]

"Eva Ivanovna: can it be you?"

Seen in profile – quite simply divine, and her bosom – perfection.

Between buildings, under a sign hung for "Sosipatr Sidorov,"[169] filling the passage, a sparkling crowd: with gold teeth, pince-nez and monocles.

They stared in the windows and ate with their eyes a fine lily-toned mixture of muslin and surrah[170] with fans; right next-door was a sparkling downpour of gems; of clear rubies and yellow-mist beryls, and garnets the color of rum, and a lace of small emeralds; all, in a word, a roulade made of faceted light; and the crowd stayed and watched how the redlight sparked up, then the green: and they'd startle and gasp.

---

168. A fragrant natural resin found mainly in Somalia, said to have a balsamic, honey aroma. Not unlike frankincense and myrrh. Also known as opobalsam.

169. Sosipatr Sidorov's Linen Manufacturers was a well-known Moscow business and this location, Petrovsky Passage, was one of Moscow's prestigious shopping destinations.

170. Surrah, a soft, twilled silk or rayon fabric.

Just amazing!

A smallish brunette, quite remarkably beautiful, squinting one eye at the brilliance; a mustache and top hat, nicely equipped with a monocle, wearing, wide-open, a coffee-tone fur coat, while squinting his eyes at the brilliance he saw in her eyes; from the door: came a hump-nosed and sideburned man, wearing a pince-nez and earmuffs and holding a box, small and wrapped (bought for *his* ballerina); a grey-haired old lady, all dried-out but stylishly dressed: in a toq; held a bright purse, clasps polished-up.

Writers and critics, and counts, and some merchants and traders, some shaved and some bearded, and mustached, grey, and blue-green, and women in coats and nice tops, from the right to the left and the left to the right.

And they walked, in both twosomes and threesomes: and splashed on their hems and made noise, looked at earrings, and clutched at the hats, twirled their canes, gripped their briefcases, held their packages, sorted through gloves – there were suitcases, fur tails, a boa; they gave way, permitting each other to pass; but they crowded the exit; and left for Varvarka, Stoleshnikov Alley, Spiridonov, and Lesser Nikitskaya Street.

And behind them came carriages, carts, and sedans.

A woman there, shielding her face with a muff, up and ran from a spot in the light to the black cubic head of a car; she was raising her skirt, which was rippling her "dessa" silk; running behind her a gentleman pressing a glove to his ear; then the driver, while risking his skin, turned the wheel; and the engine, which stank of spilled gasoline, roared.

Then a fat-reared and furious coachman; his cushion flashed red as he cut through the crowd, with a white-maned horse hitched to his carriage; he flew to the end of Kuznetsky where lights grew much weaker: then out through the greenish murk.

15

"Mitya, you lie consciously; I don't lie: who would I lie to? Lie to my 'god'?"

She moved closer: eyes twinkling.

"I can't lie to 'god.'"

On the pillows her warm little body had pressed a clear shape.

"And yet everything in me feelsfalse."

In the heavens, the Pleiades surely will rise: it's already high time to sleep; no more stars for the night, go to drown, to be tortured in sleep; like now, off to her dreams, which were muddled and heavy.

"Everything in me feelsfalse because I drowned the nymph: I came here from out there."

Her eyes showing her total surprise (what a girl!),[171] and while sticking a cigarette into her mouth:

"You won't understand this my dear!"

After stretching her neck she shot smoke through her nose. And again:

"Out of there and came here."

And then throwing her hand straight up over her mouth, swiftly spiraled the cigarette, watching the glowing loop:

"How would I know," she had lost the attention of Mitya's wide brow.

Then she lifted the cigarette; narrowed her eyes with the pleasure, smoke curling up.

"I did not understand what you mean: 'out of there'?" And the smoke had encircled her, dissolved into threads:

---

171. Bely's parenthetical description, "what a girl," or *prosto devchurochka*, again alludes to prostitution. In this case he is basically saying that she is, in fact, just an unwell girl with unbalanced, muddied intentions.

"I just feelfalse," she said, as she nervously twitched both her shoulders and lips.

For some time Lizasha just knitspun her words to make missiles; it seemed that a fine and invisible lace hung all over. A weaver; then crossing her legs like a pretzel, surprisingly casually showed him her knee; and again with two fingers reached out: for the ashtray.

An ashbit fell off.

"Yes, let's end all this idiocy; what can I say; I'm a fool, don't you think?"

Then he felt her long fingernail touching his hand.

"I can scratch."

He moved closer; but she moved away; but played with her hair like a nymph.

"Now sit still, just like that."

And then suddenly tilted her head.

"Time is a cannibal: eats people like snacks: it's disturbing!"

"So why're you talking about this?"

She looked, eyes aglow:

"A nymph told me."

Then, Mitya saw: rumpled and tiny, a paper scrap fall on the floor (from Lizasha's own pocket); he looked automatically; saw a few symbols he knew: and the hand seemed familiar: saw integrals and an equation..."Where is that from!"

Then he stretched out one hand for the paper.

"Just what are you doing?"

"That paper."

She saw it and grabbed it up:

"Give it, it's mine."

"Just a moment; that looks like my father's handwriting."

He grabbed; and she scratched him one.

"Ow!"

"Keep your hands off it."

"No. And just how did it get here?" Lizasha was cunning:

"You left it yourself last time: fell from your pocket...You dope!"

That was strange, and again things were senselesss: how did the paper end up with her "god"? Then her instinct insisted she lie: tell him he'd left it: so she just acted surprised. "Why'd you do that?" She lied, unexpectedly: not for herself but for... Could it be that for "god" she must lie? Does "god" lie? There she stood, right above the abyss.

She fixed the abyss with a stare.

Then they heard a distinct and loud creak from the back of the curtain.

And Mitya could hear someone there; took a peek at Lizasha, who, standing, was looking at him: but right through him; he turned and he shuddered on spotting Mandro's manlyoutline: as if he'd snuck in with the twilight, his face quite well-groomed, he was groomed to a fault.

Then he swiftly marched in, with grey horns, strong browed and wellbuilt, as he flexed just a bit his heroic-sized shoulders while stripping a glove he was chewing his lip with a sourpussed look that he tried to relax.

Threw a glance at Lizasha and Mitya: and said with his toothified maw:

"Hello."

Mitya assumed that he browblacked, black coal, for effect: then he turned on the switch: a clear lamp on the ceiling shone brightly.

"You're with Lizaveta Eduardovna, sitting in shadows; the sounds would suggest you're discussing your dreams?" his harmonium played.

But he gazed with funereal eyes, a hard look that could kill conversations.

"I'm not pleased with, little Alyona, your nymph, no," and scratching a sideburn, he whistled.

Then sat.

But this sitting, for them, seemed a torturous contest: could someone here out-sit someone else: Mitya... Lizasha? Lizasha… Mitya? Perhaps von-Mandro could out-sit them both; he remembered the rumors alleging that he had allowed himself too much with one young female gymnasium student: Lizasha's girlfriend.

It was said that at one point in life he'd partaken in sodomy.

16

"Dinner is served!"

Von-Mandro stood and looked around sourly.

"*Eat*, let's go eat."

And his nicely-groomed sideburns walked past them and almost right through them.

They went to the dining room, yellow-oak panelled; with carved fluted columns lining the walls; an impressive buffet; and a table was set with a cloth of snow white; and the crystal and glass shone; each place had three glasses, a green, and a gold, and a rose; and a vase; with red fruit; there was wine; to the side, on a table shone: silver, a wine cooler.

"Noodle soup," tempted Mandro, his lips smacking.

He tucked in his collar a napkin: he mmm-ed; then he looked at Lizasha with care and surprisingly gently.

"You don't want to eat?"

"Ah, no."

"You should take chloral hydrate, Alyona."[172]

---

172. Chloral hydrate, a nineteenth century sedative with high rates of addiction.

He signaled a servant: the servant then toweled off the bottle, and placed it back into the cooler.

"Yes, yes, young man, meatballs.... I guess it depends on your taste..." bare fingered he wiped off his lip gloss, "...your virtue depends on temptations."

His fingers had lip gloss.

His eyes misted over; all toothy and long-armed, his sticky lips close to Lizasha's. He turned at the waist toward Madame Voulezvous.

"How are things with the bat now, Madame Voulezvous?"

"Well, I finally figured it out, it was Fedya, the cook's boy, who caught it near Moscow: let it go in the house... I had noticed for quite a long time: that it smelled!"

"That it smelled?"

Von-Mandro's head dramatically shook; he adjusted his napkin.

"Just why is it, young man, that you won't try the grouse; taste it... I tried all kinds of meats at your age."

He turned to the grouse.

And Lizasha hit him with the end of a white napkin.

"That's for you."

He surrendered.

Mandro ate his grouse with quite obvious pleasure: he stretched to the cooler: for wine: he poured Mitya a glass, to the brim: a gold stream.

He extended the glass: gave a warm look: the look turned to ice; it was clear he could take him and juice him.

"Clink glasses!"

He started to speak more sincerely.

It happened that way more than once: like they'd reached an agreement: or if they had not, they soon would; this depended on Mitya himself; while Lizasha would serve as the guarantee; in fact, no agreement was needed: things were quite clear as they stood.

They clinked glasses.

His gestures displayed, nonetheless, not just violence: but damage, disturbance, dictation of terms.

At the same time, with lips chewed and bloody, her smiling expressed her submission: it seemed they conversed with their eyes.

"Now the drama is over."

"What's that, your glass empty?"

"Again?"

"Well, let's clink!"

"Eduard Eduardovich, I, I: the drink has gone right to my head!"

"You are not getting drunk."

But he sensed, as he drank more and more, there was some kind of something that showed in Lizasha: that undefined something was there in the atmosphere: something invading her spirit… and evil.

A home with real atmosphere!

Lizasha sat with an expression of innocence:

"Mitya, it looks like you've had quite a bit: no more drinking!"

"Leave him be," Eduard Eduardovich waved, condescendingly wagging a finger.

But Mitya appeared to be drunk.

"So, your father, how is he?"

"Are his papers at home?"

"At his desk?"

"What?"

"Does he work all the time?"

"Tell me, when can I find him at home?"

"Is he healing?"

"Bad luck!"

He stayed cool as he stretched a refined hand (and ruby burn scar) for a pear.

"Oh Lizasha, Lizasha," young Mitya's mind boiled. Then he noticed Madame Voulezvous and Lizasha had vanished.

"Lizasha!"

Mandro tried evincing sincerity; it happened this way more than once: like they had an agreement: or if they did not, they soon would; and it seemed this depended on Mitya himself; while Lizasha would serve as the guarantee; moreover, conditions were unneeded: things were quite clear as they stood.

17

His head spun: had the sense his subconscious was hollow. The wine? Or Mandro? He'd forgotten: a loud noise in his ears; he remembered one thing, no conditions were needed: and things were quite clear as they stood: he awoke in a guest room; he'd likely been out for a while; he had suddenly come to his senses: in front of a mirror.

Who *is* that?

His mug red, a bed head, his arms dead; in a chair, he was rocking; encircled in lion's paws, gold: he lay back: his face burning, with oatmeal for brains, with an urge: for Lizasha, discuss his damnation; that's why he was there.

Like a dream, Lizasha appeared.

Her eyes, like rising flood waters, ran up and over him: she stood there wearing a cute brown dress, topped with a pinafore (black), at her back was an emerald screen, with a gold-winged bird spread on its panels.

"You, Mitya, are drunk."

"You see, no, that's not it, I'm just very… you know."

Then he staggered and grabbed for the chair.

"Well yes: you said that already."

"Lizasha, see, no; I did not say a thing: came to talk; you yourself know I said nothing."

"What do you mean?"

"Well, I did it, Lizasha!"

She looked at him totally shocked:

"You did! You? And so what did you do?"

Then she took his hand, petted it.

"I forged my dad's signature..."

"No!"

And Lizasha caressed his cheek, fingers like ice, while her eyes, a bit warmer, just gazed into space.

"You unfortunate boy."

Then he clutched her: she moved:

"No, sit quietly... God knows... you're drunk..."

Then her face grew severe and she turned, and saw Mitya move toward her: so she stepped back, away, toward the curtain.

"No."

He grabbed her hand, she pulled away; he did not let her go.

"Oh you wretched young wretch, little Mitya."

She dove off away through the folds of the drapes, left her hand in his grasping palms; putting his head to her hand, he kissed it all over; she struggled and wriggled her hand as she tried to get free of the drapes:

"Let me go," she exclaimed, small voice pained, an alarm bell behind the drapes' folds.

And immediately swift steps toward the voice.

Her hand was yanked free.

In between the drapes' folds he bumped into... a fist, knocked him painfully back, and while splaying his fingers, he slipped: was thrown back: the drapes' folds tore apart; then a ruby, a cuff, and a ruler flashed: whistling through air, its edge slicing two fingers.

His fingers were cut with a slapping sound: soon they were covered in blood.

And a sound like two angry flies came from behind the drapes.

"Ha!"

And a silver-horned head, matched with two blue-black sideburns; emerged in a grimace.

Then Mitya broke into a run: and on top of the sound of his steps was an echoing slap.

He bumped into a bald, little gentleman.

Mr. Bezitsov was knocked back to the door.

He saw von-Mandro, that his mouth was equipped with white shining teeth that played off his beaver-brown eyes: he shook hands in a pose he'd worked out in a mirror.

Acetylene lighting, a mercury-blue; a bit rosy: from ad-shine at play: all the headlights looked green: all the windows were closed; and up higher grey gloom where the barely perceptible, almost impossible lines of the cornices softened; cold snow slapped on eyelashes; both red and unthinking, he crossed the road, wounded, his fingers were burning; his spirit was chock full of worms; his cheeks were both burning, veins throbbing.

He ran, swept by snow, swept by wind: everything sprinkled with snow, all the fences and corners and roofs: the snow powder shone brightly, formed wings of snow in the circles of light from the streetlamps; and everything roared; and people ran by and they brushed by and walked, both in twos and in threes: and some walked all alone: and they came from the left and the right to a place where bright light played its part: where a woman walked by in a caftan of squirrel: a fine lady, who, hiking her skirt, "dessa" silk in pale cream, had walked out of the light; and behind her an officer, caped, with rose stripes on his breeches and piping in silver.

A marten-fur coat, with luxurious black and white fur, took a car that looked just like an angry and barking pug sweeping its lights like a nose which disturbed, momentarily, those in the beams, with bared faces, gold teeth.

The little man ran.

"What cold!"

And the frost found and lilified noses.

Lizasha had gone to her room: where she thought about Mitya; she pitied him: though she did *not* see what happened: Madame Voulezvous did.

For naught could be kept from Madame Voulezvous.

18

Biterbarm stood there, affectedly flirting and fawning; Madame Evikhkaiten arrived: he affectedly wagged both his elbows and backside.

"That's *entweder* not *oder*!"[173]

There, screened just a bit by a green-backed *dormeuse*,[174] stood Madame Evikhkaiten; adjusting her dress like a debutante holding her skirt: for a curtsy.

"Just marvelous: *entweder* not *oder*"!

Entveder, dressed up in a new blue-green greatcoat (white-sashed), interrupted:

"But this time, you goofed, Biterbarm: all my ancestors lived on the Oder."

That's fate!

Biterbarm was a field full of pimples; teeth and gums; and what else? He liked sports: though not tennis, but football; he said of himself: "I'm a true hyperologist."

"Listen," he turned to Zehn, "Kuverdayev's big scandal? Is it true that in class he got thrashed?"

At that, Zehn, a skinny-legged student enrolled at the Kreiman gymnasium, lively, a dandy, his face too made-up, said:

"Oh, yes, something happened!"

"Just something?" said Entweder, surprised. "Got his ears boxed quite thoroughly."

"Why?"

"A scandal, quite sordid!"

---

173. In German, *entveder* means "either," while *oder* means "or." This seems to be wordplay, perhaps the punchline to a joke with a sexual connotation that does not appear in the text.
174. A divan with no sides or back, or a sloping half-back.

Zehn stepped back a bit; he'd already been fooling around, hanky-panky, with Vassochka Puzikova; after all, everyone said that he had the money to keep her.

But God only knew.

"Mademoiselle Bobinett?"

At Mandro's, for some reason, they all called her Vaska, quite simply. New guests were arriving non-stop.[175]

Lizasha was wearing a lilac-shade dress sewn of satin with trim done in lace, and low cut, with no gloves; her bared shoulders shook; chatting politely with guests; she enjoyed a quite light-hearted talk with Arkady Ivanovich Grai-Pereperzenko, son of the merchant, an artist who wrote the étude "Golden Autumn Parting," belonged to the circle "Dmagog" (why "Dmagog"?); was a part of the group "Berendeyev," he played a most tasteful rendition of a romance by Vertinsky,[176] he called Baltrushaitis[177] a friend, was dubbed "Sandro" (again, that is, why was it "Sandro"?); he nicknamed himself Botticelli Ivanovych: and was called Botticelli Ivanych;[178] was clean-shaven, stout: he had glasses; long hair; and he wore a silk scarf tied with flair.

Madame Evikhkaiten: surrounded; the ceiling's faux garland encircling the room was hung with a green Chinese lantern; Madame Evikhkaiten leaned on the dormeuse, demurely adjusting the sea foam of lace on her dress; and someone was fanning Madame Evikhkaiten; and, clearly, Bezitsov was jealous.

---

175. Note that the circumstances around Kuverdayev's "thrashing" remain unclear.

176. A.N. Vertinsky (1889-1957) a prolific poet, composer, cabaret singer, and actor who travelled and performed extensively around the globe but returned to the Soviet Union. He exerted tremendous influence on twentieth century developments in Russian vocal music.

177. Jurgis Baltrushaitis (1873-1944), a Lithuanian symbolist poet and translator who worked in both Lithuanian and Russian and was a colleague and friend of numerous Russian writers.

178. Sandro Botticelli (c. 1445-1510), the working name of Alessandro di Mariano di Vanni Filipepi, an Italian Renaissance painter. Perhaps his best known work was *The Birth of Venus* (1486). Bely almost certainly includes him here because he was rumored to have had illicit relations with minors.

Eduard Eduardovich, tryingrealhardtobenice to his guests, took Bezitsov in tow, Merditsevich too, took them aside to a bar with liqueurs and some sweets, and inviting them said:

"Try a drink, it's genuine 'Old Khan's,' a treat, straight from Persia."

Merditsevich then stupidly joked:

"My wife calls me a cockroach; I say I'm a cockroach; and just everyone knows it, they call me one too."

As a man, he was always a bit of an insect: but a powerful merchant: about him they said:

"Just affected tomfoolery!"

After he left, Eduard Eduardovich strode to the guest room. There, trios and duets and quartets of people near trios and duets and quartets of fine chairs in a tasteful arrangement. He threw a phosphoric and sparkling, child-killing look straight through Zay's head: made Lizasha's heart thump.

Lizasha was smiling unnaturally, flashing her eyes a bit strangely; a puppet: her shoulders were bare, thin and shaking, she ran and approached Biterbarm:

"Hyperologists, like you, must find noises like these hard to follow…"

Lizasha was waving a wide-open fan when some sideburns, well-oiled, passed between them, and almost right through them, and smiled at Lizasha quite gently.

"Enjoying yourself?"

She shuddered, as if she might say:

"I'm afraid of you."

But, her face answered, eyes flashing.

Their eyes met and melded: Lizasha looked off: then she stood, her mouth open (the pools where she drowned had appeared). Eduard Eduardovich, after he spotted Madame Mindalyanskaya, quickly approached her; Lizasha's bare shoulders shook; quickly, she blanched: Botticelli Ivanych inquired, most upset:

"Are you ill?"

"There's no air here, but no."

"Well, you're pale and you're shaking."

Lizasha just laughed: and she laughed, and laughed louder and louder; laughed louder 'til tears filled the holes in her eyes and spilled out: she ran off.

As Madame Mindalyanskaya, wearing a white shiny dress, rushed along the parquet with her lace; and her profile – divine! Merditsevich, all slathered in lotion, talked lotion; and Biterbarm affectedly wagged both his elbows and bottom at someone.

The hands of 12 squinting old men were all holding up laurels: above them.

Alone, on her heels in a corner, one shoulder bared, shaking, Lizasha both smiled and cried, not knowing just what was the matter.

19

In front of a mirror, Eduard Eduardovich wore an expensive new leopard-skin robe, in a murmolka,[179] (a gold stripe on a red field), with a cigar from Havana in one hand.

With his other he smoothed down a hair.

He put down the cigar and lazily lifted his arms, the robe parted: a mirror reflected his body; unclothed, so he looked black and white; he then pushed up his sleeves; on his arms, thick black hair; he was covered with hair that was darker than others': his wife used to say:

"If you saw what I see...you're hirsute like a beast."

There were rumors: he beat her.

He made a slight motion; adjusted the hand that held the cigar just to see his reflection more clearly: a multi-drawered cabinet was set close to hand; he'd arranged the whole room for his gestures: he knew, with the lily-white wallpaper background, (the bedroom so lily) the robe stood out better, real leopard.

He furnished his gestures.

He smiled to himself, with two fingers withdrawing the butt from his lips.

Then he lay back in bed.

But he just couldn't sleep; and for hours he'd tossed and he'd turned and he'd fidgeted: finally, sloughing the quilt (a lily shade) back he sat up, and looked at his black-haired and white legs, back lit by mercuric moonlight; he felt all around for his slippers; and wearing his robe he went out in the hall, which was empty and bathed in the lively mercuric moonlight.

---

179. Murmolka, a traditional Russian hat with flaps held by buttons or loops and often made of velvet or brocade.

Her bed springy and comfy, Lizasha sat; bending her head to her knees, with her black hair let down; and the quiet had calmed her: that worked just the same night and day:

Around her high brow
Like clouds, curls of black[180]

At times, there was rustling (a mouse, bugs, a cat?): and it frightened her terribly – a bit: she could not sleep at night: but dropped off right near morning: she let the cat into bed, a fluffy Siberian: the cat meowed; and it sometimes just meowed in thin air; lots and lots of times, then she got up, out of bed, crossed the rug in bare feet, to the door, just to let the cat out.

There was no cat.

It sounded like someone was outside the door; so she opened it, leaned out, and screamed: right there, standing in front of the door, just imagine, was "god." And his breathing seemed pained as he smiled a pained smile to himself in the dark.

She was baffled, so much that she stood there in front of him open-mouthed, wearing a night shirt: he showed some confusion; and angrily left, as he glared at the doors in the hall (to Madame Voulezvous's room):

"Hey, shh!"

---

180. From *Poltava*, a narrative poem by Alexander Pushkin about the Ukrainian Cossack leader Ivan Mazepa and the Battle of Poltava in 1709, where Sweden fought Russia. In Part I, nobleman Vasily Kochubei's beautiful daughter Maria is in love with Mazepa, her much older godfather. When their secret love is discovered they elope.

The doors to the neighboring rooms: Madame Voulezvous slept there, opened; she leaned out, a condul in hand with her hair up in curlers, a powdered white face, like a clown's.

"Who's there," shrieked Madame Voulezvous, "I just can't see a thing: is it you?"

"I can't sleep, so I'm here, just me wandering 'round..."

"I'm not dressed," said Madame Voulezvous.

And the door to the neighboring room quickly closed: for Lizasha had realized that she wasn't dressed: in plain view of her father, who looked right through her: and she slammed the door: saying:

"You, 'god,' truly are something: you wander the deepest and steepest black darkness! You frightened me."

She considered that: then, a knock.

"Who's there?"

The door swung wide open: and there stood a figure in grey, in mercuric light: someone had turned the switch on: there her "god," was bare chested and wearing his leopard-skin robe and a murmolka, standing uncertainly:

"May I?"

He sat by the bed, a bit nervous, and frowning, and timid, and trying to manage his gestures: and to keep some small ways from Lizasha; he'd come in: to clarify things; and perhaps to calm her and himself; or, perhaps, to torment: both himself and her; he did not even know why he had come; and his lips shook a bit; once she'd pulled up the blanket a bit on her bosom, Lizasha just sat there surprised; then she lowered her head to her knees: her soft hair fell across her shaking thin shoulders; she timidly waited for what he would say; then she stretched out a bare hand to her night stand: to take out a cigarette; suddenly, she was afraid of his silence; she gave him a girly, small cigarette.

"I have my own." And then he handed her a cigar:

"Smoke."

He got smoke in his eye; but endured:

"I came by just to say a few words, clear things up."

And then, after he thought a bit, said:

"My dear daughter, things just weren't right between us all this week."

Then she lifted her cigarette: narrowed her eyes with the pleasure, she loosed curls of smoke.

"And perhaps I was mean: but our minds are complex, a real laboratory: mixed-up."

But she was confused: and her words were confused.

> *Around her high brow*
> *Like clouds, curls of black.*

She reached her hands out to him: he took them, licked his lips; and started – just you imagine this – clapping the palms of their hands together:

"Fine, fine! Where were you? Off at grandmother's. What did you eat? Hot, hot cereal. What did you drink? Fruit juice..."

But there was something unreal in a 45-year-old man, not generally willing to play, in a game of this type with a grown-up; Mandro understood this and turned as he dropped both his hands; his brows knitted, not down, but went up, moved together up over his nose; and this mimicked two hands that were joined at the palms; in between them were wrinkles like teeth that were open and biting his brow.

As if singing *"Miserere,"* his forehead made noise. She thought: "Strange: why talk now, late at night, when it could have been done in the morning?" And things grew uncomfortable: then, the door scraped a bit thanks to Madame Voulezvous: she said, shuddering:

"I have a fever."

She saw that he frowned and she smiled. Then, maternally, she soothed his forehead with gentle hands, calmly.

"My head!"

"Oh my Sister Alyona."[181]

"Can," she looked in his eyes, now dark black pits, "can your sister Alyona…"

"What!" he startled.

"Call you brother?"

"Ivan?"

"Yes!"

Unexpectedly pressing his hairy head into her chest, his breath burned on her brow just like acid: sulfuric.

"No, better not."

He recoiled and flushed just as red as a ruby then ran.

Just imagine: that night he grew bilious: next morning he'd turned a dark yellow, a lemon-green face.

20

Light wind blew.

Boys from everywhere came to Prechistenka, came to a yellow, three-story; above all its windows were set snouts of beasts; and below all the windows were balconies; round columns curved from the walls in between all the windows; and under the pediment: a black iron sign with gold letters announced: "Gymnasium of Leo Vedenyapin." At the entrance a doorman stood watch, dressed in black, with brass buttons.

This is where they came in.

---

181. See footnote 140 on page 106.

And was where they removed their coats, climbed the stone stairs with green carpets, to a balustrade boasting ten shining white columns, elaborately carved, on square rails nicely framing an opening: down in the front room: 'round the balustrade, silence; a crystal knob opened the door to the rooms of the director; and there, Vedenyapin hid out behind the white door; and from there he would leap out; to here he flew; this is where he led study halls, headbreakers.

"E... e... a... a... o... "

At times there was squealing; at times, there was crying; at times it was totally noisy: an elephant's roars.

A second door stood right in front of the stairs, and it led to a two-toned and columned room bearing a sorrowful icon (in a small dark recess winked a red lamp): a staircase led up to the school; there were bars; "vava-vavava" the boys and the lads and young men raised a roar on their break in black coats with black belts and black pants; and they leaned and they shuffled on back and forth: singly, in pairs, or in trios, and even quartets, with joined arms; quite a rumble; and loudly the 200-head-throat cried out; "va" adding strength, turned to "v v ooo," which then sharpened at times into "vvuu."

"U–u–u... "

The grey-brown attendant, neck wrinkled, quite old, walked through loud "gaks" and some "sherks" and said:

"Shh... Just look what I have!"

He led out a class clown: and that loosed an unpleasant phenomenon: general howling.

Among those gokking, and uselessly booming or wandering and crowding, milled Mitya Korobkin, who worried and twitched bandaged fingers: showed up at the school: just to suffer: expecting to pay for his forgery; the payment was horrible: life from now on would be fractured in two; 'til today, a gymnasium student; tomorrow, who?

A vagrant...

While nervous-perverse, Mitya's heart felt the worst; and just why did he suffer? Because his forbearance was finished, he had stopped putting up with remarks by his classmates:

"Hey, Korobkin, Korobkin! So tell us Korobkin! Have you read Tolstoy?"

"Nope, haven't read it."

"What the hell, and a professor's son! That's why he forged it!"

And someone had said to him once:

"This is progressive you know: a paralysis affecting thought centers."

"Well, what do you think I should read?"

"At home, there's no literature: mathematics, philosophy, as much as you'd like... No Tolstoy, and no Pushkin: well..."

"Literature, Mitya, you know, yes sir: basically distracts one from science: you'll have plenty of time to read..."

Mitya knew he'd suggest *History of Physics* or *History... of the Inductive Sciences*.

"Read this one, Whewell:[182] most useful!"

"Well I'd read Tolstoy."

"Well, Tolstoy, you know, rationally speaking's a blabbermouth..." After that, Mitya ran off down to Sennaya Street: to Ostrovsky's free reading room; next, he completely abandoned his classes; and he brought in notes he had written himself to explain his own absence from school: the signature forged; the lie lasted a year; an assistant twice, very suspiciously, eyeballed the signature: once he looked carefully, then tilted his head: but kept quiet, suspiciously shoving the note in his pocket; then Mitya turned red; a week passed since the assistant suspected him; he'd sadly suggested:

---

182. William Whewell (1794-1866), an English polymath, scientist, philosopher, theologian, and historian of science.

"It would go better if you confessed to it all: and the notes."

And then Mitya swore before God: but he didn't believe him.

"I'll show him: let's see what our good old Lev Petrovich says."

So Mitya was frightened and vanished: he avoided the school for a week; for he knew that a storm had been brewing; and he'd be expelled in disgrace: Lev Petrovich just scared him: he was tall, stooped and thin, with a rough grey combed mane, a clipped beard and gold glasses, a blue coat, the director was just like Attila the Hun; a grey mustache hung over his lips, which were able to open as wide as his ears and could bellow out elephant roars and display his black tongue; his ears twitched at high speed; and he sometimes when speeding past trailing smoke looked a bit yellow, his cigarette holder was amber: when students got out of his way they all bowed; and his skinny cheeks sank in his cheekbones; a handsome, fine nose held his glasses, up over which bulged his two eyes with their bushy thick eyebrows; a bony brow sloped to his thick hair; long arms (longer than normal) that lent him the look of a hybrid: a lion, a stallion (or ass) that was mixed… with a little jerboa.[183]

It seemed, all in all, Vedenyapin was ready to leap over heads out his door and right into the crowded front hall (a soft "scratch-scratch" was heard and then someone was caught like a mouse: misbehavior, he'd sit for an hour); Vedenyapin could freeze like a motionless corpse; but a corpse that could jump like a hurricane: motion and words, a full spectrum, from roars up to… puerile tears; yes: wind and storms! And a death-like calm; he went to extremes: and his face was an odd mix: of clearly a monkey, an ass and a… Zeus (god-beast).

He inspired horror.

And he inspired a generation.

---

183. A jerboa is a mouse-like rodent found in Africa and Asia with long hind legs used for jumping.

At the school one true cult was instilled: Vedenyapin; before all his lessons young students all crossed themselves.

21

Mitya, distressed the whole previous night, with a scared, racing heart hung around in the hall; Lev Petrovich arrived in the mornings at ten; what if he stayed at home: or slept late?

Vedenyapin rushed in.

And Mitya, lips swollenandfat from his chewing, stood outside the teachers' room: Mitya bowed but Vedenyapin did not.

The door slammed.

So, he knows!

His blood froze.

Then the doorman, in black, his buttons of brass, rang a bell as he ran down the hall, it went: "Ring!" And at that, the rooms smiled as they opened their doors: and the rooms, a whole row down another hall, shuffled and shouted from many throats, banging their desks.

Mitya could see up ahead: all the classrooms along the next hall: and beyond them a room; and beyond that the doors to the teachers' lounge: open.

The teachers had left for their classes.

A priest in a cassock, dark brown, swam by quietly swinging his gradebook (a thin green one where grades were recorded); and Pyshkin, enormous and limping and brushing back grey tufts of beard and of hair was firmly pronouncing his plan to go to room 8; the thin Latin instructor appeared.

Vedenyapin, reserved and dressed neatly and bearing himself like a corpse, rushed to class.

But no, Mitya did not go to class; he considered his whole situation; he thought of the books.

Yes, the books!

It was 14 whole days since his father had spoken with him: had he guessed it? How could it be otherwise?

But he had expenses: he bought this and that: a new textbook, a notebook, a pencil; his friends (one and all!) had some coins in their pockets; not him; and he didn't know how to insist or to wheedle.

"Just give me some money."

"A ruble, oh please."

He was sick of the squawking.

"Again? More new textbooks?"

"You what? You used-up a whole pencil?"

He started with books at the market; he sold them; this money bought books and some pencils and pens: he developed a passion for flowery eau de cologne: he applied it before he went to Mandros'.

Von-Mandro's!

But when Mitya recalled the events a day earlier: his heart skipped a beat once again. How banal and how horrible! The cuts on his hand were annoying; his father's mean silence was wrong; he was scared: Vedenyapin would kill him.

The horror!

Then Pyshkin trudged up to the blackboard to bang it with chalk for a while; they were scared; but three students did homework down under their desks; and a mumbler named Slobkin was nicknamed "the snout" (what a snout), and he raked out his thoroughly picked nose there, right at his desk.[184]

If he held up his snout at an angle, just right? You could see his mouth lined with his breakfast.

Class ended: they gushed out.

Addressing his students, a grey-haired math teacher was finishing up:

"If we multiply the numerator," he rose on his tippy toes, looked from bottom to top, "say, by five; then the bottom must also be multiplied," he sat and he smiled, "by five too..."

Then he poked a boy's chest:

"The result?"

"It won't change"

"And if we," he scratched his chin, " multiply the top by..." he ran to the corner: to spit.

Once he'd spat, he ran back.

" ...the denominator..."

Mitya walked down to room five.

Vedenyapin was finishing class: and it seemed he was handsome but his face had been covered in whiskers much like a thick brush.

Or perhaps a baboon.

He jumped out of the room and like a jerboa he rushed: to the lounge for his amber-stemmed cigarette holder, set firm in his mouth, for appearances.

---

184. Slobkin is a made up name that I substituted for Podletsov, a fake name used here by Bely. Podletsov is a play on the word *podlets*, or slob.

He could shame them and drive them out too if he wanted.[185]

And out they all went in the crowded hall: break!

The bell: classes dispersed; the boys left inarush, went off head over heels; the whole multileggedcreature then shuffled quite loudly and found empty rooms; and it broke into years; and the years came apart into pupils; each sat at a desk to shout something or other.

The teachers then trickled back into their rooms.

Disillusioned, a Frenchman walked haggardly into a cat concert,[186] the room filled with the first years; the Latin instructor walked past.

Vedenyapin was rushing to class with a confident muzzle and sweeping fear dust-like before him; terrible! Closer and closer...

With trembling hands all the students then made a quick sign of the cross; at that Mitya snatched up a loose book and he stiffened his spine as he blushed:

"What will be will be!"

Then...

25 pairs of petrified eyeballs ate-up a cheek-boned and furry-haired sketch of a face, two cheeks with deep hollows that flew in and landed while flashing the circles of glass in his specs.

Then he sat, one leg bent: flared his nostrils; and stretched out his lips; then they vanished: some kind of a stripe!

And he loudly exhaled.

"Ah, well, you!"

And he stared straight at Mitya.

---

185. A nod to Tolstoy's *Anna Karenina*, where Anna fears how Karenin will respond to her infidelity.
186. Cat concert: common expression in Russian for a crowd of derisive, howling students.

It's starting!...

It seemed he'd leap over the table and desk from his chair; like a predator falls on a ram's spine: to slaughter the ram.

22

But no leap: he sat just like a question mark.

"Well, sirs?" A whisper took wing...

"Slobov!"

Then he grabbed his bent knee with his hands, and he pressed the thick brush on his cheek to his knee:

"What?"

"I can't hear you?"

He licked both his lips and he sat, his nose running: "You're done!" and he penned with some flair a huge D. And so Slobov returned to his desk. At that, Mitya thought:

"Why? What of me? Not a word about *me*?..." So he *still* doesn't *know*: but of *course* not or he'd..."

Then his heart sank: "He knows."

"My good Baer, recite!"

While approaching his desk, Vedenyapin grabbed *A Lev Vedenyapin Reader* and using the end of a pencil flipped through it, while jotting in places notations or question marks.

24 hands made the sign of the cross on their chests; but the 25th chest was not crossed, and it pitifully swayed: disappeared: for the D had infected him fully with worry.

"Korobkin!"

He stood up.

"Recite!"

And under his chin Mitya's Adam's apple bobbed ominously, maybe four minutes: Vedenyapin kept silent; and then, just like rays of light, wrinkles began to play on his dead sunken cheeks:

"Good!"

It was done: his hands reached for the grade book and entered an excellent score:

"So he still does not know!"

Vedenyapin glanced tenderly at his voluminous tome, *Vedenyapin's School Reader*, while licking his chops at the sight.

"Time to read."

He jumped up and twitched his head; tossed down the open book.

How did he pick them?

Unclear. It was known that he got through to all of them; seemed quite forgetful; but even injustices served higher justice; a "D" scrawled in pencil, and shouts were smoothed out; but an A, which he knew how to give in a way that his students turned red, just like crabs, while they panted from happiness, made everything, everything worth it.

Their fear was redeemed by rewards: introduction to poetry.

Suddenly, scratching his head, Vedenyapin requested:

"... Korobkin, I left my part four of the reader..."

He dug all around in his pockets.

"The key: go run down to my office: and open my desk; in the right side top drawer is the reader."

Once outside the room, he ran down the stairs; through a door: Vedenyapin's; a table and shelves, and some busts, then he fumbled the key; but the key did not fit: he tried both ways, no fit.

So, what happened?

He stood, not prepared to return.

And then, suddenly heard a small noise at his back. His heart sank: Vedenyapin just stood there; kept silent; the boy's Adam's apple bobbed.

He knows.

Then just silence. And after the silence, a voice:

"Well, Korobkin."

An arm fell on his shoulders:

"So what do you think now about your misdeed?"

"And have you thought it through?"

Just like men throw themselves off of cliffs at a run, he then hurried to talk: he included it all, even bits that he'd kept from Lizasha: despair had helped loosen his tongue.

In response came an audible:

"E... e... a... a... o... o..."

Vedenyapin sat back and he listened, he puffed through his nostrils; and dug out a hair, small and silver and raised it to one eye; removing his glasses, he looked at the hair.

Then he sniffed it and tossed it:

"This incident stays... e... e... a... between us."

He started to speak about truth: and how wisdom and fear were related; and that fright packed a punch: tore our spirits apart: but light gropes its way out; Vedenyapin's way. His mind, sympathetic, would press to their chests, go right in, know them clear through and through: he had spent whole sleepless nights up in sympathy, Mitya's pains hurt him before they awakened in Mitya's own mind; he'd long guarded him, wanting to shake him and take him: awaken him; thus did Zeus, when incarnate, an eagle, attack: and seize Ganymede![187] He struck: and they

---

187. In Greek mythology, the boy Ganymede is described as the most beautiful mortal. Zeus, in the form of an eagle, rapes Ganymede then abucts him to serve as cup-bearer for the gods

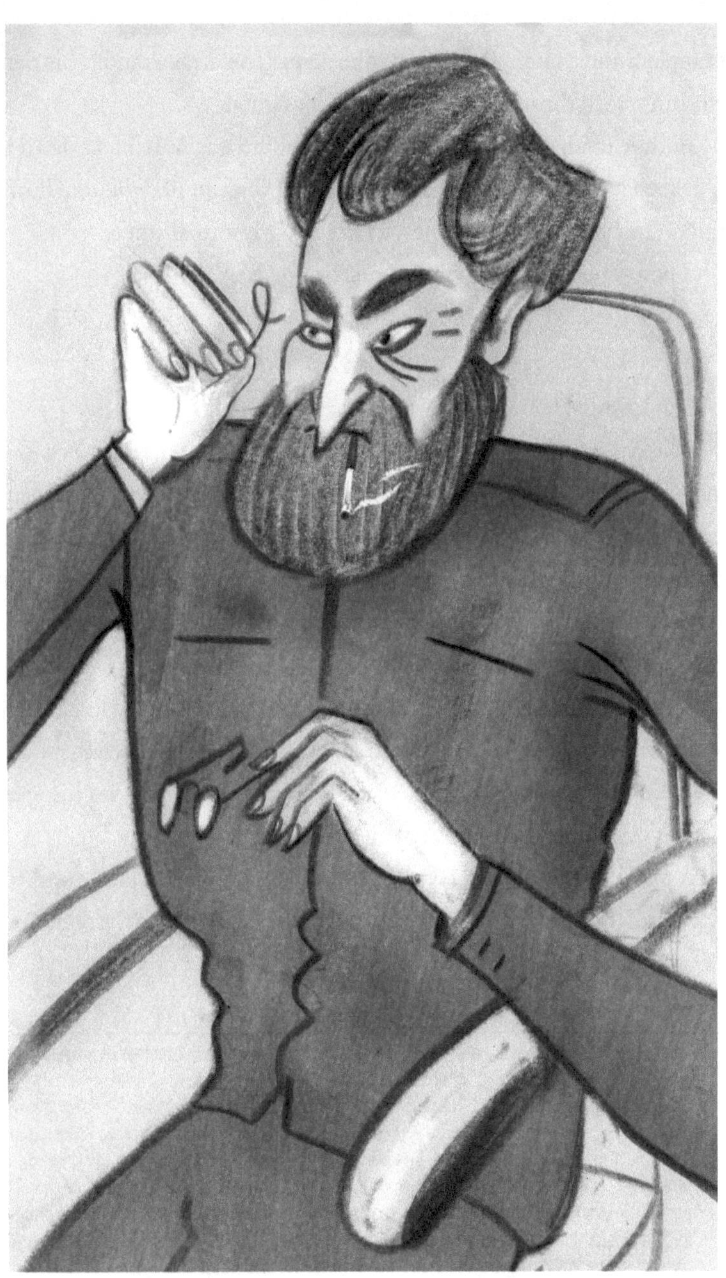

"This incident stays... e... e... a... between us."

grappled: and shattered the truth like an egg, he drew grandly, his pencil stub traced through the air: a symbol of goodness.

Both Mitya's eyes bulged, and it seemed he was walking at dawn in a field that lay fallow; distinctly felt rays of the sun like the touch of a finger; he heard wordless tunes, a familiar, primordial voice.

They announced: school was out for the day.[188]

23

Sundown![189]

The sunset, like Indian topaz or fiery yellow-toned rubies, was fading when Mitya walked out with his love for the truth up in flames; and he knew it would go on for days, stupefaction: the houses tookcolor; on the unwinding evening the factory tossed up some blackclouds; it seemed like an eye was there peering out, lit, from down under a narrow, gold-cotton and lily-side cloud.

A man passed, plagued with blisters; you'd call the oldcodgerabum and a blue-nose, an end-stage old alkie: a swollen face, whiskers; and if you looked under his cap; you would gasp: oh his eyes, yes his eyes! They were shining like rubies. You'd hug him!

A fencebum sat talkingastreakoffilth; and you could say "good for nothing." But *then* he was spotted: a waif walked up gently; squeaked "Daddy."

---

in Olympus. The myth has been called a model for the Greek social custom of *paiderastía*, a socially-acceptable erotic relationship between a man and a youth.

188. Beyond the direct mention of Zeus-Ganymede, the final paragraphs of this section include what appear to be veiled references further suggesting that Vedenyapin raped Mitya. Walking in a fallow field "*po polyu pustomy*," can be taken, if read literally (and considering the context), as "empty sex" with the operative word being "*pol*," a noun that can mean floor, field, or sex. The phrase "a familiar primordial voice" in Russian "*golos iskonno znakomyi*" not only is a bit of tongue twister, it appears to be a play on *gomoseksualnost* or *gomoseksualizm*. The phrase "*urok otmenyaetsya*" may be a toungue-twisting play on "not erotic."

189. This entire section can be read as an extended exploration of Mitya's troubles coping with the stress of the rape combined with a family life that offers no hope of support or understanding.

Oh "Daddy"! A man in a chair sat there slumped, with two crooked and splitfallen shoulders, both the dirty old belt from his robe and his house coat gone maculate:[190] like he lived and he worked in a pillar of dust, yellow pollen, ripped drapes, with his beard bound from bottom to top, and his ears in a bandage.

"Well: my arm has been sore." And as someone just recently said:

"He won't talk with you: that's just his way."

Then he wanted to run home: lay down at his feet, laugh, and cry.

And a lady, her hat with blue feathers: another in blue; but everyone seemed to be angry; their muscles grown all through with tumors; their faces were stretched into muzzles.

He imagined himself in front of a mirror: there, in the mirror, his muzzle, so stupid and pimply and sweaty and smacking its lips: and his body grown angry, haphazard: just like the haphazard affair back at school: rip them up! His grief, it was nothing, would fly off away like the curled-yellow smoke from the trash heaps, to niceblues in the distance, where the sky, much like cotton, dissolves in the sky, where a giant, a glow in his hand, cast the dregs of his drink in the heavens creating a multistar.[191]

Mitya forgot how he got to the square: he was feverish, head like an oven and fueling the flames in his eyes: but he knew he could not go straight home, he had *no* place to go; had no home; he did not turn for home but went looking to find a new place; where, he didn't know, or if such a place even existed.

Perhaps his next home could be found in his heart?

---

190. Spotted, stained, used in opposition to immaculate; Joseph T. Shipley, *Dictionary of Early English*, Littlefield, Adams & Co., 1968, p. 405.

191. The Greek Ganymede myth concludes with Zeus granting the boy eternal life by turning him into a constellation, the water bearer, more widely recognized today as Aquarius. A later, Roman re-interpretation placed one emperor's boy lover, Antininous, in the same position in the sky as Aquarius.

Which at first became filled with remorse for his life, for himself: or his self? But he was not there: his "self" was reborn: Vedenyapin's own words; was his "self" Vedenyapin; or possibly somebody else; like, perhaps, that old man: but then why did he chase him? His "self" was not Mitya, but every last bit that regrets, that can shoulder regrets: his humanity.

Thus spake Vedenyapin.[192]

Go back: and find Vedenyapin: and kiss his gaunt hand, not at all for his mercy: but because he had laid Mitya's haphazard problems to rest;[193] it all would have been carved on his gravestone; but now it was obvious, Mitya was torn out of Mitya: he'd discovered a warm and faint beating inside his own body: his heart in his throat; like a babbling small child had reached out a small hand: like one recently born.

That he'd been forgiven was *not* what upset him: it was that inside the cleansed one a new one was born.

And a silver half-moon, that seemed mother of pearl, shone: and clouds hung there barely just visible, like embers that promised, "that's all, that is all."

Only what?

"What's wrong Mitya? You're crying! In tears! So I ran here, Prechistenka, right there behind you: I shouted..."

"Lizasha!"

---

192. Bely is alluding to Nietzsche's *Thus Spoke Zarathustra*, parodying Vedenyapin as an immoral superman.

193. Bely has some very clever phrasing here, which I cannot hope to reproduce in English. He uses the Russian verb *sorvat*, to tear, as in rip up the file with the compromising material on Mitya, while readers may, at least for a split second, see the verb: *sovrat*, to seduce, or with slight amendment, to lie (related, certainly). The crux of the word play falls on two letters in the middle of both words, "r" and "v," which, given recent developments in the story, are easy to transpose and confuse. Compromising with the original text, I use the word laid, which in addition to the sense of "putting away" or "ending" has the slang sexual meaning of intercourse, and also sounds somewhat like the word lied. The entire sequence starts a few paragraphs earlier and is telegraphed to the reader by repetition of the unusual word haphazard, *tyaplyapoe*, which Bely uses heretofore as a marker for Ivan Ivanych (in descriptions of his nose).

"Today, I heard everything: really a mess!" He recalled not a thing.

"Well, so… What are you talking about?"

"It's about what occurred at home yesterday: please forgive "god"; he is just not himself: and it's killing him; he's not like that; I'll explain: come by… But no, don't come… I'll come over myself… Just as soon as I heard, I rushed over to school to wait at the door; I don't know, when I saw you I didn't approach: but then chased you.

He said his goodbyes to Lizasha: but she did not touch him.

The sun burrows down into the earth. And the wings of invisible birds chase the sun through a black sky: with stars: but a star is a bright flaming day; and the starry skies show many daytimes, suns rising, and suns never risen; let night spill its dark on a colorful street; let the blackest of words grip and hold things: that's life.

But the sun will come up!

On the fence 'round the square, right in front of him, leaning, a passer-by, bundled-up, wearing a worn and grey cloak, its tails blown by the wind; an old cap trimmed with fur slouched up there on his head; with a cane like a stick the man tapped on the road; and then Mitya looked under the brim; and the passer-by scrunched his dull eyes: shabby, head shaven, he turned full away: and his face, just like fur that had faded, lost color, dissolved: into fur that had faded.

He's blind.

"Allow me?... I could... help."

But the old man just mumbled, spoke rudely, uncaring and angry, down into his fur, and when trotting across: he looked close.

And he realized that he'd just seen himself: and today he was walking a path to the grave.

Oh if it came to that, if...

The sky, much like cotton, dissolved in the sky.

CHAPTER 3

KNOWNOTHING

1

A door faced in brown oilcloth; oak shelves with a yellow wool cover; a hall in bright colors: along the grey floor were small circles in patterns like white and brown eyes; in the hall, there were doors to the left and the right, and diagonally; it felt like the doorbell would ring, and dear Martha would let in events of the day: and the doors would be opened.

"So don't take the chain off the door: you should ask first who's there."

"Professor Korobkin's?"

"That's right."

The door squeaked: and a woman peered out, she was squinting, face tired; her hands primping her yellow-green spinach-toned dress: at her waist hung a chain with a watch and a charm.

"Well who's out there?"

"Just some gent with dark features, requesting Ivan Ivanych."

The woman then stepped out of sight.

"And the name?"

"It's Mandro: von-Mandro, Eduard Eduardovich…"

Gave them his card.

Just then Mitya had poked out his nose; from behind the door, rolling his eyes and afraid: Eduard Eduardovich broadly and tenderly smiled, like his ruler had not left a scratch: and then Mitya pulled back; and then out from behind popped a pale girl, thin, wearing a blue blouse (embroidered), and berry-red skirt, her eyes squinting suspiciously at his fox trim and sable hat: blindly and kindly.

Mandro bowed and thought:

"The whole clan!"

The young lady left, her skirt flaring, a flower; went off down the hall; while she chirped.

On the left, out of sight, someone bumbled their way to the door; from the sound of a rip he knew something got caught on a nail. Through the door flashed a cowlick that swayed in the gloom and then vanished once more; with a bark:

"Just a moment!"

Some kind of a slob had then squeezed out the door while he tried to get loose from the nail, and he stood and he stared with his arms and legs awkwardly splayed and dramaticallywinked at Mandro: then he left.

Soon, a second collision occurred in the hall with a coat rack.

It was then Eduard Eduardovich knew: the professor was standing before him.

So how did he look?

The man clearly had not cut his hair in some time; it had grown out in bunches; face sagging; nose squat in the hills of his cheeks: so out-landishlytopsyandturvy! He always seemed ready to sneeze; his eyes, settled in trenches, looked ready to shoot while his glasses defended them; his walrus mustache and beard were both beastly, ferociously browned; and, unseen, his lips smacked; his round forehead resembled a stone, and he looked fully able to knock it through walls; so, beastly,

ferociously browned, it was the head of a giant; but he was small stat-
ured: no neck; one slumped shoulder; the other pulled up toward his
ear; his body was bent out of shape; and his arms were too short; one
behind him, the other wrapped up in a sling; he twitched, tossing a
pencil; his belly bulged out, one leg thrown right, one splayed left; a
yellow-brown jacket; a yellow-brown vest; starch abandoned long since.

A black bow tie.

A shortie, his head cocked.

There, he thought: well, what a picture!

Assuming an innocent pose he said:

"Please allow me to introduce myself."

"What?"

The short little man turned an ear; then he put up a hand near his
ear, and he eared:

"I can't hear you."

But clearly, the doorbell displeased him: he'd rear up his ears, try to
hear; but Mandro was in no way put off by that fact.

"I am closely acquainted with Mitya... and being a..."

"No, just one moment: with whom do I have the great honor?"

The shortie crabbedup to the front; with his baggy and dirty coat
flapping; he stretched out a hand; blocking the glare: from Mandro's
full selection of teeth (or, to put it more accurately: dentures).

"Eduard Eduardych Mandro."

Eduard Eduardovich saw a brown stain on his fingertips; clearly, the
famous professor had recently colored his hair.

"You're most welcome."

Then he tossed in the air a sharp pencil and caught it; both sideways and flat-footed, knees never bending, a hitch in his step, he
entered his office.

The floor had been polished but had a grey rug, with moths flitting; his desk, a real mess, books piled; dusty drapes: spiders; all dusty and dirty; a blackpawed chair, and angled, not flush with the wall, and; another, identical, but further out, blocked the way (clearly, it tripped people).

Oh yes, a real nothing!

Encroaching brown dusk made the brown-yellow tomes in the brown-grey shelves almost invisible; some sort of blanket (brick apples on black) was there scrunchedinaheap on the black leather divan. He thought:

"What could it take to wind someone like this 'round my finger!" Mandro smiled and entered the office with confident steps and his shoulders spread: fully at ease!

"Oh well, yes, your young son..."

At the words "young son," squinting, the famous professor's red mug grimmedagrimace.

"Your son comes to visit Lizasha, my daughter."

The professor suggested he sit in the chair that was nearer the door; then he sat down himself with a slump; and Mandro looked around: a real dumpydisaster, with scattered loose papers and books; and a scamp of a mouse scratched away.

"I'd guess, basically, you're tired of Mitya... Please do have a seat old man!"

So, Eduard Eduardovich sat on the edge of his seat and he leaned on a table.

"Mercy," he joked, with good cheer in his eyes, "oh, your son is so nice!"

And he looked just completely disarming!

The professor's eyes skewed; his expression concerned:

"My son, basically: everything's clear..."

"Oh just what are you saying!"

"H... he... he..."

"Mercy!"

"But no, it's all clear: my son..."

Pounding his fist on the desk:

"You can multiply him," he sprayed spittle, "by zero as much as you'd like, he will still be a zero."

His bark boomed.

Then Mandro lit a cigarette, pointed a finger and balanced his temple while striking a carefree and calm pose; he scratched at a sideburn; the back of his hand moved expressing an offer: a smoke?

"Our two children have known one another for quite a long time: so I thought it an honor to pay you a visit..."

"Well, I'm most pleased sir..."

"to bear witness to awe you inspire all over..."

Mandro set his sideburn on fire; and the smoke started smelling (unpleasantly).

"I may be a businessman, but believe me, I know that Professor Korobkin is...

"Stop it!"

"...Professor Korobkin..."

"But no, sir!..."

"...Professor Korobkin is Science's pride."

The professor's head turned while he snorted, and sniffing Mandro he knew; that was the problem: Mandro's sideburn.

"But I do have one thing: though, it's really just bosh." The professor tap-tapped with his fingers.

"It seems, but the world is all rumors, you're working hard?"

"Yes, sir: a bit."

"Bearing fruit?..."

The professor just pawed at the mess on his desk.

"Have you made a discovery?"

"What?"

The professor reached out for a handkerchief; took it, and laying it open upon his soft palms 'neath his nose, crossed his eyes.

"The discovery, I heard," von-Mandro said, lids batting, "well sir, is significant; and, so they say, will perturb all technology; everyday life..."

The professor then sneezed just as loud as he possibly could; and the handkerchief wandered across his huge thunderous nose and got all his attention.

"and railroads..." He balled up the handkerchief, put it away.

"Unexpectedly, quite, I just happened to speak with a man representing a mighty industrial giant, their interest is keen in your work!"

On the edge of the desk the professor just shuffled his fingers a fraction.

"Unable to come here himself, the man asked that I make a proposal, but just between us."

The professor kept mum.

"and to say, once more, just between us two..."

Mandro then delayed for a second, then said all at once in a blink:

"They gladly would buy it..." Then after he looked all around, he restatedmoreslowly:

"...their interest is high..."

The professor procured a fresh pencil: he sharpened the pencil; he splintered the pencil.

"Oh, dammit! It cracked!"

"It should suit you, I'd dare say," Mandro once more widened his eyes and exhaled a thick cloud of dense smoke, "please excuse me for being so blunt: just how much would you want?"

The angry professor's eyes narrowed; his glasses flew up to his forehead; he opened a drawer; it was packed: a safeplace for his papers! He pushed papers aside; found three notebooks: inserted his nose.

And dismissively waving said:

"What's that? Just what are you saying old man? What I have here," and he banged on the notebooks, "are just a few formulae... nothing more..."

Clearly dissembling, he drilled on the drawer with one eye: it was obviously *not* in the notebooks.

The drawer seized Mandro's full attention:

"So: there!"

He spied with one eye.

And then drawing together his brows he leaned, pushing them toward the professor to pressure him:

"They are proposing a very respectable sum." The professor, a thoroughly nice man, grew furious: his eyes flashing fury;

"They're offering..."

"What?"

"300 thousand."

The professor's eyes flashed just like lightning: celestial brilliance, a manfromthestars.[194]

"400."

"כְ!כְ"

He looked, both his eyes rimmed with blood, just like Tommie the dog would at times when they pried a real stinker from out of his jaws; and Tommie would howl and he'd flash his bared teeth from his nook; but then he'd give it up; and he'd sigh in defeat; the professor was similar:

---

194. Here, Bely offers a foreshadowing of a major theme from *Moscow Under Siege*, the next book in the trilogy: Korobkin as a man so talented it is as if he has come to Earth from the stars.

"No, sir…"

He won't sell: he won't show his hand!

"440."

Evening murk was replacing the grey-lilac-yellow dried flowery colors.

"500."

But horror fell out of his eyes as they goggled.

"It's clear, my good man… that I haven't discovered a thing."

"What's that?"

"Well, if I had, then I would, sir, re-sell it…"

"Why, dear Professor?"

Unsettled, Mandro scratched his sideburn.

"That's just the way it is!"

"You're not so inclined?"

"And it's all here!!!"

He squirmed.

"I won't try your patience," Mandro had then toothed. And he hurriedly, nervously, pushed back away from the desk, thus expressing his anger…

"Perhaps…" he looked over encouragingly:

"…you'll think it over?"

Backed by dark green wallpaper, he sat stone-faced, lips downturned, an acid expression.

It seemed to Ivan Ivanych the light had been swallowed by mist, that his previous clarity now was all yellowed and rough; his conceptions of human affairs and of life had consisted of – here we will say on our own – dark and unpleasant shapes, murky yellow-grey, orange, and saturnine red; all the rest was covered in some sort of faded and moldy blue blots; but now torn all to pieces; and everywhere bottomless, inky-blue dark.

His decision was firm:

Von-Mandro!

While Koroobkin was thinking, Mandro, with his sideburn, was sitting distractingly, fatefully right there in front of him; he had the scent of a subtle perfume; bitter almond; he rose to depart.

And again flashed a toothy big smile:

"Oh do please come and see me at... I would consider a visit the greatest of honors."

And looking away, his sideburn turned forward, he left; the brown twilight was being consumed by the not brown of night; in the gloom the professor sat fully immersed in his problems: both Nadya and Mitya!

2

To tell the whole truth, the professor was fully prepared to find out that his son was the reason the books disappeared; and as soon as he healed, and unknown to his family, he paid a visit to Gribikov, who had been waiting: the books, bound in yellow and dark brown, had stopped up his thoughts for some time.

With great pleasure, and slowly and painfully, Gribikov told him how Mitya had pilfered the books: all of August, September, and into October; from time to time, getting up, Gribikov smiled with two teeth, and his oral cavity open; his eyes had turned mean: a hyena.

And it was as if the professor licked mustard; although he put up with the pain; then he went down to see Vedenyapin: to put all the pieces together: so, sir: his son was a sap! Vedenyapin suggested the problem was money:

"Did Mitya have change in his pockets?"

"Of course not!"

"Did he ask you?"

"He asked me for nothing."

"How did you, old man, push your son to this sin? Differentiating, you just completely forgot that your boy had matured; that he had to have something to put in his pockets: young..."

Yes, he was grown; and had pawed up a girl; but then after all:

"He stole."

And for two days he mumbled; his legs and his arms splayed akimbo; the third day he went to his son; and stood over him:

"Why did you shame yourself, brother?"

Wiping some schmutz on his robe he just sighed and returned to his office: the shelves there were all out of place, and the chairs at an angle, not squared with the desk:

"Oh those cleaners again!"

He left Mitya to stew for the sake of appearances: he would forgive him most clearly!

The silence continued.

"Well, that's what you get!"

Mitya annoyed him; stayed home; and was loud: he was tired of faking: and sick of enforcing the silence; he'd gone to his family in hope, for the first time, to be part of the family's affairs; it turned out that there wasn't a family; and, so, he put off the decision:

"I'll wait: they're not ready to hear the real truth..."

Mitya had gotten a look in his eyes: they showedtruth; but he'd never find words; had no place to begin;[195] his mother pretended; and his father ignored him, as if trying to push him away: he'd talk back:

"You're a hypocrite!"

Mitya got punished with silence.

---

195. Bely's verbal creativity is at work again playing off the common expression, "*klin klinom vybivat*," or "a wedge must be used to knock out a wedge." In other words, starting a process can be difficult. Forceful methods are sometimes required. Here he invents a verb to suggest that there is absolutely no crack or weak spot to jam in a wedge to help Mitya.

They noticed: formerly sort of a fool, he'd become a bit brighter: now he'd argue and even tried logical thinking: did homework:

"Well, look: he's a mess: does he study?" the professor had barked: nonetheless, with surprise, he observed: "Well he may, in the end, have finished some books; but he has noheadforalgebra, after all, basically!"

Mitya now brushed his teeth; earlier he'd been quiteaslob; but he'd fixed-up his jacket; he looked a bit better; his pimples subsided; his cheeks were not grey likeaskull; and he wasn't unpleasant to look at.

And the professor knew why: Vedenyapin.[196]

But Nadya was different.

She wore a blue blouse and her skirt, with a kitten embroidered, was wrinkled; she loved her canary; she lounged: and she chuckled on endlessly; not even catching her breath; but she felt like a rock had rolled onto her chest; in the dark she would sweat; but some *kvas*[197] helped; though now, she lay curled in a hook on the couch.

She was being capricious.

"Nadya, you're quite a complainer!"

"Well Papa, I just want to scream!" Her heart screamed for something that couldn't exist.

Kuverdayev unmasked, a degenerate; Mitya, a crook; as for Mother, well, no, it was best to keep quiet!

Tried smoking one time: her head spun: and she coughed 'til she bled; so that "they" would not learn of the blood, when she coughed she

---

196. Clearly, Korobkin has no clue about the rape or Vedenyapin's real thoughts.
197. *Kvas*, a slightly fermented drink made from rye bread (0.5-1.0% alcohol). It is popular even today across the former Soviet Union and Eastern Europe.

ran off to her room, brightly colored, the addition, who'd been there? The armchair was damask, silk backing; the floor was all covered with squares: a cute rug; she reclined on a couch with her face on a cushion, distracted and sunk in her thoughts: Kuverdayev prefers little boys – and for her? So she suffered because he turned out to be such: all were such here in "such" a Moscow, now carried off by the flood to an unknown abyss. That was Moscow.

With homes by the bale: and with people sealed in their whole lives; and in Moscow, a pile of bales; heaped-up huge loads; who would drag them all through?

Time!

And time, like a many-humped camel, scraped by. It was knackered, collapsed on its front legs: as it staggered it kicked over piles; and wrecked house after house; and soon Moscow would be just a pile of ruins: when?

In a jiff!

Her moans were like harpchords compared to her hack; she was torn by explosions of coughing that wracked her young life and her lavender scent; such a "life" had the stink of rank cabbage; her clock coughed away.

Take a look, there's blood caked on her handkerchief!

Dreaming one night Vasilisa Sergeyevna heard:

"Save yourselves!"

"What's that?"

"A poisonous woman in Snuffsneezer!"

Frightened, they'd blocked themselves into the dining room: outside and under a red cloud, and touching her head to the window, there stood a large woman, blue glasses, she grew to a horrible size: in the lenses: they went out in the corridor, latching the door, but they knew that out there stood a woman in moonlight whose acid breath killed.

She awoke to dull pain; and her hair was all damp (and a mess); right beneath the pale lemony blooms on the wallpaper; and she sat in a bright chair and fell into thought; stood in the bathroom and sighed; while she tried to make sense of her dream. She felt ill: just as if she awaited a time in her clear and well ordered life when something would be revealed: something caustic.

All morning she sat with her head in her hands; and then later she told the whole house:

"I am writing my memoirs."

Like a lost sheep, she wandered the rooms all disheveled: she brooded, was downcast, and sat by the window: her sorrow enclosed her like curtains.

Mandro's arrival had raised quite a ruckus; Korobkin had taken it badly, he thought it a thumb in his eye: and he felt that he'd seen von-Mandro once sometime and somewhere.

He yanked out the drawer: and riffled the papers he kept there; he poured the chess pieces all out on the table: and set up the board.

"PerepuKiyerko, oh dammit! If even just Ratsetserko came by!"

So he toyed with a pawn.

And then suddenly stood: oh, things were such a stewofamess they would never make sense; things were totallyscrewy. And, dammit, he'd found, not quadratics, but, dammit, that cube functions reigned;[198] and he puffed out his cheeks, swelled by formulae; threw himself into a mountain of papers; he trashed drafts with curly-cue writing; and obviously, illness had forced him to rest; his whole mind was renewed; and he wanted to work on the principles for discontinuous motion; he found in the process provisional peace.

There he stood, his eyes fixed, and hard-headed, and whispering things to himself from the door to the cabinet, the cabinet back to the door while he leaned into turns as if giving himself a good push.

"This discovery clearly: upends all our science."

"Can improve all our railroads...

the army...

the navy!

so, we, brother, Van-Vanych..."

He went from the shelves to the cabinet, and spun like a top. Then it suddenly dawned on him:

"They're still on my trail."

Then he thought of the man's blue-black hair; he'd sensed when the plumbing was fixed: that Mandro.

"Oh dammit!"

He carried his hunched-back right out to the door; locked the door with a key; groaning heavily, crouching, and lifting the rug at its corner, he took a small piece of parquet from the floor; and the notes were still there and still safe.

"Still here, and still safe!"

At the door his eyes narrowed; the shift in his eyes showed concern; along with Mandro something new had crept into his home; no, Man-

---

198. The suggestion here is that cube functions are inherently more difficult to solve than quadratics (squares).

dro was not good; and he suddenly wanted to check it himself: get a look at Mandro.

"I should visit, it's clear that this calls for good manners; there's Mitya; if children are friendly, the parents, well, visit."

The brownish-red embers of daytime burned out: as they fed the black-maw of the night.

3

Fighting terrible snowy wind while it was growing both colder and darker with whistles and howls: one could see a cast iron fence (iron spikes welded to iron paws); standing a scattered guard, trees with their flashy and snowy manes combed by the wind: and a walnut stone house, sitting inside a fence of repetitive squares, raised on powerful columns: and stripes in between all the windows; that seemed to be topped off in whipped cream; and garlands both molded and carved hung nonsensically: pears and grapes.

It was a cake, not a house!

As if inside a cake, Zadopyatov sat down.

At the second floor windows the wrinkled drapes clumped; with a woman in glasses behind them, with barely just visible locks of grey hair, light and dark, with some greenish and yellowish tints; two blue lenses rose up from behind the panes, horribly large; and then everything grew quite confused: the grey-walnut house seemed to collapse in the cold and the dark and sink down in its inky dark windows; the freeze marked its spot with loud howling and whistling; the square disappeared; and the gates blew wide open; the fences were broken...

The small shreds of smoke that were blown by the wind from the chimney rushed off.

But he wanted to wait until everything cleared, and the grey-walnut house and its windows appeared through the trees, and until two blue lenses had looked in the window.

Anna Pavlovna Zadopyatova, a corpulent, round-headed matron, appeared in the window, a watering can in her hand; she was watering withering crocuses; taking a break from her writing; a stern and hard woman, and honorable, she preferred I.I. and P.I. Petrunkevich to other Cadets;[199] and the nickname they gave her was "Iron Heel"[200]: once, Nikita Zadopyatov's most dedicated teacher Oldov, now deceased, said of her:

> *What a beast! All womens' whips fly*
> *Lashing sheep but hitting lions too…*
> *Nikita Vasilevich, our beloved guy*
> *Daily suffers Anna Pavlovna's shoe!*
> *Be you local or from a foreign land*
> *this cross elicits groans of fear*
> *'cause fate's braided leather strands*
> *long whip even Zadopyatov's rear*

---

199. I.I. Petrunkevich (1843-1928), lawyer, politician, and a leader of the Cadets, elected to the Duma, brother of M.I. Petrunkevich; M.I. Petrunkevich (1846-1912) activist and member of the Cadets, elected to the Duma, brother of I.I. Petrunkevich; Bely may have gotten the second brother's first name wrong

200. Regarding Anna Pavlovna's despotic inclinations, Bely may be referring here to the Jack London novel *The Iron Heel*. Published in 1908, it told of a dystopian future where the United States is ruled tyrannically by an oligarchy, headed by one character "The Iron Heel."; A second level of humor here plays again on the fact that her married name is Zadopyatova, formed from puns on "butt" and "heel."

Her face said it all: it was covered with moles, it was reddened and roughened, her lips had gone thick, and her second chin bristled with hair; hair was piled, green and yellow up high on her head, and was fixed to her forehead: her hair pins all over the floor, on the rugs; and the glare from the bright but stern glasses replacing her eyes was amazing; her dress had been sewn from a greyish-red, berry-tone, low quality cloth with stitchwork all filled with unusual figures; her shoes had no laces, she grunted while putting them on (you would stopper your ears with two fingers).

She dragged just a bit with her heel on the floor; and she limped (she was bow-legged) using a stiff gutta percha-tipped cane; she had "pipifax"[201] purchased at Kohler's at home, and she kept a stern eye to make sure things were clean; and where needed she hung a small sign "Keep Things Clean," with a jet of hot steam she deloused the wicker frame bed, though the place was lice free; and once every two weeks she attended a meeting of the "Society for Propagating Technical Knowledge among Women."

She often took courses on sewing.

For years she had suffered from nosebleeds; had asthma attacks, when she'd flush to the roots of the hair on her head and the downy soft hair on her chins; for Nikita Vasilevich Zadopyatov thoughts of this average lady were linked to the queen in the drama *The Death of Tintagiles*; and it was not clear: if she'd founded the shelter: "A Newborns' Retreat."[202]

---

201. *Pipifax* is a euphemism for toilet paper. The word was widely used in Russia in the ninenteenth century, but it fell out of favor in the 1930s. There are competing theories as to the word's origins, but most revolve around the verbs "to pee" and "to make" in Russian, French, and German.

202. *The Death of Tintagiles*, a play published in 1894 by Belgian playwright Maurice Maeterlinck (1862-1949): a nod from Bely to an influential member of the symbolist movement who was awarded the Nobel Prize in Literature in 1911. In the play, written to be staged with marionettes, the Queen, representing Death, has complete control of her people and servants and kidnaps and kills Tintagiles despite attempts by his his two sisters to save him. He is captured by the

The queen from the drama *The Death of Tintagiles* kidnapped newborns.

Lately she'd grown more severe: and was plagued by more nosebleeds; as if that weren't enough, though quiet already, she'd grown even quieter; the rage in her eyes when she looked at her husband had tripled, quadrupled; there was something cruel there behind it, that something resembled revenge; her lips smirked with sarcasm whenever Nikita Vasilevich outlined his thoughts for an essay.

He started to call his discussions with her "my remarks":

"Here are my, so to say, marginal notes," he'd announce over breakfast, while shelling eggs into a glass.

Now she stopped conversations as if she had something to hide; and the lines of an unopened notebook stayed empty and useless: Nikita Vasilevich timidly squinted; he dug in his heels in the silence squared, cackling silently:

"The drawer with my treasures is locked. And the key is quite safe."

She kept silent but caustically drilled with her eyes.

She'd been trying forever to get at his letters; that drawer had been locked with great care all these years; and she was surprised it was locked; all the rest were left open; and she knew what belonged where; 'cause she organized all of his papers; this drawer had outlines and notes he wrote after he'd read some Musset; from Chaucer he'd filed some aphorisms; there, too, were some notes for a cycle of lectures and folders with greetings he'd written to sundry officials; it also contained all his letters to France, Wells, and Paul Boyer, who'd been guests in these very same rooms; and some reference books; but just one drawer was locked.

Queen's servants and brought to her castle. Ygraine pursues them to the castle door. Tintagiles cries for help from behind the door, but Ygraine is unable to open it and he is murdered by the Queen.

And not once was it unlocked.

Her doubts and her pain had grown stronger; for years they had hidden beneath the blue lenses of glasses; they'd sprouted; matured: the seeds of her malice.

4

Nikita Vasilevich sat down to write a long "essay"; he covered his knees with a blanket and folded one leg sort of awkwardly under; the string on his pince-nez and a lock of his hair swung; he tried to breathe deeply to have enough breath to blow dry his fresh lines; he reread it and crossed out a part; and then after removing the blanket he patted his belly and stood for a bit on the rug as he teetered just slightly, one foot to another; he tilted his fish face down toward the spittoon in the corner: to spit.

Then he spat.

In the whole situation surrounding him, something smelled rotten.

For freshair the windows were open; the ventilator screamedblue all day and all night; but it couldn't airout all the stink; it smelled deathly sweet, much like a corpse, and a bit like a cookie.

He looked around sadly – nothing new; nothing had changed!

His superlargeoffice had windows with speckled drapes, walls with old paper, gone yellow; and everywhere, black specks; and black chairs; their covers striped dimity with patterns in yellow and red, wrinkled and stained with the traces of heads that had leaned on the backs (peoples' heads seldom were washed in professional circles); and cabinets, five, with their doors nicely inlaid – mahogany; they gave off distinctly the smell of an aged piano.

And busts: there were Molière, Granovsky, Ibsen.

What else?

A sick crocus that Anna Pavlovna missed when she watered that day; near the window she sat in a chaise longue; this was the spot from which she had spent years in the window enjoying the view of a frieze on the pediment: danticles clung to the columns supporting the rosey house opposite.

Nikita Vasilevich sat down to write, with the strap of his pince-nez let loose; and started to cover the paper with scratches that looked much like spider legs; truthfully speaking, his thinking felt perfectly horrible; just not at home with his thoughts; and his mind was arranged in small furnished rooms; in one today; and another tomorrow; his method of thinking was quiet (and almost subconscious): his books were just like a hotel; a whole series of hallways with doors for the rooms; this is Kareyev's; Granovsky, Dzhanshiyev, Goltsev, Yakushkin, Machtet, and Alexei Veselovsky all had their own rooms; he had only a mess; he would live then he'd die and he'd leave a big mess.

He stood up.

As he puttered around he would mutter, hair wild, while pretending that he was conducting a score with a pen in his hand up above a fresh draft in his chicken scratch; wearing a roomy, black robe of thick velvet set off by grey locks.

"So, let's raise it," he muttered, "oh, yuck... their own heads..."

"Higher..."

"With heads held high..."

"Ugh, yuck..."

"We shall bear all our sorrows."

He was composing short phrases.

"Oh, what are you mumbling about," Anna Pavlovna asked from her seat.

He responded unwillingly:

"I'm here writing... composing..."

"And, well?" with a sneer.

On the table she set down her glasses, severe, lenses blue: and her eyes were both learned and stern, filled with sparks, and were bulging and blinking from nerves.

"I'm here writing," he smoothed his disheveled old duster (she called his grey hair an "old duster"), "that in Russian Imperial lands opportunities are boundless and hope for the future infuses the air; let us raise," as I say, "our heads higher," he read the last phrase, "and with heads high, now go..."

Here he put down his draft.

"That is not your idea..."

"Just what do you mean?"

"It's from Brandeis..."[203]

She stifled a yawn with the back of her hand.

Then he grabbed at the yellowish hairs of his mustache, displeased with her comment; he said not a word but he felt that he'd lost all the taste in his mouth: life was somehow smashed flat; and he knew: that he'd built not a thing, while he'd bragged for 25 years that he'd taken the bull by the horns, and had captured the bear:

"Give him over!"[204]

"He won't go."

"Come yourself!"

"He won't let me."

Nikita Vasilevich Dzhanshiev, Goltsev, Kareyev, and Yakushkin had grabbed the bear, while he yelled from the pages of journals and books that he'd won; they believed it; and they even wrote of it; wrote about him in some journals abroad: Léger, de Vogue and Boyer;[205] but he

---

203. E.K. Brandeis (1847 -1931), a Danish playwright.
204. A popular Russian children's tongue twister.
205. B.M. de Léger (1848-1910), a professor of Russian language and literature in Paris.

thought with his 12-pocketed kidney, not his brain; he was a man of his times, and he filtered his thoughts by the hour in small drops, like a measuring glass.

Barrels of phrases; he split them apart.

He plunged into the article, considered himself a true martyr; he tired; stole a glance at the clock and decided to leave; with no warning he trotted his fish face right out of the stuffedwithstink room.[206]

"What are you doing? And where are you going?"

She fumbled a hairpin.

"To a meeting."

She acidly curved up her lips:

"Not today, it's on Friday."

He noticed he'd left the small case for his pince-nez, went back to the table, there only to see her whole chin press her neck, and she showed him her second chin too; a true horror: it seemed that she saw with her lenses not eyes; two enormous glass lenses, so blue they were black, they let through no expression at all.

And beneath them?

"Not that one, another big meeting."

She sneered: and insultingly, cruelly, and vengefully vented:

"What type of a meeting, that's clear… and perhaps you are meeting with Agasha…"

He did not challenge this jibe, but his eye lost its gleam; then he made a hugefist but relaxed it: to smooth his mussedhair (he had dandruff); so screaming with both eyes he turned his fishface one more time, and he found the spittoon: to spit.

Spat.

---

206. Cuttlefish are related to squid. A'cuttle' is their internal shell, or cuttlebone. Cuttlefish range in size from 6-10 inches, have large eyes, eight arms, and two suckered tentacles.

"You say Agasha?... Agasha worked as a housekeeper; here the whole time."

"That's not *all* of the service she rendered."

"Well you managed her... anyway that was ten years ago."

He was afraid of her fierce, savage jealousy; he flopped in his chair: used some curlyandbraided expressions; then, raising his eyes, with their bags like dripped wax, he leaned back, palms magnificently raised, in a pose reminiscent of King Lear, which he had reviewed more than 30 years past in *Artiste*.

He rushed from the stuffedwithstink room.

She opened it: using the key that she'd found: ay! Then an asthma attack; she could hardly get hold of herself.

First, just like Nora, she thought she should leave; or, like Ella Rentheim, stay and take vengeance. Or, wasn't it Ellie?...[207]

Well, Ibsen confused her.

In the drawer there were: first, some eleven poems Nikita Vasilevich sent to one "Sylph"[208]; and a twelfth. "To Dear Sylph" was a playful verse (she did not trouble to read it); but she did read four lines; here they are:

---

207. Nora Helmer, a main character from Ibsen's *A Doll's House*, a play that was significant for its critical approach to nineteenth century marriage conventions. Nora leaves her family. Ella Rentheim is a character from Ibsen's drama *John Gabriel Borkman*, the story of a family brought low by its patriarch's crimes.

208. Paracelsus, a Swiss-German alchemist and physician, coined the term "sylph" in the sixteenth century to describe an air spirit, one of four spirits governing the elements. Bely was probably aware that this scheme was incorporated by Rosicrucianism and was found in later hermetic texts. He may also have been referring to a parody of the idea by Alexander Pope in *Rape of the Lock*, where he suggested that sylphs were formed of the humors of cantankerous women. This would be consistent with Vasilisa Sergeyevna's personality.

When I have a strong urge
for a black birthmark so fair:
well I kiss at its verge,
the black birthmark's fine hair.[209]

Second, from sweet yet naïve dark lily and azure-tone envelopes, she took out a number of notes that were drenched in perfume: reminiscences, promises of trysts, some confessions of love; and short poems.

Like sowers out sowing
Fresh seed in the spring
When you really get going
Your grey beard sure swings.
This loosens my heartstrings
To tender love's feeling
To think of my fingers mussing
your hair: on your head.

Over the signature, "Sylph."
All this rocked her: a punch.

5

He went out to the door with his hair smoothly-combed, white and curly; a suit; and he'd jammed his foot into a boot like a rock.

A servant fanned out his fur coat.

---

209. The birthmark and hair make Sylph unmistakably Vasilisa Segeyevna.

From behind the door Anna Pavlovna leaned toward his back with her head; what a shiny old mess, with her yellow-green hair 'round her cheeks and her ears: she turned dark (as the blood filled her temples); a hair pin fell loudly; they stood facing each other so tensely it was as if they were waiting to see who'd fall first in a yawningabyss.

He ran out.

And the rumbling grew; sounded like someone was wrecking a roof; a bombardment: wind howled! The sky smiled at the sunset: an azure transparence; the sun watched a cloud; quite a shinyfine day of a day: and the playfullysparkling ice emphasized everything, breaking, refracting and shining rays right in your face.

Then he slowly examined the square: he lived on a small Square (the small Squares in Moscow included: Dog Square and Calf Square).

He saw square after square; a small house, it was lilac, white-columned (an Empire);[210] the roof a broad oval, was almost a faux-cupola; on the bias a grey fence stood out; at the corner, an olive-shade seven-floor house filled its space, built in cubes; it stepped out for five floors; and it threatened to fall on pedestrians' heads; and the house stretched off into the alley, hard pressed by a row of identical coffee and sand and grey homes that had six-sided half-towers, cubes reaching out; from a distance, a knight could be seen way up high in a niche with a spear as he slayed a fierce dragon above the tall corniced eight-story cube.

Huge enormities, not buildings.

In only one place could you find a small gap, by a group of wood houses: they were fragile and small and totally grey, rotten, and somewhere between a slate shade and a lighter slate grey; and all three were two-stories; a fourth that was pressed up against them was rosey, and

---

210. Empire, an architectural style prevalent in the later years of eighteenth-century classicism. In Russia, Alexander I, who invited architects to Russia to spread the style as part of the long term wave of French influence, was its primary benefactor.

just one and a half floors; imagine; they hung up above; and, so, it was time to demolish the gap and the difference in height; the owners themselves did the work; they received quite a payoff to spoil the spot.

Nonsense!

Out windows turned grey by the grime of too many springs, rushed Rieger and Bruckner and Brahms. From a huge home next door, faced with tile, with a grand entrance hall in severe northern style, with a doorman and lift, could be heard a fine amateur choir in a version of Bortnyansky's *Quiet Light*;[211] choirs would all gather at "Kuzma on Little Hooves," known as the brown church, each Sunday for concerts.[212]

Rasputin had once stayed the night in this home; Manasevich-Manuylov waltzed here one night; and to mark an occasion an evening was held there for Sabler.[213]

Houses in clumps; and their owners had sealed themselves in and stayed put 'til they died; now all Moscow was piled-up clumps: just a heap of big loads.

"Hey there, driver: Petrovsky!"

At the walnut shade house the door opened: and Anna Pavlovna walked out in her waterproof, no fur, and the fluffiest hat, held secure by a scarf of black wool; and she leaned with her hand on a cane; with a wave, sleigh and driver were summoned for her from the corner; she sat and she pointed ahead: Zadopyatov's slumped back in a sleigh up the street:

"Well… um… Follow that gentleman, driver!"

---

211. D.S. Bortnyansky (1751-1825), born in present day Ukraine, this Russian composer is best known today for his sacred choral works, but was prolific in a variety of forms.

212. Bely has some fun here with the Russian Orthodox practice of naming churches.

213. I.F. Manasevich-Manuilov (1869 or 1871-1918) an agent of the empire's special services and senior political advisor.

The Arbat: where the manyleggedcreature shuffledonin; clouds raced across Moscow's manyheights;[214] Nikita Vasilevich thought; too soon, Christmas was almost in front of their noses; ...and that meant the term was now done.

Arbat Square!

People were everywhere; all in one place; and the multileggedhuman came shufflingrightin; and a cop in the street stood and cussed a drunk lad on the sidewalk, and, then, boxed his ears; dressed in a cloak a man grabbed a huge hat while he yawned and he waved at the square, a Spaniard: the poster at Movie Theater "Kino"; and a woman down under it waited in fur; and the creature, both turners and straight-ons, proceeded off into the lightofthebright shining snow; all eyes squinted; store signs sparkled brilliantly "Kohler" and "Blank."

A city with sparkle.

Nikitsky Boulevard.

Zadopyatov, a Muscovite, knew all the buildings; right there was the memorable, former Talyzin home; later Tolstoy had acquired it; and then, in the end, Sheremetev; there, Gogol had struggled to write: Zadopyatov's own literary memoirs lay there in plain sight.

Then a toast came to mind; quite well known, he had made it; the toast flew through Moscow, went in his collected works, tome one; Turgenev had shaken his hand for that toast; and Fet too loosed a snort; Prince Meshchersky in *Citizen* published a comment; but Katkov kept silent; while it got a big welcome from old Grigorovich from Ukraine;[215] Vasilisa Sergeyevna Kekareva,[216] still just a schoolgirl, re-read and then

---

214. Legend has it that Moscow, like Rome, was founded on seven hills.

215. *Citizen*, a Russian political and literary journal with monarchist leanings published in Petersburg from 1872 to 1914; M.N. Katkov, (1818-1887), a Russian journalist and editor of "Moscow News"; D.V. Grigorovich (1822 - 1900), a Russian writer; N.I. Storozhenko (1836 - 1906), Russian writer and journalist.

216. The future Mrs. Korobkina, the professor's wife.

copied the toast and she fell right in love; she discovered her future: the portals of publishing companies and homes; she spent Mondays at Usovs', and Tuesdays at Ivanyukovs' hearing "maximkovalevsky"[217] long speeches, her Wednesdays were spent at Olsufev's (with Lev Nikolaevich), Pisemsky – Thursdays, and Fridays with Vsevolosky (and Yanzhul, Nos, Shenrock, Yakushkin, and Nikolai Ilych Storozhenko), a real live legend, Nikolai Ilych, about whom Ivanov and Ivan Andreyevich had both lost their voices while fighting about the "Committee" affair that left Chekhov in trouble.

Those were the days!

At the time he, a young lion and framed with a curly mane, still black, distributed slogans, which was like putting a thumb right under Storozhenka's nose; and Veselovsky's nose too got the thumb; and a lot of the boys came to pay their respects: Gershenzons, the Shulyatikovs, the Stolbichenkys, and Freeches in crowds, and they humbly attended his "holy pince-nez"; and he was called "golden tongued " and a "font of ideas," and "sound coin when you traded ideas."

But today he was labelled (albeit by hacks): a small paper scrap... that... values his... silence!

Lemonade liberalism turned oh so bitter; it cleared out his bowels now like castor; it changed about 16 years earlier; the *libretto* expressing Nikita Vasilevich's thoughts had been sung by Stolypin, and now Protopopov was singing the tune:[218] and if taken together their words should have led to machine guns on Petrograd's roofs; and then they would have cursed Mother Russia and finished things off with a streak of fine phrases: from Paris and Prague; oh but now, things were done, and he

---

217. Maxim Kovalevsky was a Moscow University professor who was sacked for his subversive views. He was a close friend of the writer Anton Chekhov.
218. Peter Arkadevich Stolypin (1862-1911), Minister of Internal Affairs, Chairman of Russia's Council of Ministers from 1906 to 1911; Mikhal Alexseyevich Protopopov (1848-1915), a literary critic associated with *Russian Thought*.

stood, a caryatid, a liveried lackey who worked for the State while he posed in protest up above the Cadets' fine front door.

He'd become an old man, was passing old haunts while *en route* to an old place each month (and from four or five o'clock to seven or eight); for 25 years (a prostitute passed; with a beaver-clad suitor); yes, yes, well whatever you'd like!

This was ideological intimacy.

At the head of Tverskoy were the multiple walls of some towers that topped off a home like a castle: and Mikhail Vasilich Sabashnikov during the previous year had outright refused to accept his new book (it was being put out by some teat-suckers);[219] Nikita Vasilevich rode with his lips pursed, down past the towers: the publishing house had been headquartered there.

But that building burned down.

Zadopyatov looked down the long boulevard; above, in the halflightoftwilight, flashed small grey snow flakes; a young boy was chucking out snowballs; the wind rose; and blew, tearing leaves off of their branches; the Polyakov and Golokhvastov homes barely just visible; Herzen had lived there; he'd probably strolled on the boulevard; Chaadaev most certainly; maybe, with Pushkin himself; Zadopyatov was not a confirmed fan of Pushkin: he left it an unanswered question. He glanced at the place where a Bonaparte Marshal had kept an apartment, beyond the old chief of police's home, known today even to all; Kologrivov first built it just after the great fire of Moscow, the former Kurchagin building: to here, at one point, Solovyov's land, his home, and his gardens extended.

It burned!

Here's, Strastnoy![220]

---

219. Mikhail Vasilyevich Sabashnikov (1871-1943), a powerful Russian publisher.
220. Strastnoy Monastery, a religious and architectural treasure not far from Moscow's center, torn

While approaching the spot for the, so to say, meeting, his breathing got heavy; despite his advanced years he felt fine: two decades and more he had felt just the same old unease, exactly right here at this point; agitation, though completely expected because: a fine lady awaited, sincere and most honorable; and etc., etc....

Hm!...

An unpleasant scene played on his left; his nose turned to the right; and there too something nasty: the "street," that is, all that was part of the "street." Where's the "excellence"?

Someplace we're not!

From the sleighs that went past them it seemed as if someone's fat body had tapped on his back; and the city, all lily and black, just then blurred: to a mix, of both darkness and lights.

6

The houswife who rented the room put her ear to the door and heard: "Yes..."

"And Kareyev once said, ooh-ooh-ooh," and the divan squeaked, "that progressive ideas are like stars in the sky guiding all eras and peoples..."

"You wrote the same thing in *Ideals of Humanity*," a woman's voice drowsily droned.

"But I state..."

"I will say *à pro pos*,"[221] interrupted the woman, "that when Milyukov,[222] wrote from Bulgaria..."

---

down for "road reconstruction" by Stalin in 1937.

221. Another mistake by Vasilisa Sergeyevna.

222. Pavel Nikolayevich Milyukov (1859-1943) a historian who headed the Cadet Party and became a leading political figure of his day.

"And I answered him, just like Pavel Vladimirovich,[223] with some comments by Chuprov[224]..."

"That Goltsev delivered..."

"At Storozhenko's..."

"I'm saying just the same thing; Milyukov wrote you a..."

Crackling, her corset.

The housewife who rented the room put her eye to the keyhole and saw: ay-ay-ay-ay!

Ay!

A lady, perhaps 45 or 50, agespotsmarking her face, and in lipstick, had bared her whole chest, as she sat with that tasteless man primping in front of a mirror; and no dress at all, a small corset with greyish blue ribbons, a short silk skirt in *"feuille morte"*;[225] a typhoon-colored dress was thrown over a greyish red, yellowing sofa; and there on that very same sofa Nikita Vasilyevich. Imagine!

Nikita Vasilyevich sat there, uncrossing his legs, with no coat, pants, or shoes: then, in front of the woman he started to strip, with a groan, long white underwear, stained on the legs in a very rude tone, while he shared a short phrase that he'd written at home:

"Oof, *chère amie*,[226] one must endure all these hardships, the everyday life of a writer..."

He got it off, standing before her: bare legs.

The respectable lady, embarrassed, rushed over a rug that was reddening, ran for the bed curtain, wrapped in a skirt that revealed two sticks (legs without hose) in translucent blue socks; from behind the bed curtain her voice, quite dramatic, rose, stopping a speech by the tragic old man:

---

223. Zadopyatov apparently mis-states Milyukov's patronymic. See the previous note.
224. Alexander Ivanovich Chuprov (1842-1908), a Russian economist.
225. "Dead leaf" color, a brown.
226. "dear friend," feminine

"*Oof, chère amie, one must endure all these hardships,
the everyday life of a writer...*"

"There's a smell here..."

"What kind?"

"I can't say that it's *pleasant*."

So he pursed his lips slicing a word: which he tossed:

"Cabbage."

"And strongly..."

And in truth: it did stinkofoldrotten cabbage. He trod to the bed; then panting and thumping ensued:

"Oh, my dear..."

"Oh, my Sylph..."

"Oh, oh yes, oh, oh no..."

Then the talking just stopped: and a spring loudly squeaked.

In a passage that led from a yard to the boulevard, portly, and wearing a fluffy hat tied with a kerchief, a woman leaned hard on a cane, pressed herself to the gate; then her two dark blue lenses, which hid her real thinking, examined the snowpiles.

Just what was beneath them?

Nikita Vasilyevich always had been a most honorable knight; he did not divulge secrets: for decades kept mum: and so we'll do the same; keep the name of the lady a secret; her family name too; for in short, she's a wonderful, honorable, glowing persona!

She appeared once again, as she smoothed out her wrinkles:

"Oh, I'll tell you, I'm tired of all..."

Then the largisholdlug went and belliedrightup to her:

"Under autocracy, oof, it's not easy to live here."

"Oh, no, it's my husband..."

"Your place in society ate you up..."

"You know positive societal stimuli aren't available..." said the fine lady, caressing then grabbing his pinky:

"We're leaving..."

She peed: with her eyes.

Then he jerked his hand back with a start at the thought that she might kiss his finger: his stomach just grumbling and groaning while he covered a belch with a flowery comment:

"Alas, as I said just today, we will hold our heads high, we'll go on...

And then she interrupted him:

"Hand me that bottle."

"I said that we're leaving..."

"The powder..."

"Oh, woe..."

She cut in:

"Well let's hurry!..."

He widened one eyeball:

"A wife's not a *shoe*..."[227] He jumped up.

Then he hastened to pull up his underwear, almost as if she had never seen him without it; and then groaning, he stretched out a foot through his pantsleg; she took out a mirror from a striped bag and powdered herself; and again one could make out:

"Kareyev!..."

---

227. Bely uses a common saying here to show Zyadopyatov's frustration with his marriage: Wives are not shoes – put them on but they're hard to take off.

"Chuprov!..."

"Milyukov..."

They pranced a parade of beliefs; and revived in a tangle a smear of their years; and she'd fed on a smear of his thoughts, she'd read only the third, then the second, and fourth Zadopyatov collected works volumes.

The first of the volumes was missing.

"It's time..."

"And just where are you going?"

"An evening appearance, 'Free Aesthetics.'"

A fat lady felt blood as it rushed to her temples when, practically knocking her down, Zadopyatov came in from the courtyard; behind him arrived a fine lady, about 45.

"Oh there she is, 'Sylph'!"

Her skirt shone like a yellow typhoon and red wave; and a veil, thick and speckled, did nothing to make her look different; eyes sort of black and her mouth with red lipstick; and someone was watching her, horrid for sure, from behind: with lenses not eyes.

Two enormous round lenses so blue they were black: and expressionless.

7

An evening of "Free Aesthetics"! Then someone announced:

"Zadopyatov is here."

"Where, where?"

White-haired and, thanks to the looks and the glances, inspired, Zadopyatov, brow creased, stood there looking a writer; his appearance included a barely detectable swing of the loop on his pince-nez; and his mustache remained a bit damp from the weather; then after he stretched out and clenched the fat lobes of his backside he trudged, watched by Rachinsky, up to the huge seat of honor and stretched out his hand to one Hedwig Sergeiva Zelaninka, a writer from *Journal Parisien*.

"I'll bite your elbow," squealed a hunchbacked young girl to a hunchbacked young poet, then said that she wanted to locate a giant who didn't exist, but who wandered the cloudtops in Bely's work "Symphony."[228]

Thought Zadopyatov:

"Where am I?"

But when he saw Dobronosov, from Kazan, a professor of literature, he quickly calmed down.

Nikita Vasilevich had planned and prepared a small talk for "Aesthetics" about the light drama *The Death of Tintagiles* (just look at the themes he had switched to); whatever he did, he had to remain with "Aesthetics": in case *Russian Thought* openly pushed him away; the same *Russian Thought* that he'd ruled back when Goltsev was editor.

That Bryusov, that Struve!"[229]

And placing his pince-nez atop his resentful nose showed he was struggling to fight with his bothersome thoughts about Bryusov; he had clawed the man badly at *Russian Thought*; Bryusov was *Russian Thought*'s editor now.

Then he thought:

---

228. Bely's *Northern Symphony (First, Heroic)*, Moscow: Scorpion, 1904.
229. Peter Berngardovich Struve (1870 - 1944), a Russian economist and writer who became a well known politician.

"I should try just a bit, and well somehow or other... and Bryusov and I should..."

He squinted one eye absentmindedly, watching a lady: with beads in her ash-colored hair, and a birthmark, her eyes were made up; and her dress a pearl grey; her age also pearl grey; and said she liked nothing that was; but she liked things that weren't; and even then not them all; she conversed with a young man with medals; Zadopyatov was very distracted, he fingered his blinking and twitching face, making his forehead dramatically wrinkle, then smoothing it: fidgeted both with his thoughts and his backside: his words were not plumb! All his phrases were weak; he'd composed polyhedrons of thought; but in fact all his hedrons were worn and were shrinking to nought; not surprised, she glanced cooly and acidly, her face showedheranger; she challenged a youth who was smirking and wild-eyed (and looking for trouble).

A Pole spoke in broken-down Russian; a Russian responded in broken-down Polish; and then someone strolled past with a stony, stern face; he stood with a smile in a stony pose, tending his smokey-blue hair.

"Iyulichev!"

Bryusov!

Extending a paw of a hand, Zadopyatov gave Bryusov a sugarylook (though it seemed a bit acid); he had a subconscious fear he might be driven away from the meeting because of a certain old "essay" entitled: *A Messy Hack.*

Bryusov, however, just asked about work.

"Well, I'm writing a mass market book."

And his eye, what an eye, glittered.

Self-importantly rubbing his belly and stretching his bum, Zadopyatov paraded the poet past all of the wives up in front; and while gracefully lifting the backs of his hands with an accurate bend of his elbows, he shifted his pince-nez up onto the bridge of his nose.

"And so what are you up to, directing?" He tried and he failed to refocus his eye while he blinked his bare lid.

"Me, oh, no, you see" Bryusov was squinting, and kindly, "in our little 'Circle' these marks look a bit off to me."

In response, Zadopyatov just belched.

For a second time Rachinsky jumped up and sucked in some air, and then coughed out his nose puffs of smoke from his cigarette, led Zado-pyatov away to a seat in the front; then, in greeting, two people stood up: a writer he'd not read in many years, Fantysh-Zalensky, and also the author of *Terrorized by a Fury*, a novel, one Peter Alekseyich Vodanov.

"Allow me," a lady stepped over, "to make introductions… please meet Balk…"

"Mozgopyatov," she mangled the name while holding an opera glass out: Zadopyatov.

He knew: she had not read his work; he got angry; broke out in a sweat; with joints creaking he sat; his bad eye seemed to wink.

A small whirlwind moved out of the crowd; Troyanovsky, through some kind of magic jumped out with panache, he was smooth: rose to open the meeting; the merchants' wives, wearing long dresses and filling the first row; a tiny young poet whose spinewasallbent stood: to recite his own poem; to dazzle with gestures; with a nervous and feminine gesture he shifted his fashionably too tight coat; further, with verve; then, right after, the critic, Safteyev, entirely unprincipled, to-tally liberal, armed with the mightiest brew of vocabulary, clenching a cigarette holder, fine tuning ideas (he was fullofhimself): mosaic-ed, his thoughts.

In a word, a real mess.

Zadopyatov sat consciously pursing his lips, and with such a curved belly, and such a curved mess of a bottom, had an itch in his hemorrhoids; he suffered and fidgeted.

Suddenly he stood to speak: a genuine prophet of truth, and he stood there, artistically batting his lashes:

"Allow me," he slowed, "that is… dear… hm, hm… ladies and…"

"…gentlemen," then inafountain, "to express… hm... a thought…"

Then he sputtered, eyes locked on a lady: not listening!

"… thought…"

And then someone stood up and walked off as they fussed with their hair…

"In my books I expressed; that is…:" ay, the girl hunchback had bitten the hunchback male poet: his elbow!...

"…and that is…"

Here, Zadopyatov just belched: hid the belch by repeating the phrase "and that is."

"and that is: works of literary brilliance are written when under the obvious influence of some conception of progress, which…"

Here he equipped his fine words with a metaphor:

"like guiding stars serving all times and all peoples…"

And so on, and so forth; he drooled on forever; his ending the words:

"Please allow me to summarize this with my poetry."

Eye bulged, he recited:

The word from the press
Is "hurrah" for success
The idea of progress
The idea of goodness!

Blindingly good!

Then he stopped and he looked all around the room silently, thirsty for praise; nodding his head, an expression of pride; it seemed everyone there had abandoned him; just Rodentalov the docent respectfully shook hands; the composer Iyulichev played; Zadopyatov stood up; then he flashed a rude gesture, and got the hell out of "Aesthetics," where they failed to honor an older, sad gentleman with such a worried appearance it seemed that his forehead was permanently bound like a book (simply something nonsensical happened).

So, Zadopyatov, a general (retired) and a liberal (retired) in the end as a thinker was dragged out to pasture.

Oh how did he get to this point in his life!

Intermission: a whirlwind of people.

Some kind of a glittering woman was showing off rose-colored hair with a yellowish tint, when she spotted some sparkling; she walked with a soldier in formal dress uniform sporting a haughty expression; a large diamond glittered, its large mass was set off by a cloud of surrounding bright jewels; and a circle of sparks danced in greenlight and yellow with sparkles in redlight, some sparkling blue next to some purple-rose next to a fluid, rose-lily; the soldier proposed that they madrigate; she did not answer; a ring sparked and dazzled his eyes.

As he wiggled his elbows he walked a fine tightrope behind her: a pleasant, well dressed, most polite and quite friendly man: Onchenko-Dronchenko, centrifuge operator.

And a balsamic smell followed them.

8

When Nikita Vasilevich fought Anna Pavlovna, *then* Nikita Vasilevich ate all alone in his office, and coughed in a fist above a tangle of papers with scratch marks; and even while eating he sweated his many-tomed work; and, in general, felt inconvenienced; he liked, for example, his jam without seeds; it was fig; there was *no* fig; and Tatasha the servant poured cold tea, served stale bread.

Just recently he had been eating some lamb all alone; "she" had kept to herself: for what reason? In general, she'd started to squint just a bit with one eye; and he would have liked saying:

"Your eye looks just evil!"[230]

But then, after all, she had no eyes at all: and her glasses annoyed him; invisible eyes always forced him to work out the subtext; later he knew: she had kept to herself; and sitting behind the closed door, her deep silence enraged him; while an enveloping, ceaseless hum filled her mind.

Nonsense!

And once, in his office, while working, he thought, quite depressed, how she'd thrown in his face:

"You had models!"[231]

"We lived with Agasha!..."

Just that day, when he was preparing to go, she'd stuck her head into the hall and he got it: "Agasha" meandered in every direction within her brain's vessels.

He cringed at her merciless jealousy.

So, more than once, he'd whipped his face into a proximal proxy of order with help from a mirror, and padded the hall to her door with a condul: and standing right next to the portal he'd beg, try to speak with her softly; she'd answer with snores (with her nostrils and snores); and then, later things stilled, which would strengthen his will.

Then he'd flee with the condul.

---

230. Evil eye; alluding to *likho*, in eastern Slavic mythology, personification of bad fate

231. Anna Pavlovna employs a euphemism in Russian that is hard to match in English: *modistichki*, or milliners were associated with the sex trade. Here, I use "models" for the same reason. The implication, of course, is that Zadopyatov frequented prostitutes.

He, honestly speaking, felt terrible: failure at "Free Aesthetics" the final blow, hitting him right in the pocketbook; his pride took a hit, more than one; and another blow: *Russian Thought*'s pages in need of more words, swum away.

Two thousand!

No small sum that.

Dreaming, his nose fell away from the driver; where time was a mix of black spheres that contrasted with white from the days; the black spheres shrunk way down; and then Calf Square appeared in a white sphere, in multiple multitudes; and he sat in a sphere's center in multiple multitudes; the sphere split up in multiple multitudes.

The black spheres ensphered things: then day after day they got smaller; the days became darker; each day was more shadowed. The wind banged a sign. It was tossed all around.

Each day the wide ocean of darkness expanded; he saw an old sloop (he called "Argo") and he sailed to the sun, then behind it; the sun, he called "Golden Fleece,"[232] wrapped in mysterious gloom, was then shaken and tossed out. Again he got bumped. So he woke. "Hey go easy there driver!"

A street light and a wall of a white-sided house that was cut at an angle in half, a black hat and black hair; and someone, both huge and dark, rose from the earth toward the sky. Who and why?

Then he realized that it was a shadow, his own, that flew down the wall of the white-sided home; it was thinning, and stretching,

---

232. *Golden Fleece* was a monthly literary journal published in Moscow from 1906-1909. Its title and guiding principles were heavily influenced by a young Symbolist poet, Andrei Bely.

and greying; he formed out of a shadow again, tossed out there and under the sky.

Multiple multitudes: he, an old liberal (retired) vainly tried to charge through the front doors of a publishing house where youth rules, absolutely no luck, here's a draft for you Bryusov, he threw it right back; yes: his teeth were worn out: his whole spirit; his face too; but given time teeth can grind stone.

Then a house, a rock pile, marched past threateningly, showing a grey-walnut side that was facing Calf Square: and the door, like a crack, bared its teeth:

"Stop!"

He was trying, it seemed, going past the front door, sliding down the long grey walnut side on a contour of black, to jump up on the roof, so, once there, once he'd stomped on the sheet iron roof with his heel-shadow (on Anna Pavlovna's head) he'd go poof, disappear, but the house had a corner and the corner cut off the whole head of the shadow man; then, on the grey walnut side, there was something enormous that silently slipped off away and down into the earth.

Blackmawed, the building's front doorway devoured him: perhaps Anna Pavlovna ate him?

<h2 style="text-align:center">9</h2>

"Where's my lady?"

"In her room, all alone..."

He took off his fur coat; he walked down the hall to his office; here, he used his split vision: one eye watched the wall; and the other looked down at his feet on the floor; up ahead, walls of grey-blue exuding pure evil from out of the gloom; and a hall edged with columns; a turn in the hall with a clock getting ready to chime near a door; and although Anna Pavlovna's started, *de facto*, in back of that door, she seemed to be one with the door; the door was her, and saw all who walked through the hall to the front door; and could see into the door to his office; this last door faced her door, relaying his actions, and even when locked; a most terrible door; and behind it such a terribly unpleasant woman: who obviously knew how to peek through a keyhole.

A poisonous woman!

While passing the door, as if passing the lair of a beast, he methodically forced a quick smile, but only his lips and then just for that moment when he could be seen; so with fits and some starts, and not with that smile, and on tiptoe, he snuck to his desk through the columned hall, grabbing the door knob (not "that one," the office door); meanwhile, behind him the mouth of the corridor yawned like a pit.

The door, with a sealed face, attentively watching.

If not for this he'd have squeezed all his fingers in fists; all the same, they were shaking... to make one; as if they knew, and as if he himself knew that years more of refined torture awaited: and saws and a drill; it would happen when he, groaning, moved up; and he knew: in the depths of the hall sat a fat woman, ready to chase him each midnight down all the hallways of life.

He entered his superlargeoffice.

He exhaled, and wrinkled his brow, lit a condul: and woke up: he listened to "her" as she walked by the door.

It was "her" as she walked with a condul, returning to bed from a certain most urgent spot: meanwhile, behind her, repeating her gestures: a fleet but worn-out little person:

"My Annie!"

"My Annie!"

"My Annie!"

Guarding the door with a neutral expression, hers was slammed with a "whack" in his face; and a "click," and the grate of the key ground his guts!

"Yes, that means it's serious: but why?"

He transformed: exclamation point mouth; and a question mark eye; all his gestures were colons; a condul flame comma too; but, nonetheless, he delayed at the door; then knocked softly; he turned; went away; and returned while he tugged his fine curls; but he just couldn't do it; he brushed at the string from his pince-nez as he bent at the waist, grey hair loose, and dramatically tilted the yellowish spot on his mustache up (he'd read this in his own work); it then became a bit chilly and toxic, diseased, epidemic.

He stared at the very same danticles outside the windows; all lit by the streetlights; their contours ran off in the long dark blue shadows: and mixed with the darkness.

"Oh, this is a moral attack..." while he scribbled he worried; his hands had the puffiness shown by sclerotics, and lay on the arms of the chair: his view fell on a drawer that he'd always kept locked; but he didn't notice that someone had come; she had limped down the hall as she dragged her bad heel and she clicked with the tip of her cane; his attention was fixed on the drawer, which protruded a bit: and that meant it was open.

His face was a blank:

"What can that mean?" Her cane and her heels clomped.

He opened the drawer, but the drawer turned out empty: his "Sylph" things were gone!

A thick folder appeared from from behind: and from over his shoulder:

"Ho!"

"Ho!"

"Looking for something?"

"Ho!"

Outside the windows, the sound of horse hooves: in the distance, the clatter of metal.

He didn't dare turn: she would sneer! Then she laughed in a bass from her belly, her bust all aquivver; she peered through her lenses, then jabbed in the needle.

"I read you sing songs there with 'her'!"

Then her hair, quite a mess, fell and hung on her shoulder.

"I... I..."

Then she licked the hairs grown on her lips:

"And I read how your pinkies get licked, and a balding head nuzzles an old feather duster..."

"My friend!"

But a second, old, yellowgrey snake had unwound:

"You still want to be sweet, you old bootlick!"

A flood of tears rushed down her breasts, smooth taut spheres.

"Yes, I ruined my life...What's it worth?..."

"You say, 'squeeze out the lemon and then throw it the hell out'? Is that why you married? And now you would kiss your foul lemon..." she fussed with the edge of her blouse and she stunk of her mouth wash. She gargled with Odol.[233] Her breath smelled like fish.

Then he started recovering:

"My friend, always, no matter what," and he stuck out a hand.

"Leave it: don't foxwithfalsepraiseme."

"But our history," attempting to ride out the storm.

---

233. A variety of oral care products have been marketed under the *Odol* brand name since it was developed in the early 1890s in Dresden by Karl-August Lingner.

"I've got medical training, I know 'her' whole story: all rotten."

With perfect gentility the scene played on out:

"I repeat, that our history..."

"Ho!"

"Time is a witness, excitable friend: like it or not, it's been 30 whole years of our life."

Then he winked. What a man!

"Time's a witness!... You've cheated for 25 years!"

"What a drip..." he thought, grabbing his nose; and then widening his eyes.

"Ah!... Then why'd you get married?... Your writing? Acquire a muse?... Ho! But your muse is a shrew!... Do you see what you've come to? You both should get medals, a Stanislav Star with an Order of Saint Ann chest ribbon: a servant who stayed 20 years!"[234]

So then facing a pelting, her hail, he turned to the right, then the left: a bit helpless.

"I just want to..."

"Shut up!"

"I..."

"You're making a fuss, ho-ho, you, and your greatcoat, embroidered in gold, with a protest in mind, and you're wearing your ribbon!"

In truth, at a ceremony, he had recited *The Sonnets of Shakespeare* in greatcoat, a sword; and his medal.

"You've spokenyourpiece... Want to play me a tune on your lyre?... Like a nail on a board... Grew a beard on your little idea, got some silver and grey in your hair, then you chewed up some phrases, and sweetened farewell celebrations, ho! And an honored official: you look like a lily...

---

234. The Imperial Order of Saint Ann, established in 1735.

but act like a patriot-monster![235]... And the Petrunkeviches:[236] what do they say? They say you're an old cabbagey cabbagehead,[237] covered with leaves, not real thoughts: you should cut out that cabbagehead; wormy part too… And she plays the Melodikon, great with the mouthpiece![238] So speaking quite plainly, that pro-did-toot."[239]

Stand for this? No sir: excuse me!

He rose with some dignity, posed melodramatically, but it came out small caliber: then he slipped down past her glasses' blue lenses and awkwardly turned down his eyes at their feet; then she spit and she smeared it by swiping her shoe:

"You just wait: and they"ll give you a medal: not laurels but whips on its obverse."[240]

He winked boldly and glanced at his shoulder, as if trying to prove to himself he was "boss"; and here, accidentally, he saw on his shoulder a hair from a woman, not yellow-green; black; so he hurriedly brushed it down under his feet; but he had, locked away, a fair bit of this hair, that is, only if "she" had not taken it: "she" could have all of it, if "she" would just leave him in peace! Oh, but "she" would not leave him in peace; her revenge would take years; oh no, "she" would not use just one bullet, but pellets of lead from a shotgun; a leashed life awaited him; he would be pressed into slavery.

---

235. Anna Pavlovna's rant refers here to Gamzey Gamzeevich, the nickname of L. Topolev, a member of the Black Hundred, an ultra-nationalist right wing group.
236. This may be a veiled reference to V.M. Purishkevich, a right wing politician and one of the organizers of the Black Hundred, noted for his monarchist, anti-semitic, and anti-Bolshevik views.
237. The cabbage-head insults refer to so-called "cabbage patriotism," a term for jingoism often used in association with groups like the Black Hundred.
238. A melodikon is a keyboard instrument not unlike an organ with the relevant difference here being that the air is supplied though a mouthpiece similar to wind instruments, such as a flute.
239. Anna Pavlovna uses the same word for flute that Bely toyed with at the book's start: *dudka*. The references are to Zadopyatov's anatomy and marital infidelity and Vasilisa Sergeyevna's technique.
240. The whips here are yet another reference to the Black Hundred.

Just imagine: he slid from the chair, put his knees on the rug, with his head on her knee: and his paw on her leg and the "old feather duster" set down on her fat leg; she waved a huge palm and she puffed out her chest; smooth taught spheres.

"I'll put salt on your tail, my unfortunate bluebird." He sat, and he flattened his nose in the palm of his hand and tried squeezing out sobs, an old man, so unhappy and ugly and caught with the evidence!

In his superlargeoffice he froze for some time near the armchair; the columns and danticles gracing the rose colored house filled the window: the house, piled up rock; then house after house, piled; and façade past façade, and then Hades past Hades; the doors were like cracks; from the cracks came out monsters. How frightful! Just like the old law:

Crushing,
and dangling, façade past façade,
hung right over a Tartar in flames!

Then he rose...

And he knew what was there; it was hidden in back of the door; she spun webs, in their center a greasy she-spider sat (she-spiders devour their mates); he started to shake; then ran off: small, disheveled; although, if he bolted how bad was the bite of the whip?

"I'll grab her and bash her, a hammer!"

But, scared by the thought, he returned to her door: tumbling head over heels, a yawningabyss.

And the door kept its silence.

The queen from the play *The Death of Tintagiles*, half-turned and dragged him right off to her lair: no escape; and she'd kill him.

She's fat!

They walked out and right into a nasty and snowy wind blast that blew sleet and deep cold, while it whistled and howled: the end of the house, and the cast iron fence, and its pickets, the entry, the trees as they cracked in the wind; with the air now refreshed, a mane of snow settled, the walnut shade house had appeared from the storm: and it formed a square pattern; its details appeared; there were fruits on strung garlands; in each of the windows were conduls that flickered in shadows (a beard and night cap), to be torn from a body there outside the window and frozen right through with one eye stuck out into the night; and then visibly: a window shot out a black cone formed of shadow; the black cone, with no hair, voice, or head, from its base took off flying out into the cosmic murk; then, and exploded there, up in the cosmic murk when, at its highest point, it was torn off: Zadopyatov's heel.

The heel lost its shadow: the condul went out; in the yard, where the shadows exploded, snow flickered.

And from there could be seen how things thawed to pale puddles: the entry, the trees, and the chimneys and roof; and the walnut shade house, just as if all its windows were dark, it was crumbling into the cold, could just barely display one wall's corner, a nearly invisible line, as it turned grey-white, then white, then it flickered and vanished.

10

He sketched out the formula, turned to the students, and poked out a finger!

He'd gotten much better and quickly; but still, he was rushing to make up the time he took off; in November-December he'd caught up on reading; it was nearly mid-winter.

He banged on a formula:

"Spheres are a multi-dimensional form," and he sketched out a sphere, "from which can be cut sections of various shapes," he wiped trembling fingers, all whitened by chalk, on his frock coat, hung up on the blackboard's top edge.

He was catching himself: in the year before last and last year he'd managed to finish; this year... Professor Nebo Nikolayevich, known as a lazy slob, cut him off:

"Any decision about the Mlipazov affair?"

"Well, basically..."

"And the inquiry?"

"Rebuffed."

The professors' buffet was quite lively:

"Zadopyatov, however is..."

"Leave Zadopyatov to me..."

"Well I think," Professor Nebo Nikolayevich stifled a yawn with the back of his hand, "that Mlipazov's wrong, and that Peremeshcherchenko too..."

"How can you, old man," he half stood, "so carelessly..." off he walked, waving a hand.

Like he'd swiped a fly out of mid-air:

"The boy-minister's itching and wants us to move: but the problem is not with Mlipazov, it's with Blagolepov!"

Professor Nikolayevich made a mistake!

Nebo Nikolayevich was a professor, a surgeon; he knew what to slice; he would run to the operating room; with a song on his lips he would grab for a scalpel amidst a large crowd of assistants surrounding the patient, though he would be cursing from nerves; but in surgery he'd fall asleep; and he dripped, indiscriminately, mucus on everything.

Also, a fan of Armenian poetry, an interest explained by his wife: an Armenian; the issue was not with him, but Ivan Ivanych.

A surprising fact: the professor, conservative, after he'd posted three notes to the minister "boy" that had outlined education reforms (left unread by the minister) joined the opposition, right after deciding that basically, Minister Blagolepov (his student) was only a follower; Mlipazov was spit: a plow-brained, flat-headed professor with bad skin and nine warts, world famous for working with anilyne dyes; he was leading a shameful attack on Professor Peremeshcherenko; he was a specialist; iso-nitriles of rotten fish (iso-nitriles stink); then Professor Peremeshcherenko got a summons from Petersburg; but Korobkin commanded: resist the request; Zadopyatov moved cautiously through university politics, starting just recently, since he had joined the Academy; he kept the inquiry in mind; but the votes split.

A battle awaited:

"Please don't make a mess of things, Osip Petrovich," he said to Savkov.

Savkov, an applied mathematician, who boasted a chestnut trimbeard and a lead personality, was cause for concern; but not like the round-head, Professor Kokovsky, all shiny and pale, with a look just like death, a false prophet, pronouncing his words most melodically, softened some consonants,"kh," not hard "g";[241] a translator, both an-

---

241. Kokovsky has a southern accent in which hard g's are replaced with an h or kh. Readers may recall that Mikhail Gorbachev, who acquired a similar accent in his youth near Stavropol, was ridiculed for it by Moscow's elite.

cient tragedies and slogans that students devised when they fought for their rights; as a whole, mathematicians and physicists under Ivan Ivanych's leadership waged a campaign meant to counter Mlipazovist charges; a caustic short poem had been going around. Here it is:

Mathematicians quietly
Herd to the fight,
Integrals held tightly
Like spears, upright:

"We are square roots,
Called by rhymes' unction,
Yell it loud, stomp your boots
We're smashing log functions!"

That Professor Korobkin
Kindling our hunger to fight,
Staying whole he set to workin
Used "square roots" as sights

Seventh root, basically, solves the puzzle.
Finished eating Blagolepov's lunch
In Blagolepov's well-made muzzle
he'll throw a well-made punch!"[242]

The famous professor plunged into his notebook to study his schedule: and under the heading "December, the year (the date, such and such)" was the first point: do his grades; and a note in a beady, small hand: "If it's possible, catch them red-handed," they'd gotten around his defenses; they'd used his nearsightedness; chose friends who could

---

242. Playful name creation by Bely. Blagolepov and throwing a punch by combining *blag*, good or well, and *lepit*, to strike or hit.

differentiate; dammit, some boys took exams for themselves and for others, weak students; he wanted to catch them red-handed: he held just a small piece of chalk; he would mark those he'd quizzed with the chalk and then watch for the cheaters.

His second point was: "Anna Pavlovna"; beady, small writing, "Return all her letters."

In anger, he pounded a fist. Then he rose and he hurried and slid like a pawn as he slipped by Drapapov, an old man, his neck badly bent, who sat twitching and wrapped like a bandage around a whole chair; oh, and, damn, Anna Pavlovna, dammit, had sent him that letter; with anger and obvious obstinance she'd described all Vasilisochka's[243] blackest betrayals; a package with proof had been firmly attached: the address (12 Petrovsky Boulevard, apartment 12, rear entrance), and all of the letters she'd sent Nikita Vasilyevich (azure and lily-grey envelopes, filled with the scent of "*Coeur de Jeanette*"[244]); Korobkin was lit with a startling fury at, dammit, "that monstrous old broad": (He called Anna Pavlovna simply "the broad": he would snort that Nikita Vasilyevich married a "huge broad"). So, first, and regarding this matter, he wasn't upset; he was worried about his discovery, Mlipazov, a math congress scheduled in Bern, final marks for his students, and Mitya's malfeasance, and even Mandro, or the fact that his office had roaches, not this; at the thought he remembered: Vasilisochka's age; her yellow-grey sacks were not breasts (she would sit in a tawdrydisplay by the mirror); and second, he'd already freed Vasilisa Sergeyevna; third, (most importantly): he was aware of all "this": and had known it for probably 15-odd years, since the time an anonymous letter informed him about his old friend and the place on Petrovsky. It's clear! What did he have to do with it?

---

243. Korobkin's pet name for his wife, Vasilisa Sergeyevna Korobkina.
244. A scent created in 1899 by Paul Parquet for the French company *Houbigant Parfum*. In 1890, Alexander III appointed *Houbigant* perfumer to Russia's Imperial Court.

So, in the "broad's" deeds he saw only irresponsible handling of papers: no more:

"Oh, that broad!"

And then, after pounding his fist on the table, he fled the professor's buffet; that startled Drapapov; he'd only just grabbed Tverdokhlebov ("The volume of sediments..."):

"Well, the classicists love, old man, punning on slippery questions of love; but romantics just clammer, I tell you, about poor digestion."

"What's that you say?"

"Yes, yes!"

Professor Drapapov spoke Arabic, Persian, Korean; wrote poetry: Tadzhik. In the distance, the zhzhing of voices.

11

He sat at a table; and started to call out the roll while he lifted his glasses a bit as he looked at their noses: Yanitsky, Yanents, Yantsev, Yantsevich; Yantsevich's turn: his answers were written; he explained them. Ivan Ivanych, there squinting, looked down at the formulae, swung his legs under the chair and then slapped his knee hard with his hand.

"And so, after all, no!"

"What then?"

"You don't know how, my dear sir, to interpolate."

No, sir! The student was lost.

"Tell me, what does interpolate," patting his knee with a hand and for emphasis using his nose and his tone, "mean?"

He answered himself:

"Well it means, you insert the unknown in a series of values, all known, they're your givens: well, there you are sir..."

Then he called the next student while raising his glasses:

"Yaponsky!"

The eyes down there under his glasses were blind-blind: he stood and he turned to the board with true hard-headed obstinance; scratched calculations and mouthed calculations; Yaponsky, head down like a bull, he let go; as he stared at his sleeve with the same strict attention he'd pay to a fly; and ignored all the thicklygrown X's.

"Oh, yes, sir, an integral," he said, and he poked it.

"That's one, of course," squeaked the youth.

"Measures the…"

"Size."

"In relation to what," he tried digging.

Much louder, he answered himself:

"It's an infinitesimally small part…"

He brushed back a lock of his hair like a horn and then seized the boy's sleeve with a hand:

"You've been caught. You're not Yarikov!"

"What?"

"You've been marked!" The boy twitched:

"Well I don't understand."

"You've been marked by my chalk!"

He stood up from the table, and said to them:

"Yarikov's chalked!"

So he asked:

"You're not Yarikov: no, so who *are* you?"

"Frizakis!"

"I marked you," he showed a small cross on his elbow, "a cross means you've answered: and I drew the cross."

He had secretly marked them with chalk while reciting: and then, when he called them, he checked their sleeves first: inspecting: a cross?

Well he'd caught one (was craftier).

In this particular memorable case he had proven observant:

"You're marked, yes you're marked, so move on, please Frizakis!"

"Oh yes: he came up, but I'd marked him with chalk," he recounted at lunch with his colleagues.

He was pleased with his catch, and he gave an account to them all; then he went to the meeting: the council already was at the green table: Drapapov, Savkov, sociologist Krylesov, Zadopyatov, Kokovsky, and Prof. Nebo Nikolayevich: Rector Beznyet, white-eyed, with a shaved lip, on his neck a white carbuncle, opened the meeting with lisping and shuffling his papers.

"Nikita Vasilyevich," after the meeting Korobkin had touched Zadopyatov, and leading him off, deferentially but firmly, even quite cheerfully somehow, cut in with real emphasis, "please, over here, sir!"

He pushed a small packet off into his hands.

"What is *this*?" Zyadopyatov looked over: seemed thinner and greener, and the bags that hung under his eyes looked much paler:

"This went to the wrong place: to me; but your address is here, it's for you, sir... And cutting away, he rebusied himself with a book:

"Third point: see von-Mandro."

Yes, it's already late; and a pity, Mandro would be busy; he'd wanted to check: take a look at him; basically: well, if the children are friendly, the parents do visit.

The brown twilight was nearly all gone, consumed by the anti-brown night; he sat shaking, alone in a cab on the way home to Snuffsneezer: thawing had loosened the snow: made the winter go rotten! The stones came uncovered that dark and damp day.

What can you do: it's no city, no it's ahugesloppypuddle, it's Moscow!

12

At dinner, recounting the ambush while clutching a napkin, he crunched on some juicy-brown duck:

"Peerless duck: edible."

Vasilisa Sergeyevna's tone said:

"You're being a pig," and she pointed to crumbs on the table, "a place mat?"

He looked at the ceiling: and prickled.

"You smell of burnt paper and sealing wax: put on some *eau de cologne*."

"It's clear: I am no stinking lout: why should I wear a scent!" he declaimed with his forehead all lines.

He was sick of this nagging.

Then, bump, his chair rattled: he didn't see what he should do: that is, snatch up his plate and escape to his office; instead he had fought her; poor Nadya had always been anxioustohelp; she often was worried; and she had a cold, and a cough; and not dressed for dinner; she suffered from shortnessofbreath; he sighed at the sight of her, just like his Tom, the deceased.

His external appearance suggested blank thoughts; while his glasses suggested some thinking, the rest of it, no: so he sat and he ate; and then later, he wandered the house; he was not in the mood for his math; papers in loads sat awaiting review; he started unloading; the discovery, there, hidden, was huge, revolutionary science for the world; while a tuft of loose hair hung down over his compass's point; he sat tracing a circle; his head was all tingly, an anthill.

He suddenly stood; and displayed all his hard-headed obstinance, whispering under his nose from the cabinet to the door from the door to the cabinet:

"They sniffed it out!"

At a sharp turn he swung out a hand; it was like he was slapping himself in the face; just because, in his mind, he had taken a smack from that sideburned Mandro.

Like an icewater faucet full blast he was seized by a chill.

So it seemed all was quiet: like always, the quiet was worse: so he pushed those thoughts off; but he feared an ear up to the wall, or an eye at the door; or, he'd confess, a small figure right outside the window that he could not see but who'd come, and most certainly: soon!

He'd been standing one day, with his back to the window: when up on the wall its light rectangle winked; from the shadow of someone there outside the window; he turned much too fast, and blood rushed to his head, for a second obscuring his sight: but the window was empty; however, the shadow he'd seen in the light meant that someone had looked in the window; a shadow just couldn't appear by itself; and he couldn't believe that a shadow could fall on the person who cast it, that those who cast shadows were shadowless, or that dark shadows could curse, that the Tartar was found and unmasked and would fall; all together with... Moscow.

But that's not the point: the real point here was that he'd once stuck up his nose in the window at just the same moment that someone else stuck their nose up, it was someone who'd been on the street, small and dark; a small man with a dog's nose or a dog with a man's face; they'd have bumped one another: the glass had divided them; "dognose" flew off from the window, had totally panicked; and fled.

And besides that, who knows?

Such confusion, oh dammit! So strange he'd remembered: and strange this annoying, persistent, pure nonsense returned so much later, it was nonsense on wheels! In his thoughts, rolled all sorts: there were people with carts that had tires, and on buses and automobiles: Androns, Evlampyas, and Yakovs (or *what* were their names?), those that roll off with Andron, when Andron sets off in his chariot: all there in his tired old head! As if someone, on purpose, had steered weird ideas near his ear.

He'd become resolutely convinced:

"My dear sir, the discovery is something that 'they' would not hesitate stealing."

"Things are clear now!"

"'And 'they' know a treat when they taste it."

"He'll, dammit, come here to see me, some Mordan, oh yes..."

"They..."

Who are "they"? Are they Androns, Mandrons, Mandrys, Mandragorys, Mordans? That's nonsense and, basically: he'd failed to extract the name's root; and, even more senseless, the root that he got was Mandro. Well then, what did Mandro have to do with it? That he had come 'round to sniff, that was one thing; a kid, that small doghead, was sitting right outside the window, and that was another thing: had he returned? And then third, there was...

Once: with a napkin in hand on his way to his office, he noticed that Darya was dusting a spot that had never been dusty; she'd pulled up the rug; she was down on her heels at that same bit of flooring, right under... right under... which.. tss-tss! Then seeing him coming she wiped the parquet; he escorted her out, locked the door; and inspected down under that square.

And it all was just fine: all the sheets still were there... all in order!

He took them out, checked them, and stuckthemallback re-arranged, re- arranged them once more... and then hid them completely; but he could not find peace; and so time and again checked the lock on the door; like a child! He should take all the papers to Nadya; decide things with her: and go down to the State Bank: and rent a steel box; things were getting unreal: like some objects standing and swelling: a nightstand not standing but swaying.

Just everything swayed: all of Moscow's foundations were even now foundering, shaking, had proven unfounded.

Cold drafts in the rooms blew and braided together and threatened to swirl in a whirlwind; for now, it was hidden and clinging to Moscow's warm nourishing breast; you could surely say Moscow had breast-fed no serpent: instead a huge whirlwind, worldwide! It consisted of whirlwinds: with each little whirl in a room, they first quietly twirled in the dust; then like snakes they all slithered off, stirring up all of this nonsense, and tossing up papers and making some people sneeze; weaving and weaving together, and growing and rising and fracturing ceilings, and tearing off roofs: and one shining October day... we will speak more of this later.

Korobkin explained it: fatigue: too much work; he had pushed to the point he was sleepless; he tossed and he turned; got no rest; he did math in his dreams, but completely a new way; in truth, it was totally different; a new calculation; he differentiated speech, paying attention to sounds and not sense; and re-integrated; not in his forehead, but more like the back of his head, in his spine; and then once, when he woke in the night, he had found himself integrating; muttering all through the night, he was carefully trying...

What kind of ridiculousnonsense had he done as an "Andron"?

Popfizzles and fizzpops in the knot on the back of his head!

Oh, I do need, I need, yes, sir, basically, rest!

The complexcombination of all he'd observed – the doghead, von-Mandro, the shadow – "popfizzles and fizzpops" – resided right there in the knot on the back of his head: with his blood building up; and the sound of the words "popfizzles" and "fizzpops" – "zz," "zz," – a buzz in his ears:

These "popfizzles" were blood backing up in his brain. Thus, he concluded: once decided, he could, after all, rest.

One night, sleepless, a condul in hand, his thickheeled bare feet scuffled across the parquet like the dog, Tom, just wandering; here, he bumped into the cause of his worries or (nearer the truth, a contrast to his worries)... Vasilisa Sergeyevna; paleverypale: in a nightshirt with skinny goat legs and a condul; like him, she was walking:

"What, Vasya, my Vasya, up wandering?"

He batted his eyes.

"Is it you?"

"It's my eyes!"

"I can't sleep."

A few words, left unsaid, flashed between them. He thought:

"Yes, Vasya, so look…" she wentquiet, he wiped off his hand on his robe, "she's not playing with, rationally speaking, her eyes; she's not moving her arms: blinks her eyes just the same, no regard to position... It's clear: oh dear Vasya, my Vasya...

He went back to his office:

"So, basically…"

Piled some papers: stuffed drawers.

He dreamed: there were cannibals feasting on earlobes.

So basically, rational clarity rusted: Aristotle the Bright down to Heracles the Dimmest: a world that was strewnwithdebris!

And quite frankly, Professor Korobkin had lived in a world built in 2-D, not 3: and lived not with his "I," which had "N" real dimensions and Tommie the dog, too; but Tommie, the dog, was long gone: he had died; he'd been placed in a hole in the ground: like a comet his "I" rushed up into his skull made of "N" real dimensions that peeled, like Nikita Vasilevich shelling the eggs for his breakfast; and from "N" real dimensions of shadows and two fundamental dimensions (like a tray, we live on a flat surface) there started to form, from a well known celebrity and a most gentle dog, a man.

So he stood at a crossroad!

Rotten old winter!

The rotten old winter was shining; a warm day; December like April; he remembered his humoungous old hound: he hove back on his haunches and mourned, hung his chin on his hand; a brown jacket and yellow-grey vest; he sat hunched down beside the room's yellow-brown curtain, cut through by a yellowish column of dust motes all swarming the sunlight:

"Poor Tommie, a goner!"

The sun sobbed a shining and large-dropped cold rain; a real sun shower showing a saint had departed this world!

But the yellowest cruelty arrived with the evening; in the green-grey of twilight things settled; the black-maw of the night then devoured them all.

13

Clouds raced across murky old Moscow.

A drip icicled down to the street; out there everything icicled: snow had been chewed into spitwater puddles; and stones could already be spotted; and the grinding of cobbles by wheels had begun; and weirdos, and womenroughedup by the street, and washedupoldslobs threw their garbage and offal and trash in between the grey, green and rose-colored old houses; crouched, blunt, stone and wood, with strange speckles.

The gawkers kept watch all over; their windows, and doors, and their gates.

And a bluish short fence, and a lily short fence, and a rotten short fence: and between them annoying old ice laytthererotting: the fences defended each house from the houses next door; up above, it was clear; a free space with a view and a factory chimney exhaling blue smoke; here a five-sided tower stuck up: it was blue; and there, from a distance, a window-faced factory loomed: they made textiles.

The factory factoried smoke.

Then some kind of a snot-nose walked up to a battleax, skirt hem all muddy:

"Oh, Grandmother, can it be true that a dwarf lives on Snuffs-neezer?"

The woman adjusted her coat:

"Well!"

Out of the yard, where oldwomenslinens on clotheslines were blown by the wind, came an answer:

"Of course, the guy mopes all around and spews nonsense."

Then, *crack*, a guy shelling some nuts on the corner, "a destitute bum: and his clothes are just rags, nothing warm..."

"No nose and nowoman..."

"A *liar* and drunk, he's just hopeless!"

Then, senselessly, someone there pounded a rock tomakegravel: a wide and curved alley was soaked from the sidewalk's wet runoff.

A greybearded merchant, in tails, a bit dressy, barked:

"Braggart."

A man walked up: scraping a loose lock of hair:

"I saw dwarfie."

"Well?"

"What?"

"Boy does he have a mug!" They all cackled.

Then Pepikov whistled a bit of a call, kind of festive:

"Hey you, now I've gotten things started: you newfangled joker!" He extended his fingers to catch Pereprotov:

"It's mine, just for you: have some thoughts? Is it working?"

The group grew: and gathered: Muyashev, Sikazin, Upakin, Yelchi, Dukhoventov, "hurrah for old grandpa Mordan" (someone's nickname); the neighboring alleys were empty and quiet; but if you came here: the street was quitenoisy: there were shouting and teasing; a flockofloudcrowscawed and circled a church spire and cupola; grey, a cloud started to smile, with an edge turned geranium; clouds were aligned on the rays of the sunset.

Porfiry Petrovich Parfetkin[245] rushed out from his first floor apartment (a curious man):

"Can you tell me one thing: is he Gribikov's dwarf?"

"Well now if you don't smell him you won't even recognize him." Novoderezhkin got all insulted:

"Well thank you so much: only I don't use snuff, I don't smoke." It grew silent:

"Old Gribikov sits there, he's doing just fine."

"Grabs the bone (from the soup pot), that's still not enough..."

"So, so," Porfiry Petrovich Parfetkin (a curious man), "so, he's greedy?"

"It seems, I suppose, he loves money?"

"That skinflint just sits on his strongbox."

"Who pays for the dwarf?"

"Von-Mandro."

"Tell me, why does he pay for that stinker?"

"The reason: well screw you!" He showed him a thumb, right down under his nose:

"All the better, that's something to talk about!"

It went on and on, and they spoke with the street people; a gawker stood slit-eyed and staring; a taxi wheel rumbled against a rough cobblestone's forehead; some sleet flew at first, soon a sticky snow slewed; then the group just evaporated; horses were led off, pedestrians pranced their own dance steps while drifting away.

They all ran off to tend to their lives in the lily-black.

---

245. A nod to Dostoyevsky and *Crime and Punishment*.

14

Buzzing like beetles they babbled at home; where they baselessly dribbled foul gossip.

"A dwarf with no nose roams the alleys: and lurks and makes trouble."

Porfiry Petrovich Parfetkin went out to see Khelefonov that evening; they say Telefonov was in a chikchiri,[246] Telefonov from number 28 whose daughter was proud of her old, it was claimed, family name, from the gentry: back during the reign of Alexander II, Telefonovs had worked for the state.

He opined:

"I'd keep him in sight," he said, rubbing two fingers together.

And Parfetkin, "no matter his tricks."

"Ah, ah, ah?"

Telefonov: "Well that's how it is!"

"Ignoramus!"

"You're joking!"

"Ah?"

"What?"

"Yes, that's it!"

Things are clear: "Heh, heh... Flies smell a corpse!

They repeated the news: and rumors moved on house to house.

All the way up to Princess Kitaisky.

An aside: it was here that a house had been sealed-up for two decades, Yudif Nikolaich Kitaisky twenty years earlier had choked on a bone; he appeared every night and he choked once again, the same house that had therefore been empty (the princess Anastasia Yudifovna and an old woman resided in *San Tru de Iglais*), from the house, boards

---

246. An ethnic hat

were stolen: Anastasia Yudifovna from *San Tru de Iglais* returned; it was long overdue: then they waited; and when they came out on the street there were oohs: My God save us from flatterers, she wore a man's hat and pants; in her hand was a cane; her voice sounded as if it came out of a barrel; there was down on her lip; she announced that she wasn't a she, but a "he," and that they were all wrong to call her Anastasia Yudifovna; what can you say? Well, with nature she played hide and seek; she'd need surgery to be: Anastasy Yudifovich.

This probably frightened the ghost; and he vanished: the haunting was done; but some wretches appeared.

It was strange: when the princess was asked in an interview, "What does your majesty do to keep busy?" she said:

"I'm in the army...".[247]

"Excuse me?"

"That's right."

Explanations commenced: and then later they'd learned that the army was real but not made for killing; instead it saved lives (alcoholics and crooks), and the general commanding the army, a "Boats" or a "Coats" (who knows) was some kind of a miracle general, kind to the core; the police for some time looked askance; but got past it: she handed out leaflets, and brought wretches home; where she suffered the wretches. With respect they would tell her:

"The dwarf in the house on Telepukhin: a stinker, a pauper, no nose."

But the princess had listened, and closely; took notes; they soon saw: that the dwarf had arrived; and behind him, and rolling her eyes, was the princess; and then at the door she insisted: "Oh, please, come with me."

---

247. As will become clear later, Bely refers here to the Salvation Army.

The dwarf, who was thinking the worst, soon absconded! But, nonetheless, she got him home, then she stuffed in his pocket a leaflet; she forced him to sing."

It's you, my Lord Savior,
I called and you heard.
I'm just a rank sinner,
A man of this World!

Thus they would sing for themselves; it was said, they had medicine to rub on his nose; rub it in, it will grow.

And then emptier gossip: the dwarf had caused trouble; right out on the street where they'd spot him and gawk and then spit:

The streets that we roam
the dwarf Yasha calls home.
With a certain same one
Chinese princess has fun
Won't smoke near her door,
But they'll play at amore.

He got infested with lice: took to drinking.

15

So, look!

Why did Gribikov say this to everyone out in the street?

"There's a dwarf here…"

"Oh, what's that you're saying?"

"No-nosed."

"!?כְ"

"He just mopes: he does nothing."

He didn't know why, like he didn't know why he had sat there for 20 years in the window: just noticing what and how, understanding what was what; if he failed to connect all the dots he'd just guess; while attempting to tie things together: for wisecracks and jokes.

For entertainment?

Two decades with nothing to do: he might open a bottle or bring out the bucket; he was tired of clipping his coupons, blasé; at the same time he curiously watched all the lives he could see; yes his interest was sparked: there were politics, all types; is Mitya Ivanych now pilfering books? And Varvara Platonova, doesn't she live with Bobkov? Well, and this "Uncle Kolya" and that "Uncle Kolya."

What kind of an uncle is he?!

"And so what if they think I'm a thus and such, they're just food for the lice!" He hung out the window, and out into life: others' (not *his* after all); life was interesting; only unclear and nerve wracking somehow.

He conducted intrigues: out of boredom.

"Oh, I've got a punch, got a punch..." let me at that professor: it's like this... "Your Mitya Ivanych is pilfering[248] books, sir!"

But it did not work: tossed him out by his collar.

By what rights was that dwarf round his neck? Well, he'd gone to Mandro; hardly knowing himself why: Ankashin, Ivan, the one fixing the plumbing (at Mandro's) had relayed to him, "Mr. Mandro, who's quite wealthy, has someone to help, and is seeking a room." What? How? Who is Mandro? And just how do they live? Is there money? An office? He sniffed it all out, looked it over: and looked himself right into a fix: now the dwarf was there hung on his neck.

With the lice falling off him.

Telefonov had said about Gribikov once:

---

248. Highlighting Mitya's larceny, Bely uses a slang verb, *kolokolit*, that refers to poor people who sold stolen scrap metal to bell makers (*kolokol* means bell).

"There are snakes; they are dangerous; he simply stinks... so then, what kind of snake could he be?

Telefonov forgot: that on earth there are stinkers whose looks scare off leopards; those stinkers are guiltless, are snakes not by choice; that was Gribikov, too.

Like a corpse, he had no need for time; and his leg fell asleep; but he smoked as if racing; his smoke filled the room; and the smoke filled his spirit as savagery filled up his head; on the table before him, imagine, were glasses (a crude frame); one hand scratching his back with a hook of a finger (it was less a room, than some kind of a flytrap), he stood and he leaned as he walked like a broken down nag that was on its last legs, but it still cast a shadow[249] his eyes locked on a tablecloth half filledwithholes.

Just a miserable room!

It all stunk; and looked shabby; a trunk of neormous[250] size peeked through the mess (and it hid all the good stuff): it was covered in white; and a Tikhon Zadonsky,[251] with halo, was brightly displayed; one whole corner was roachified; paper hung off of the smoky and damaged old walls; and, like drapes, there were spiderwebs everywhere; smoke-coated, crack-filled, the ceiling had threatened collapse for some time; and another small corner was moldy.

A spider just sat there, quite fat.

---

249. Perhaps this refers to his mortality.
250. First two letters reversed in the original.
251. Tikhon Zadonsky (1724 - 1783), a Russian Orthodox bishop in Voronezh and Eletsk. Canonized, he is considered one of the great eighteenth century propagators of the Orthodox faith.

In the corner, a shelf with some wadded up napkins: daguerreotypes, yellowed, pulled out of their coral-toned frames, full of holes; they'd been broken now 20 years; stickingupout of the mess were some yellowing newspapers, *Niva* from the nineties with poetry written by Kupernik and Korinfsky as well as a popular story that always appeared by itself, by Akhsharumov and Zhelikhovskaya; yellowing copies of *Niva* and a worn-out red shoe: were down under the bed with a feather with half of its fluff torn away.[252]

Worn out drapes of a dark Chinese fabric; encrusted with fly specks; a twist of tobacco leaves crumbled; a spider; he smoked, clearly, "home-made" tobacco; the floors were uneven and covered with canvas and worn.

In this room, and for decades, they did some of Moscow's real dirty work; not professorial, or noble, commercial, or for the intelligentsia, or proletariat, but for those who avoided the main streets, which suddenly blossomed gigantically just when you turned off: went down through the network of alleys that crossed and recrossed in real knee-bending turns, and where everything vanished that ever was there; from the deep depths of Russia, from Europe's proud capitals; everything there was disfigured, and mixed, and turned upside down, stopped in the silent dead end in the center of town.

That's backalley "Moscow"! All Moscow: a web; at its center a spider, old Gribikov: wretched, immortal; the zhzh of the flies that were trapped in the web; and the web was all woven of gossip, a network of nerves and of horrors and gloom and confusion smack dab at the center of consciousness, "popfizzles" and "fizzpops"; and the professor naively explained this was caused by fatigue and the pressure of blood in his

---

252.A.A. Korinfsky (1868-1937) a poet, journalist writer and translator; T.L. Shchepkina-Kupernik (1874-1952) a poet, playwright, and translator; N.D. Akkshamurov (1819-1893) writer and critic; V.P. Zhelikovskaya (1835-1896) wrote on theosophy, one of Bely's interests.

ears; he had only to put his nose out of the window to see that the buildings of Snuffsneezer Alley were "popfizzle and fizzpop," and not from that lump on the back of his head but just everywhere.

A back alley Moscow embodied "popfizzle," a tumor, all pathwayed with streets. In a lump on the back of his head, on the back of his head,[253] sat old Gribikov: Moscow's own lump!

He cracked open the window: to let out the smoke.

As the sun set a cloud turned to nickel; the freeze hung around and the meltwater froze; then was covered by snow; and its icicles just didn't drip; a man stopped by the yellow house after he saw: the guard sat, with a blue hat, like always, a yellow-brown dwarf.

A blizzard: wind boiling and shrieking.

16

Nikolai Nikolaevich Kiyerko heard all the rumors describing the dwarf; and so Kiyerko lived in a house of white stone whose first floor was roachified, filled with the worst kind of poverty; neighboring Gribikov's yellow old house; from there Gribikov leaned out his windows and over a fence built tofendoffthecity; the buildings were linked by a yard that was shared and a mess and was covered with ruts and with dirt.

Kireyko[254] walked as he sucked on his pipe in the bitter wet mist; he was dressed in a moth-eaten sheepskin coat, wore a large hat like a bun,

---

253. Repetition also in the original.
254. Reversed letters in the original.

he was narrow-eyed, greasy, and bearded: yes, a bit of a thaw; all the days of completeandunendingdownpours were past; he stepped into a noisyandboisterous crowd; and, among all the rest, were Ivan Psevdo-podiyev Ankashin, a street preacher (hands just like pitchforks, for girls a real monster); and Klopovichenko, always a realist (he worked at the pipe plant and there, it seemed, pilfered a coat) stood in his coat (full of holes), with a big nose and muscles; and waved to Romanych.

It was clear he knew how tomakemoney:

"You dope, so just *why* did you fight for your corner when threatened: went and fought 'gainst Mandro; now Gribikov's gotten the dwarf for himself."

"Gets a nice monthly nut for that dwarf," one said.

Kiyerko sat there and listened: and people approached him right there in the yard like he owned it; and, winkingandnodding, he spoke with them:

"So, Nikolai Nikolayich, time to make peace with the flies out there?"

Kiyerko puffed:

"But the music's still playing!"

Blew smoke out both nostrils.

Romanych heard something: Gribikov, damn him, accepted the dwarf, but with us he is playing it tough on the rent; and he still sits there clipping those coupons.

"He cheats, strips you bare."

"It was fine in the summer, but now, well, he threw me right out by the scruff of my neck."

They sympathized :

"Can't get blood from a stone..."

"Eh!"

"You pay for the truth, you pay for the lies." It was raining complaints.

"As for this," puff, puff, "surely you see that they're rich!"

Then Nikolai Nikolayich's eyeballs traced out a twin line.

Puff! Nikolai Nikolayich drew in on his pipe, puff puff, "wait: and you'll live to see it."

Professor Korobkin was wrong to tell everyone that "Tstserko-Pu-Kiyerko" had slept his whole life on the divan; he rushed; he had things to get done; and in part he paid visits, imagine to whom: Evikhaiten, Emil Leontyevich Mileiko, the Pole, P.P.S., he met too with the Menshevik Klevezal; still more often he ran off to No. 6 Rostov, close to Plyushchchika, where the Bolshevik Pereulkin was living, where questions were settled by comrades Kanizarovym, Zhikova, and Grokina concerning the concept of value and issues related to Bernshtein.[255]

What's more: Nikolai Nikolayevich Kiyerko wandered; it looked like he comfortably shuffled then smoothly appeared, it seemed, everywhere: factories, meetings for workers, and underground presses; he poked his nose in at committees, and agricultural groups, statisticians: Kiyerko might show at a bourgeois salon, or be seen at "Free Aesthetics," where else? He'd arrive, and joke just a bit, and then vanish; though he was discussed very little; he was "kiyerko" (with a small k); and "Aesthetics" did not know he went to a club for professors; and there they did not know how close he was tied to the workers: "Kiyerko," "Sir," "Puk," "Tsetserko-PuKiyerko," who was he? A rumor was going around that he worked as a government agent, that he showed maximalist sympathies; neither was thought to be true. But remember one thing; that he roamed among brains; and he pounded in everyones' heads, big societal issues; in "back alley" rooms he would

---

255. Eduard Bernshtein (1850-1932), a German Social Democrat.

sprinkle "Ricardo,"[256] "Bernshtein," "Orthodox," "*Iskra,*" and "Lenin," and "Marx"; on the streets, periodically; yes, he was great spinning thoughts; and his words were like pinpricks; you'd say he broke bones with ideas; set the compass for views held by poor folk. Now that's a strong drink! And so that's what they said.

"We are livingthegoodlife, but we might just as well shave a priest," said Klopovichenko, happy.

Romanych's pain was awake, a bruised spot on his soul; so he chased off a dog from some food scraps: a Milanese hound had escaped from its owner.

"Where?"

"Well you, you've always got troublesome questions," puffed Kiyerko.

Drizzle spat down on in his face.

"In this life," Psevdopodiyev stood up for freedom, "it's one thing to be apolitical: we need our rights you know, brother Romanych,"

Klopovichenko said:

"So and if so!"

"So and if so!!"

"So and if so!!!"

And then back to him:

"I know: you want revolution allied with the gentlemen? They'll slip a radish down under your nose."[257]

And they laughed:

---

256. David Ricardo (1772-1823), an English economist.
257. An incentive offered for desired behavior, similar, In English to the proverbial "carrot and stick," which in Russian is usually "rod and cookie." In this case, the positive incentive is a radish.

"You'll be choked on their nasty old table scraps."

"This is just what Milyukov has to say: that is, freedom is yours; but the land is still ours."

"That's enough of your nonsense," his veiny hands waved, "Milyukov offers kopeks; while rolling in rubles."

But Kiyerko, leaking thin curls of blue smoke, kept his silence:

"A thief!"

"Tell me why you are battling, comrade," Psevdopodiyev struck an imperious yet comical pose, "with the world?"

"Perhaps!" he explained, "But you might just as well shave a priest! Here, some priest hums a hymn; you believe like a bare-bottomed child: it's because all our people are drownedintheirdrink."

At that Kiyerko rolled his grey pupil around: and he grew mighty cheerful; he jumped up a bit; but his sock drooped; and squinting one eye he examined the smoke from the chimney; his other eye closed; and he sat for a bit; one-eyed.

"Gobbledygook..."[258]

Romanych was friendly, his tail to his mane, and good in a tight spot:

"Tell yourself, 'We should unite.'"

"But just where are your people?"

"You freeloader!"

"Blind!"

"What kind of a life is this: fit for a horse!"

"Unite!"

"But if some swell came along, with a belly, a fat one, a glutton; you'd lay down like a dog and do nothing, all skin and bones," Klopovichenko claimed.

---

258. Bely uses a colorful expression from Dal here. Translated as "gobbledegook" the word "gallimateyno" refers to a misunderstanding due to complete ignorance on one or both sides of a conversation.

"And that miser will tear off your hide, just you wait and you'll see!"

The word "hide," pulled the leathermaker out of his revery, "it's soaked in some *kvas*, and then buried in dung to be cured; and still later, it's ready to use."

"And you've heard all the whispers; who is he?" A worker spoke up:

"If you can't sink a nail use a punch: do what works, that's the way of a worker; and if the punch does not work, grab a file…"

"You're a gradualist!"

"He is a Menshevik. "This Klevezal, is a liar, well I'd go…"

"Make a squeak and they'll crush you!"

"Rebel! You must fight for your rights; hurry and join with the working class."

Klopovichenko tightened one hand in a fist:

"Hit the bourgeoisie in the ear and the face: beat 'em up, beat 'em back!"

"That's impossible, it won't be allowed," said Romanych with doubt as he pulled at his hair, rubbing two fingers together.

He spat.

"Allowed, not allowed… well they came and just took it they did," with that Kiyerko coughed (on the streets he used sayings).

He pithily, cheerfully, summarized; took out his pipe; and he knocked out the ashes; and nimbly left down the alley; they said to his back:

"Oh, that one is resourceful!"

A merchant was standing right there in his gate: and with cruel eyes he watched and sarcastically said:

"Get a drink…!"

A voice answered, "You wait and they'll go get a razor." The twilight closed in.

17

All the houses grew pitifully wet: and as if from their tears the dark sidewalks rose out of the snow; at which Kiyerko thought:

"Yes!"

"All the air here is stale and unfit."

"Moscow is under attack: and it's falling to pieces." He turned past a house with a shed toward the square: in the crush of the crowd and the push and the shove, well, good luck.

At the kiosks: vegetables; rotten old cabbages, cucumbers, stinking soft turnips; the wing of a house loomed out over the street: pe-pedestrians[259] crossing, he turned and he followed; but kept near the houses; the streets' traffic trafficked the streets; they were sloped; on a hillside a small house; he bumped into a lad who was shoving his way through the crowd and was spitting out shells at the spot where four hills met (from the right and the left): Voronukhin and Mukhin,[260] which, right near its top, had a new church most wonderfully built, and a *banya*, quite old, and "just right"); and, further, a bridge; a most newfangled Empire: grey columns with helmets, and swords, and some shields, *bas relief*.

Nikolai Nikolayich looked off Voronukhin and saw in the distance the point where the houses all started to thin out, grouped in pairs and in trios, with feathery fences, above them a layer of second floors; chimneys stuck through dark blue factory smoke past Bryansk station; a gable roof; next to the house, and attached to its wall, a small chapel; and shrunk by the distance, a ribbon of trees, Vorobyovskye Hills, sat on top of it all, pressed Potylikha.[261]

---

259. Bely playing with sound.
260. Mukhina Hill, sometimes known as Smolensk Hill is the higher bank of the Moscow River. Mukhina Street was nearby. Bely is also likely referring to the nearby Borodinsky Bridge, which was decorated with bronze statuary and plaques to commemorate the Battle of Borodino.
261. Potylikha refers to the spot where the Setun River meets the Moscow River. Looking south and slightly west, the Vorobyov Hills are approximately 3 miles from the spot that Bely writes about.

Kiyerko caught this, one glance.

His thoughts swarmed at the sight; and men swarmed from each thought swinging fists.

Puff-puff, an auto spread light from twinnednostrils: a smell, gasoline, with a hint of some kerosene.

Then he stopped near a park full of stink.

In the depths of a new house with skylights, intended to soar from the earth to the sky, lived Madame Evikhkhaiten.

Kiyerko went there to see her.

Madame Evikhkaiten: an ethereal lady: a gourmet, *demi-ton*,[262] liked demonology and, paradoxically, studied societal issues: she opened her home to two totally different groups; in one, Pkhach[263] a known demonist, Catholic, Mason, or Rosicrucian, whatever you'd like (he served all secret tastes!); a shaman, a Druid, a Melchizedek priest, a baptizer of women in bathtubs; some other things; members included Ter-Bekov and Voshenko, a very respectable worker who kept to the fringes of several clubs, who had studied for 15 years the whole history of secretive learnings and written a study, his respected work "Catalogue of Catalogues."

This club met on Tuesdays.

The club for societal issues met Thursdays; Klevezal chaired it; Kiyerko went, although not to agree but to listen.

---

262. A semitone, or pitch interval midway between two whole tones; essentially, neither black nor white, gray.
263. Taken literally, Mr. Pushy.

Madame Evikhkaiten, a delicate lady, her azure eyes lowered and humble, attended both sessions; but went all in bandages; a lady with ticks, and a lady with twitches!

And at Evikhkaiten's he noted Madame Voulezvous, who kept house for Mandro.

Voulezvous told Evikhkaiten:

"*Imaginez, madame, si je vous dis que*[264] my stance, as an educator..."

"Oh! That's just awful!"

"Lizasha..."

"Just awful..."

"Madame, *je vous dis que*,[265] that the girl has a nervous condition, that she is perverted...

"You don't say..."

"And he, *je vous dis que* with her..."

"Sex maniac."

"Foo-foo-foo..."

"Scoundrel..."

"Foo-foo-foo..."

"Simply a monster!!"

Evikhkaiten just blanched.

And so Kiyerko knew they were talking about von-Mandro: greyred, quietly focused.

And often they spoke of Mandro right in front of him; always eyes squinting and checking his socks, he smiled crookedly: silent; just once did he fail to refrain from a rant:

"All I hear is Mandro, yes, Mandro with no end, well I tell you, he's nothing. I know him quite well; years back we were acquainted in Poland; and while yesterday he was Mandro, he's Herr Dorman to-

---

264. If I told you that.
265. I tell you that.

day; and tomorrow Monsieur Dorman; he's like your Pkhach... and he's called Little Mandro too... He wears just all sorts of things: loves masquerades, a real clothes horse; he knows how to scuff himself up, go, as you'd say, incognito."

When the group pressed him for all that he knew he kept silent; one shoulder would twitch; as he left, he'd just measuredly puffed on his pipe.

"Well, I pity Mandro in a way: he'll get squashed! But the spider within him is already gone... You know spiders eat spiders while they are still 'Little Mandros': well and now he's a lure for the flies; he's a web..." The spiders have recently spun their webs using Mandros of all sorts, but they've gotten caught too; well there, you, if you look at it… basically: disaster is near... The collapse will be global!"

He left.

Evikhkaiten herself, with her ticks and her twitches, reported these words to Pkhach; Pkhach with great pleasure pchuckled-pchortled:

"Yes, yes, I see: and this is explicable: a unique set of astral flows, evil ones," then he dropped hints: Evikhkaiten should get in the tub with him: purification.

Evikhkaiten responded that she "understood"; her opinions were reined in the presence of guests; her behavior in front of the servants was shameful; the ether was blamed, and for everything: both near and far; and a broad with a corset to hide a huge stomach just can't be ethereal; with guests she appeared like she'd just come from Paris; but lived in a way that would likely be scorned in Ust-Sysolsk:[266] how tasteless!

She talked all the time about taste.

Why did Kiyerko go to her sessions? Who knows?

---

266. Known since 1930 as Sytyvkar, the city is more than 600 miles from Moscow and the capital of the Russian Federation's Komi Republic. This refers to the squalor of provincial life from a Muscovite's point of view.

His answer was granite hard silence: the night.

18

No wet snow; then a bitofathaw, then meltingstuff froze; and the ice did not melt; the great martyr Catherine[267] walked through in a white sheet of snow; behind her, and cackling, the frost; and it lasted 'til Christmas, lit Christmas trees, broke at Epiphany, with a frosty and merciless January, then a thaw; and an almost clear February day died.

Then their water boy, March Febralovich, came but did not drip in accord with the calendar; Snuffsneezer Alley received yet another thick cover; the frost, with new life, nipped all noses; the noses turned red; and a fence bent by snow; a man stood in a gate; and a beggar there suffered; alas, long-nosed idleness kindles inquisitiveness; Gribikov looked out the window, and ratfaced the folks as they passed.

And he pointed a hook: not a finger:[268]

"And look, that one's hat's made of sealskin..."

"With trimming in ermine..."

"He handed him silver: but there were coins there already."

Lizasha stood waiting, an ermine muff pressed to her nose: months had already passed; Mitya had not even stuck in his nose or sent news; she'd sent notes; got no answers; she thought that she might take a break; she'd kept silent two months when she ran off to Snuffsneezer, not knowing why, just to meet him.

She waited not one day, not two.

---

267. Saint Catherine of Alexandria, whose name day is celebrated on November 24. A "great" martyr is one who suffered excruciating torture before her death.

268. Play on *kukish*, the obscene gesture.

Her relations with Mitya were strange.

And she might have said "there"; and that "there" well reflected the state of her mind, which was borderline catalepsy; she sat up silently nights; she saw images clearly comprising some sort of new, second life, one in which she was drawn to dear Mitya, and filtered through all the nymph's grimaces; what could she do: it was "there" that she lived her whole life.

It was "here," in this life she endured all the pain of her nymphness.

At times she was mute; and pretended a hallway was there in the dark; and she rushed ever faster, and faster and faster; she flew and she felt the whole hallway expanding right through her, and her body seemed open, more precisely, now open to all of her corporal feelings as if she left thought in the walls of the room that contained her; she'd left her own body at home.

In her thoughts, she ran out of there, ran, ran and ran.

She knew: she'd been sitting there; but in the end she was running; toward bright rays of light; like the sun; and she rushed to the sunrise: to learn, and just, really, to know: and so it was as if her own "I" was dissolved by the drafts in the air at Mandro's; because from "there" the sun lit her, a spherical sun that consisted of substances melted straight down from her "I" that had lost all their sense in a "We."

She had labelled this solar sphere Motherland. Yes!

"Oh, Lizasha? You there?" It was Madame Voulezvous at the door.

The huge sphere was compressed to a point:

"Well, enough of your mooning." Again, she withdrew.

And again she just ran, ran, ran, ran; and behind her Madame Voulezvous ran and ran and ran and ran. This was the one way she knew how to consciously wriggle on back from Mandro's, which was just an aquarium with fish and wet nymphs like Lizasha: there was no

"Lizasha" at all; she had only to move and the sphere would compress to a point; just until it jumped out once again; for her, objects were solid; and people and lives were objectified: piles of bales, heaps of loads.

She came back from her ramblings and came to her senses, but Mitya still wasn't there: houses stood firm; and in some, they had sealed themselves up unto death; and all Moscow was piles of bales, heaps of loads; who would carry them? Time. Would it not carry everything "there"; would she run in her thoughts for some time 'til she burst with her "I"; then make a "We"?

She had tried to discuss this with Mitya, while digging her tiny self into the softest couch cushions, and raising her brows, oh so clever; she'd waited for what he would say; he had listened, no protest; she tried to say something she couldn't express:

"No, I don't know how I'd do it."

"Mitya just try, try to do it like I do: let's sit, close our eyes; and go 'there'."

So they sat: and the carpet, from Cairo, lay braiding its patterns; the parrot squawked:

"Atheists!"

Madame Voulezvous appeared: "*Excusé:* I did not know; you are not all alone here..." Lizasha's eyes glimmered with rage.

She divided all people in groups: some had not yet been "there," Voulezvous for example; then others, like Mitya had been: in a dream; she had tried just as hard as she could to explain it to Mitya, to make him a test in some kind of unspoken ritual (while they were sitting and talking), with Mitya subconsciously drawn to her; but the "nymph's pain" deep inside her refracted his image; he looked like a monster: he couldn't grasp something so formless: he thought about grabbing her leg.

She snapped fingers:

"Oh, Mitya dear stop!"

And then later, while rubbing his forehead:

"You freak!"

Yes, her friendship with Mitya was strange.

Then a bell in the church in the neighborhood rang, richandlong; a cloud opened its center of red; and sparks played in the street in reflections off ice; she forgot that she'd given already, and handed a beggar a coin:

"May God bless you!" She caught sight of Mitya.

Now strong, in a long-hairedandblacksheepskincoat, and a hatwith-longearflaps pushed up. He was rushing home.

"Mitya!"

"Oh, hello."

It looked like the meeting was painful for him. But she understood this her own way and started to ask to go with him:

"Oh Mitya, you totally don't know my "god": he gets angry... he thought that you... *you*..." then she blushed, "were insulting me... so I explained all of this to him."

Mitya had started to think for himself: no, no, no, no!

"Understand ... that by hitting me..."

"Mitya dear..."

"Hell, I am not just some guy!... I will not allow," bragging aggressively, "even your father... and I... from my school..."

He was deeply insulted.

And now he, it was clear, had done some sort of something: "his own"; he had no time to think of Mandro; for now he'd become his own man; and he'd heard Vedenyapin...

Lizasha cut in; and she asked:

"Well, how's 'that' going?"

"What are you asking about?"

She was thinking of forgery.

With conscious indifference, he told her:

"That's nonsense: it's nothing." He started again:

"Vedenyapin began... Vedenyapin announced... Vedenyapin's gymnasium..."

He'd grown up a bit: had come into his own, was a braggart, was highonhimself and dismissiveofothers, aggressive when speaking; and Mitya had said to her, consciously, casually:

"Your father visited."

Like he wanted to prove: not just "anyone" visits his home.

"He did."

"Visited my father."

Then more about him:

"Vedenyapin's fine students... At school, Vedenyapin..."

All through their discussion his toungue snakedtheair.

Once again questions: her "god" at Korobkins' house? Nor could she answer why "he" had just yesterday yelled in the phone: "Korobkin, Korobkin, Korobkin, Korobkin!" It's certain that "god's" thoughts were there in that box, the Korobkin's old home: why was that?

She saw Mitya: now stronger; his face had cleared up; and his acne was gone; he attracted some looks; he was rushing off:

"Mitya, please stay here with me for a while."

"No, it's time to get going. I'm done beingfoolish."

Suddenly showing surprising, real passion, which he'd never had, flamed:

"I want to distinguish myself through some sort of a dazzling feat."

And then, whoops! He'd turned in through their gate!...

Lizasha stood sadly: in thought: felt deprived, she missed Mitya; in spite of it all they got one another: but here with Pereperzenko it seemed there'd be no chance to speak: he confirmed it:

"You're sick..."

Lizasha had taken medicinal chalk as a calcium supplement.

Friendly, the plumber (the pipes in the house were not working) had said:

"You my dear lady, are a sesh-list."[269]

He gave her a pamphlet and said: her life "here" was bourgeois; and life "there" was the life of the coming society; a "kingdom of freedom"; Lizasha's leap "from here to there" was described: and the leap: revolution; but strangely: she felt revolutionary sometimes, like now, when it seemed that all time, once a camel, had transformed to a stallion, would knock piles of buildings right over: and Moscow to ruins, in heaps; so when would this be, when?

Let it be sooner!

Societal issues were stuck in her mind; and despite it all, it was a fact: and quite critical; spoiled her relations with people; especially with "god," she had spoken with him only once of her kingdom in "there," where all time now was rushing, to which she was running, and moving outside of real time; "god's" face wrinkled; and as a result came his friend Doctor Dass:

"You're afflicted, young lady, with nervous anxiety."

Lizasha was scared of the street; and she felt she was glass; if a pedestrian bumped her; she'd fracture. The new day was lit with a glow: and the street celebrated another fine colorful start; but then somekindofscrum was formed-up near the gate; they were sniffing the air, and had noticed something:

---

269. Uneducated mispronunciation of "socialist".

"T'mara, be warmer."

"You spouding dat nonsense"

"But looka da sky..."

"Like yuh blood!"

The glow of the sunset walked down all the windows; it browned every face; and already a fine feathered cloud floated past with a many-rosed shine; and the city sparked: lily, and then went to black.

And then Gribikov came: and crapped on the world with his eyes.

And Lizasha, in thought, had just recently taken her "god" with her "there"; but he just did not fit; and her image of him had turned out a bit wrong: like a beast, he was grinning unpleasantly, strangely submissive; a demon on earth as he witnessed her "song"; and he liked serenading her:

I'm the one that you hear
In the depths of the night.[270]

Then her thoughts grew exalted: the sphere of the sun tore her heart; that's when all of this started.

---

270. Bely takes this quotation from Mikhail Lermontov's *The Demon*, Part 2, Verse X, where the demon reveals himself to Tamara. Banned from Russia until 1860 for alleged sacrilege and carnality, the poem was first published in Berlin in 1856. It has inspired numerous other works of art including Vrubel's painting, *The Demon* (1890), and an eponymous opera (1871) by Anton Rubinstein.

19

Eduard Eduardovich said to her once:

"My dear Nymph, would you like Chinese taffeta put on the walls in your room?"

He kissed her, one sticky lip, uninvited, unwelcome.

But he interrupted himself and stepped back: Madame Voulezvous was patrolling the house for the sake of appearances; somehow her sounds always started close by; it was usually when Eduard Eduardovich was alone with Lizasha, abusing her; twixt the large hall and guest room she had suddenly turned; and he grinned; but the curve of his sideburns, the stretch in his torso, the flex in his wrists – they all showed his desire: and interest.

Thus, they stood facing each other, not knowing at all what to do with each other.

Kiss, it might seem; but Lizasha believed they'd play patty cake:

"How Papa loves me!"

At the thought that she might kiss her father she blushed; then Madame Voulezvous's swollen cheek came straight in through the door:

"Am I bothering you?"

"No."

She looked in, then she vanished.

He smiled, then he sped down the hall; and the hall was the one lined with statues of sorrowful women who stared from their pedestals, empty eyes fixed on the years that they faced, and not hearing, not seeing, not knowing, not looking.

Lizasha walked into the hall and she opened the piano, white and inset with gemstones, well tuned; and her fingers ran over the keys as they spoke with her heart; but her heart disagreed with her; somewhere afar, and joining the sweeping scales played by Lizasha, a voice rose, at times just like velvet: as though a harmonium was playing; Eduard

Eduardovich sang along with Lizasha's scales, sitting, enjoying the chair with pistachio fabric, his arms spread across the gold lionskin paws on its arms: in a beaver-toned hat and nice beaver-toned shoes.

From the ceiling's faux garland encircling the room hung a green Chinese lantern.

Then she, for some reason recalled how the ruler had whistlesliced air and then Mitya's two fingers; oh why did he do that? She wanted him back.

Her spirit just ached even thinking of him: the sun's sphere tore her heart.

Stylish heels clicked on the floor.

Victor, a dandy, then ran through the room with a briefcase of snakeskin, speaking but not really looking.

"Those Bechsteins are great: have a full and rich tone!"[271]

At the door, he then laughed to himself.

Interrupting her music, she lifted her eyes to the spot where the 12 carved old men with their rococo beards raised their 12 heads up into space; and the voice that was humming along with her stopped: Eduard Eduardovich Mandro walked into the hall and said, bowing low:

"Play me some Chopin."

His fingers (index and thumb) joined at his lips:

"Will you play for me, La-La?" He rubbed his two fingers together.

His eyes took her in.

And then everything in her ignited.

Madame Voulezvous then appeared, and she walked by Lizasha and grimaced, the eyes of a balancing act; her eyes always expressed the same thought (oh, am I interrupting?); her presence, a colon; she wanted to say:

---

271. C. Bechstein, a German piano manufacturer founded in 1853 and known for its high quality instruments.

"*Mesamis*, pay attention!"

Eduard Eduardovich, very politely, grinned stiffly, his eyes seemed to ask:

"Forgive me!"

Madame Voulezvous answered wordlessly, very restrained yet emphatic that she, in truth, didn't know what he was talking about or why he was asking forgiveness; while carefully stitching her words.

Ostentatiously treating her nicely, he gave her a brooch made of topaz.

Lizasha looked pained, and then stood and walked off; with her waist oh so narrow, her mouth small and open. Lizasha was shocked:

"What was that, what?"

It seemed that the answer was clear; it was simply a father's caress; yet quite strange; and his look at her seemed somehow terribly criminal.

But how?

It seemed that his look poured right down into her spirit; it began at that time and it mixed up her life; just as if she'd been dressed in somebody else's old clothes; but she walked as if wearing a dress; looked just like "Mademoiselle von-Mandro," one whose nostrils had suddenly flared.

The whole day Lizasha had wandered around like a lunatic; thinking expansively; played with the cat; draped its small nose with smoke; had a gleam in her eyes; and the night, hard as rock, filled the room: she was tortured: but likedherfinelife.

"Well, enough of your mooning," Madame Voulezvous once in passing remarked.

And her door knob was rattled one night: Eduard Eduardovich walking the halls, in the dining and guest rooms, just circling, hand holding a condulstick, lighting his way; and he opened up room after room with the shine of gold frames (not a home, more a gallery); subtly, their things were disguised, all the dishware and bronzelamps cast shadowy outlines of snakes, their jaws wide, then they entered the circle of light.

And the circle moved.

In its light, not Mandro: on the wall was a shadow, not sideburns – a demon.

20

Von-Mandro found a way to stay busy. He went to stock company meetings: Solomon Samuilovich Kavalever as chairman reviewed the account books; and Pansky, Jan Pansky; once nicknamed Champagne up at Strelna,[272] and elsewhere called Blackmail,[273] signed checks for large sums; and present were: Prepoladze, Ivan, the Greek Pustaki, Kadmitsy, Yevgenyevich Kapitulevich, the Frenchman Deuxperdrix, the Englishman Degury (a bronzed face), the Czech Pukeshke; all men with a nose for the practical. One might hear:

"Down at headquarters..."

"Well, it is known that..."

"The Primary Commissariat feels rushing will…"

"Contact was made with Constantinople."

Viktorchik served as their secretary: but, just a "trifle" is what von-Mandro called him, fussing with wrinkles.

The "trifle," was rushing, his briefcase jammed full: he spoke in a whisper; he sorted the papers in piles; then they looked through the summary figures; then Victorchik, no hesitation, gave documents marked with the seal of the "Company" on Yakimanka to Kartofel, from Riga; not linked to the firm of "Mandro," but instead was con-

---

272. Since the time of Peter the Great, Strelna, outside Petersburg, has been the location of one of the imperial family's summer residences. The surrounding area became a popular summer destination for the nobility.

273. Bely has an extended bit of wordplay here on Jan Pansky, including champagne (*shampanskoye*) as well as the Russian word *shantazh*, or blackmail.

nected with, think now, von Torfendorf, to whom he, while holding a sheaf of the documents, mangling his Russian, just said, incomprehensibly, rushed:

"From Mandor: To Co Mandor."

"Co" means "Company": strange, so just why did he turn von-Mandro into something named "Mandor"; was he punning or playing with words? And after all they had referred to the members of the Mandro "Company" – Kapitulevich, Pukeshke, Pustaky: "Co-Mandor."

"You are our co-Mandor," Viktorchik stalled, and then shuffled, and ran out, with briefcase in hand, which sometimes just happened.

"Yes, Viktorchik!"

Beaten-down, one blinking eye, and stooped, abitthin, young but already quite bald; there was something unpleasant about him; his eyes had real bite; at home, all his servants loved him; only Vasiliy Dergushin, a servant, a man, young, with prospects, and handsome suspected him; once, bringing Roederer[274] to the table, he'd caught just a bit of a guest's conversation: while screening his words with some sipping, Viktorchik quietly whispered to Bezitsov, and narrowed his eyes at Lizasha:

"An ecstatic, and a bit of an idiot: a great match for him.

"She's a young girl... He after all is...

"Erotically fixated!"[275] Seriously. Understand? A-ha-ha-ha-ha-ha!"

"Erotically fixated people are wretches," Bezitsov sighed, putting his glass down.

Vasiliy Dergushin poured Roederer for them, brought Roederer to Louis Deuxperdrix, Merditsevich, Pok, and, skipping the other guests, served Voulezvous:

"Just so, ma'am!"

---

274. Louis Roederer, a champagne producer, is based today in Reims, France.

275. Erotomania is a delusion that someone, usually a stranger or celebrity, is in love with you. The deluded person believes that a secret admirer is declaring his or her affection, often through glances, signals, telepathy, or the media.

Voulezvous said, "the seamstress delivered, just yesterday, Lizasha's first gown." To Lizasha she said:

"*Mon dieu*! And I already said it's too tight... Oh, Lord on High!"

She went to Madame Evikhkaiten, who vainly had hoped to replace her real mother; she'd stopped coming by; it was said:

"Madame Evikhkaiten: madame with the tongue of a monster!"

And in business dark rumors abounded.

Lizasha, Lizasha!

Recently, on his way home, Eduard Eduardovich sat deep in thought; and despite the unpleasantness, his torso felt younger while stretching and thinking: Lizasha; he smiled as he saw her eyes widen; he tried to be tender with her: as his right as a father:

"Come here my, La-La..."

Lizasha approached; with a humble but put-on expression he lowered his eyes to his sideburns; her eyes were bright sparkles; Madame Voulezvous liked to say:

"You need a girlfriend your age; we, you know, are too old... I'm just not a good match for you..."

Playing dumb, Eduard Eduardovich treated Madame Voulezvous most politely: he gave her a gift, some nice earrings.

Lizasha had once overheard just the end of a chat, Prepoladze and Viktorchik; there was a fight: Kavalever: well, what? Their words flashed:

"Available evidence says: that the job's in the bag..."

"The old man does his math night and day..."

"Finishing up..."

"And now we'll get to work..."

"And the son..."

It was clear that the "son" was dear Mitya; the "old man" was linked to the paper she found in his office; it had fallen in front of dear Mitya that memorable day; on a whim, she continued to hide the small paper; she knew that her "god" had been digging around in his briefcase.

He'd asked:

"Have you seen any papers, Dergushin?"

"What kind, may I ask?"

"Ones like these." He showed "what"; it had tiny handwriting; some math: and small letters.

"Oh no, sir..."

"Lizasha, have you?"

She kept silent: she still had the paper (a whim!).

She did not understand how Professor Korobkin was part of it. Why were the names Kavalever, Viktorchik, Torfendorf, and Korobkin re-renamed; Korobkin, Korobkin, Korobkin!

Korobkin!

She didn't like Viktorchik; feared Torfendorf: he dealt with Berlin and with Munich; spoke concerning one Lerkhenfeld, with whom he was friendly; but senselessness somehow was lurking in all this; and hanging above her, it offered no answers; she knew: he would answer, a granite-hard silence: the night!

21

Whenever Mandro left the house he looked wonderful, swathed in blue fox or in sable (his hat too); a rose or bay gelding in harness: so smooth: he went rushing through blizzardy gloom and through thaws late in March.

In his wake, a real ruckus:

"Mandro!"

"What an exit!"

"What fur!"

"What a stallion!"

But dark rumors multiplied.

Unpleasant problems were growing: Ivan Prepoladze, Pustaky, Degury, Kadmidiy Yevgenevich Kapitulevich, and the Frenchman Deux-perdrix were leaving the office, but he was held back: Kavalever remarked rather sharply:

"You're ordered to give the discovery to Torfendorf."

"Ordered?..."

"Your question?"

"It's my deal; look if I had not learned...

"Not just yours..."

"All the same. And if I had not jumped on the breakthrough..."

"You promised..."

"I'll do what I promised: my man is there watching..."

"He's twiddlinghisthumbs..."

Von-Mandro then fell silent and chewed on his lip.

It became clear, Torfendorf was the head of the firm, not Jan Pansky Shantansky; they saw Kavalever wasn't a star in their bright constellation: that his constellation was screened by some penciled-in sideburns, a huge banner: Mandro. Kavalever and problems with him were completely upsetting; but he'd posed the question politely: should they change the wax model displayed in the "Company's" window; that is, take the sideburns away, add some lipstick, and top it all off with a copy of Louis Deuxperdrix's beard.

Torfendorf would enjoy this French front. But disturbing discussions like these made Mandro sit alone; where he frowned, with brows knit, and surrounded by walls an annoying blue tone, in his office; while slumped in a huge, sturdy chair in red silk, scratching his sideburns, and silent, with blood on his lips and quite angry: from frustration and fury suppressed.

Getting up from the red chair, he grabbed up the phone: showed his teeth:

"Hello!"

"45 - 28..."

"Kurt Valterovich?"

"Please call von-Torfendorf to the phone."

"Kurt Valterovich," toothed Mandro, "it seems all is just wonderful..."

Angry sounds scratched in his ear from the shiny bronze throat of the phone at the other end.

"Yes..."

"Yes-s..."

"Well of course."

"We will fix it..."

"Oh yes, yes..."

"It will be done..."

After replacing the earpiece he sucked his lip worriedly: done with his lip, grabbed the phone for a second time:

"Please, ma'am,: 5 - 18... Thank you..."

"Hello!..."

"Is this Viktorchik?"

"Listen here Viktorchik, I spoke with Torfendorf..."

"Well?"

"So I calmed..."

"Understand that it can't be that way, it just can't: no, no, no..." and he squeezed in his fist the wool cloth on the table. "Hurry: and pressure him... Squeeze..."

"He doesn't want it?" as his triangle wrinkle itched over his nose.

"He got sick? Is he drinking?"

"And Gribikov? What of the rat?"

"More complaints?... Dammit..."

The hand with the phone shook:

"Well, fine..."

And he put down the handset.

Then, elbows set down on the back of the chair, and his temple inclined on a finger; he frowned, he kept quiet, sat handsome and thick-browed, avoiding the business that vexed him, moved on, and his tough face relaxed; and he listened; and with a strange squint of his eyes he got up and on tippy toes walked out the door to the hall, heard the tap of small feet out there walking away.

She'd gone past with her lunatic gait.

He stared, his eyes growing wide as he looked; and returned once again, breathing hard, to the table; and threw himself down in his silk chair; and pensively hanging a hand in the air with his other he twirled 'round the ring on a finger: and upset and angry, and seemingly asking himself:

"What next?"

All his fingers were shaking, his hand then replied with a broken-down drumming...

"Well, yes...Tratata! "Only one thing, one thing left..."

But, upset, the decision quite frightening even to him, he half-hopped and he stomped as he paced: from the shaking the chandelier's pendants were tinkling.

22

Sternly a servant delivered a note to Mandro.

"Who?"

"It's a man…"

Someone, a mess, came in wearing a wide-collared, long-tailed frock coat; a wide nose; he could see well done rooms; chairs well polished; he noticed a flat-chested girl as she fluffed-up her skirt, and she flashed her small teeth as she curtsied, the imp.

He bobbed his nose toward her:

"My respects my good *madame*!"

He crossed his legs and while waving said:

"So, what do they call you, if I may speak rationally."

"Lizasha."

She tilted her head to the side.

"Lizasha?"

"Yes."

With '*pianissimo*' eyes.

"I dare ask, why not Sucker?"

"What?" She felt sick.

"You, I'd guess, like to 'lick'?"[276]

She flushed:

"I don't lick, not a thing."

Abitsavage and hunted, a gleam in her eyes.

---

276. Bely plays here with the verb *lizat*, or lick, and the name Lizasha.

"A cat licks its cream... And we had a dog, Tom, who licked himself, basically, under his tail."

"Yuck!"

Then it was as if someone crushed a louse under his nose:

"What stupidity!"

They babbled, she batted her eyes at him.

"How..."

"Sixteen."

"No, I'm asking how long you have, basically, licked?

"Oh, that's nonsense!" She gave him a look up and down.

"In the past, I'd say, you were a 'sucker,' he bellowedout fiercely and shuffledalittle, "You sucked on your mother!"

She fluffed up her skirt with suspicion: well, all kinds of trash can get in!

Then her "god," who was just as emotional, captivating, jumped out with such an expressly protective appearance; he grabbed her and pressed her two hands to his chest, and then leaning his head to one side said:

"I'm so happy, Professor!" Professor?

Lizasha stood open-mouthed:

That's who he is?

And then "who" poked a finger at her and his nose at Mandro:

"I was telling your daughter," he lowered his nose on a finger, then waved it, "that she was a suckling at one time; and later, she licked up her *kasha*."

He circled Mandro, a bit loud: with his hands at his back; and his nose toward Mandro; and Mandro, in respect, sentimental, and violet, looked owlish (slow, cherry-toned), light brown and *café au lait* visiting coat and clean *crème brulée* pants, and a pale blue tie made his hair all the darker.

Exactly as if he'd completed a course on costumery. He waved toward the guest room: "If you'd be so kind!"

And he bowed like a dancer. The nearsighted professor walked in front with his hands at his back: two heads shorter; but his skull was a skull built for two; and when he lugged his head to a chair, his hand grabbed a black ashtray (of jasper, a lydite);[277] Lizasha, behind him, sat down on a divan and buried herself in its pillows; and bending her legs underneath her she toyed with the decorative stones on the table and watched.

The professor just tossed the black ashtray around in his hand, as he forced out some chatter and smiled: 'cause he thought it his role to be loud during visits; so laughing with "god" he had wiggled his ears and grabbed onto his lips with his fingers: while everything else he could manage, he couldn't control his two ears:

"Well, and what a fine," licking his fingers clean, "comic you are."

An unsavory gesture!

Lizasha had watched, eyes completely surprised, with a cigarette held in her mouth, as she thought: "the old man really calculates," "he is completing the job," "and now we'll get to work," and then stretched out her neck, blew some smoke: and she listened to what the old "finished calculating," round-bellied man said:

"If you don't like it don't listen, but don't bother lying... That is a real saying, yes, basically!"

She lifted the cigarette up to her lips; and then narrowed her eyes as she let loose some smoke curls and stretched both her hands from her mouth up above, and began quickly revolving her cigarette.

Von-Mandro lit a smoke, and sat back, crossed his legs, while one elbow relaxed on the table, the other was draped on the lion's paw arm

---

277. An opaque gemstone related to chalcedony. Black jasper is also known as lydian stone or lydite and has been used as a touchstone for assaying precious metals.

of the chair; his cigar was there tracing a half-ellipse; cigar smoke just hung, a blue ribbon, a loop that was cutting a screen with a black, golden-winged bird.

Lizasha was stunned, and she stuck out her eyes: and the paper that "god"… then the shout in the telephone handset: Korobkin, Korobkin, Korobkin, Korobkin!

"So *he* is Professor Korobkin?"

Lizasha remembered what Mitya had said:

"None like those at our place."

"None like those" meant her "god": she saw "god" as the Master Builder, Solness; so why did he say "Korobkin, Korobkin"; when after all with just as much right they could shout: von-Mandro, von-Mandro, von-Mandro; but some sort of dark secrets had multiplied; perhaps… and here yawned the ineffable; she saw the abyss.

And she sat right above the abyss.

And her "god" as if playing a role in a farce, a K.S. Stanislavsky production: *Humble Servant and Great Scholar* (in essence the farce was an interlude done for the drama *The Bird and the Python*.)

A costume designer!

The professor, hands clasping the paws on the arms of the chair, pressed his brow to its wing, upholstered in fabric with gold thread:

'It's clear you're behind in your studies; and I'd like to laugh: you know laughter's a good thing; I don't go to theaters; but I do write some poetry, simply on various aspects of life; like Prutkov's."[278]

He grew lively quite suddenly:

"See here, Annie, Anna Ivanovna, it's clear, was a servant for us: from a merchant but bankrupted family…"

---

278. Kozma Petrovich Prutkov was a pen name used in the 1850s and 1860s by a group of writers including Alexei Tolstoy and the Zhemchuzhinikov brothers, Alexei, Vladimir and Alexander; some also include Alexander Amosov in this group. "Prutkov" was best known for satirical poems on a variety of topics as well as "his" aphorisms.

Distractedly he waved a hand; while Lizasha was prancing and minc-
ing around, a bit agitated, giggling down deep.

Annie... Well, here's what I'll tell her... Barking, he said:

"Right after a bathtub one evening,"
the housemaid shared once while cleaning,
"a cruel twist of fate was in order,
soaked a beat cop while dumping the water!"

Why did he speak of this now, his first time at Mandro's?

"Things, you know, are quite flat without laughter: commissions and
lectures, hmm, meetings: and councils, and groups oh my, yes!"

Eduard Eduardovich wanted to smoke; when they spoke of such serious work, from respect he removed the cigar from his lips, though
he'd lit up the match; when their talk turned to everyday matters, he
pushed the cigar right back into his mouth; struck a match, and he
laughed, belly shaking; Lizasha then suddenly knew why the famous
professor was playing these games; and why "god" stood there prancing
in front of him playing the fool. They were eyeing each other.

Truly, Korobkin was being grotesque; Mandro rolled his eyes:

"Well, I've seen him somewhere before: it was maybe the Masons, or
maybe a baptism, da, dammit: he'd picked up the scent."

Then it seemed like he wanted to lead the discussion to something
Mandro thought intriguing; Mandro, who had noticed that something
was up, just played dumb; well that's useless, they say; does not work; I
don't know; and he tried to avoid the *staccato* with deep bass *legato*, sang
out to report on his exports of butter, Siberia to England:

"We would... they load 'ice cars' quickly... and railroads..."

He watched with eyes straight from the grave, but his pupils resembled an owl's; and, exhaling some smoke, an annoying and throaty rough cough rumbled out:

"Kha-kho!"

Something bitter appeared in his face; and it seemed that, now old, he'd become a gorilla.

The professor thought:

"Yes, yes sir": he is a man with an uneasy conscience."

He grew frightened: and just between us, he'd already made inquiries: they said that Mandro had his way with a schoolgirl; and they said there'd been sodomy too; he was there to resolve his suspicions, the product of long, sleepless nights, some with nightmares.

The nightmares seemed real: when through wide open doors, right behind von-Mandro through the sitting room he got a glimpse of an office, deep blue, an oppressive tone he'd seen once somewhere, but where? His subconscious, where orange and yellow tones found in our everyday lives were consumed by the flames?

The empty and loud red silk chair burned.

Then tea and liqueurs were set out on a gold inlaid table; a servant placed, quietly, a teacup in front of him (porcelain, pale red); Mandro offered "pralines":

"No, thank you most humbly!"

"No? I will: I've such a huge sweet tooth!!"

He flipped his hair, silver locks clearly straight up, just like horns; the professor remembered this motion and grabbed at the lionpawed arms of the chair; and he practically jumped up to run: just as if a gorilla was there, not Mandro.

He remembered it all!

"What's wrong?"

"I'm fine, sir, nothing, sir!"

His memory: a cold early morning, the first day of nice weather (now half a year back); on the opposite side of the street, in the yellow house; there in the window, not Gribikov, white and black sideburns stuck out like Mandro's!!

"I thought you..."

"Time for me to head out!"

The professor jumped up with suspicious speed, started to shuffle, and stuck out his fingers: Mandro stood up, striking a pose he'd worked out in the mirror; his anger concealed by a grimace, he nodded his head and grey horns, clasped his fingers and grinned in his fist; like he'd bit off his fingers; Korobkin was short: and he tried the wrong door!

"Not there: over here!"

Eduard Eduardovich gestured invitingly with one long arm (he was long-armed): his massive ring sparked like a ruby.

The three walked out quickly: the three ended up in the entry, on rugs, after hearing the echo of footsteps; Korobkin was donning his coat; but he couldn't see clearly (fogged glasses): his fluffy round hat lay there.

Plop, it was on!

That very same instant he felt something scratching his head: from the hat that he'd grabbed four legs reached down the sides of his head, and a long fluffy tail: when he brushed off the hat it fell down to the ground!

Then he bowed to the girl:

"Excuse me, madame! Please, madame!" But the hat had turned…

"Dammit all, Vasya! A cat!"[279]

Then the cat, after arching its back, ran right off to the depths of the hall: he had put on a cat not his hat!

Then a servant came running: his hat, and Mandro and Lizasha stood open-mouthed, holding back laughter, they stood still as posts; though not laughing, they managed to wink all around, and had tears in their eyes, and they shouted:

"Amusing, sir, yes sir!"

His brown leather briefcase in hand, out he ran, vaulting straight through the door.

23

Like spit long erased by pedestrians, he fell out the door and ran off, bumping folks with his fur coat; yes, just a bit of a thaw; and some sideswipingrain; and some half-melted ice; there was some sort of spit and some kindofakasha, some kindofamess; the weather was wet and it settled all over in puddles while raising foam bubbles; the snow had been munched.

The taxicab rattled.

"Tarvroye… rfe-rfe… starter…startar.. Tar-tar-tar! Tartars!

---

279. Surprised, Korobkin mistakenly exclaims to his wife.

"Dammit all, Vasya! A cat!"

"How, sir?"

"What, sir?"

Yes, yes it was in his subconscious: the dream in which Gribikov coughed out the window and sprinkled the ashes on months of his effort; he then saw, a day later, and in the same window: Mandro...

Then he answered himself right away, he was prey; but it could have been anyone sporting black sideburns; not only Mandro; and the window had slammed; there were sounds of leavesscratching, limbsclashing, and treescrapingbreaking.

The cold howling of cities commenced.

And right there was the square: there were kiosks, and bricks of nice tea; signs: "Belotserkovsky and Gustyansky Vegetables."

He nearly bumped into some guy: and a lady took umbrage:

"Hey, jerk: what's the rush?

Although he had put on the cat as a joke, it was no joke at all; so he walked with dark doom in his eyes, and with guilt on his conscience among all the unsightly snouts, rivers of people, mistaking an alley for Snuffsneezer (Rottentooth, really); the house was the color of chocolate, tiles, pressed clay blocks near the door and an abacus, yellow columns; yes, and a square little courtyard, square shadows; a square place of consciousness; how was it knowable? After all, consciousness *is* a round circle; and squaring a circle was something that hadn't alas!

been achieved;[280] addressing the challenge, to solve the unsolved; he got stunned by the squares; failed to grasp his position:

"Whom do you need?"

And a porter, a broom in his hands, stood before him; wrong courtyard, although he had walked just like always: 549 steps; but just once, at an alley he'd turned the wrong way; which meant this was a stranger's; small boys near some crates; where they played; the whole alley was teeming with people; it rained, oh so finely; fog clumped in the bluish-black darkness and blue-black gloom out of which blew a cold icy draft.

What was the matter?

Mandro!

And if he understood his impressions of sounds in "Mandro," he'd have noticed that: "Man" was a blue: and the "dr" was the shade of pure black that you see when recalling a dream; and the "Man" was manipulative; "dr"? That delivered a blow.[281]

---

280. The expression "squaring the circle" is used as a metaphor for trying to do the impossible. In geometry, squaring the circle is the ancient challenge of constructing a square with the same area as a given circle by using only a compass and ruler. In 1888, it was proven mathematically impossible.

281. The letters "dr" deliver a blow because they are principle components of the word *udar*, from the verb *udarit*, to hit or strike. The title of the second part of Bely's novel is *Moskva pod udarom*, usually translated as *Moscow Under Threat*.

"Yes, a blow to all Moscow!"

His words were a total surprise; then he looked all around, and he stared at the buildings' façades: they were true freaks of nature; a house made of stone, in a pile; and then house after house all in heaps, and façade past façade gone to hell; all their doors were like cracks.

It was terrifying!

House after house were all hung with the burden of time: time, a python that crushes; a load falls; and he too would collapse, and his Moscow, now hanging above all the Tatars.

"D-di-... Dig... Old-old... plain tarrtatatato."

"Tarta-mantor... mandor... Commander... the carriage rumbled."

And everything turned-up:

"Mandro!"

He recalled an event rather suddenly; a call; he'd mistakenly dialed his home; to the servant's voice asking who's there, he responded; a query concerning himself.

"Oh, yes please, is the gentleman home?"

When he heard that "the gentleman" wasn't available, he'd hung up the phone and he'd gone off: apparently home, and he only then realized that there was no reason to ask for the "gentleman," *he* was the "gentleman" (just between us, what kind of a "gentleman" is he; just look, if you please, at the "gentleman": ha! An old man: and there digging around in his fur coat in front of his home).

"Roi-rfe-ro-ro," drubbed a cab. Honked.

In the sky, constellations in garlands stood frozen; it seemed, if you looked, that a star could slide down any icicle; fall on your head; thus the sky falls on lambs; thus lambs fall at a blow.

"Dr-dro!"

The black-mawed front entryway swallowed him.

"Darya, please keep the door chained, you know, basically, rogues of all kinds are out there in the streets..."

"Yes, sir!"

"They carry crowbars..."

"Yes, sir."

"If you leave it unchained, 'he' – well, you know what'll happen – zap: right in the head."

Then he went to his office.

He looked for a spot to collapse; then collapsed, and with stars in his eyes he looked up at the ceiling; it might just cave in; and all Moscow was under attack!

Yes, yes!

Rearrange books, rehide all the papers, and wipe off the traces; he fell in a reverie, bitter, across a huge pile. Like a fly in a web he had fought with himself, piled his papers in overstuffed drawers; then dumped them again, the drawers creaking.

He picked through the books willy-nilly.

But fleet-footed time always tampered with everything, just like his Tommie, the hound; and just now it intended to tamper by ringing the doorbell quite loudly.

"Something will happen!... Oh, something enormous most certainly, there-there-there-there, it's here!"

But it wasn't a cat he'd put on – it was a crown of thorns.[282]

---

282. The reference to Christ here is developed further in *Moscow Under Threat*.

ACKNOWLEDGMENTS

I would never have dreamt of translating *The Moscow Eccentric* without knowing I had a support network of geniuses, giants, and gems. Protecting my colleagues' modesty, I will not ascribe specific types to the individuals mentioned below; nonetheless, I can assure readers that some of these folks belong in all three categories.

Boris Drayluk read and commented on the manuscript (at more than one stage) and was especially helpful with the poetry. Boris had an insightful response to any question, any time, but his greatest contribution was his constant, consistent insistence (quite persistent) that I push farther and farther, lose my preconceptions and inhibitions, and be more creative.

Michael Katz, the C.V. Starr Professor Emeritus of Russian and East European Studies at Middlebury College, was my first mentor in the field: he convinced me to major in Russian in the early 1980s at Williams College. Michael has always responded generously whenever I have asked for help, including some tough calls on this work.

Sofia Kosheleva, a Docent at Orlov State University in the Russian Federation, is a linguist and Bely expert. Sofia's dissertation on

Bely's language (and related unpublished materials that she generously shared) served as indispensable references. It is difficult to overstate their importance to my work.

Nina Murray, whom I met as a fellow translator at Russian Life magazine, has been of immense help over the years. A quick glance at the subject lines of our emails turns up horses, roosters, plants, slang and expletives, clanking chains, and a variety of other fun (and immensely useful) stuff.

Karine Noack was always ready to work with me, no matter the language, no matter the problem.

Ingrid Nordgaard read, commented with keen insight on the manuscript, and offered encouragement at that late stage in the process, familiar to most translators, when it seems wisest to find a shredder. Ingrid's thoughts on Ibsen's place in the novel were especially helpful.

Paul Richardson, my publisher, has been a friend and intellectual sparring partner for more than 30 years. Paul is unstinting in his support to his writers and translators, unsparing in his (constructive) criticism, and largely untouched (except for his taste in beverages) by his unparalleled success in the field.

Finally, let me note that any mistranslations or other errors are my responsibility. I fully recognize the *hubris* of translating one of the world's greatest writers. But, I reckon, after 90 years, no one else is likely to try it anytime soon. So, as Bely might say, why not give it a whirlspin?!

ABOUT THE AUTHOR

Andrei Bely (1880-1934), born Boris Nikolayevich Bugayev, lived in Moscow and became a novelist, poet, and literary theorist and critic. Vladimir Nabokov ranked Bely's *Petersburg* one of the four best novels of the twentieth century. Bely's prose and poetry were deeply influenced by both his theoretical constructs and, unusually, empirical analysis of his own and others' work. Bely lived and worked in both tsarist and Bolshevik Russia, and, like many of his contemporaries, spent some years traveling and living in Europe.

ABOUT THE TRANSLATOR

Brendan Kiernan is a freelance translator and political analyst. A student of Russian language and literature since 1977, he earned a Ph.D in Political Science from Indiana University as well as an area studies certificate from IU's famed Russian and East European Institute. His translation of Vladimir Gilyarovsky's classic book, *Moscow and Muscovites*, was published by Russian Life Books in 2013, and in 2015 won the prestigious AATSEEL prize for Best Scholarly Translation from a Slavic Language into English.

www.ingramcontent.com/pod-product-compliance
Lightning Source LLC
Chambersburg PA
CBHW051647180726
48284CB00006B/1901